M000311853

Also by M.T. Bass

My Brother's Keeper

Crossroads

In the Black

Lodging

SOMETHIN' FOR NOTHIN'

BY

M.T. BASS

AN ELECTRON ALLEY PUBLICATION
MUDCAT FALLS, U.S.A.

Electron Alley Corporation
The Herald Building
732 Broadway Avenue
Lorain, OH 44052

Manufactured in the United States of America

Edited by Elizabeth Love (www.bee-edited.com)

ISBN 978-0-9833807-6-4 (Paperback)
ISBN 978-0-9833807-7-1 (ebook)

www.MTBass.net

The characters and incidents contained herein are fictional. Any resemblance of persons, living or dead, may, in fact, be a violation of copyright statutes.

For Lora Beth

Impatience is the cardinal sin of youth.

Prologue

"ARRRRRRGGGGGGGG! Excedrin headache number sixty-nine!" Waxy moaned in genuine anguish.

The blizzard had ended. High pressure built up over the Yukon. To the south, daylight glowed about the horizon turning the landscape into a black-and-white film noir scene. The hull of the airplane was, miraculously, still intact and provided shelter from the whirling Arctic dervishes sweeping down across the broad plains of permafrost north of the Brooks Mountain Range, which, like unseen Medusas, could turn men to stone with a mere touch of their wind chill factors.

"Jimmi, this is not funny. Cut it out," Waxy groaned. But Jimmi the Pilot was dead, skewered by the control yoke in the crash. "Albert, make Jimmi cut it out."

Albert was not dead, but he was still unconscious in a crumpled heap behind Waxy. Waxy did not know that, because he had yet to open his eyes. He felt dizzy enough without having blurry perceptions of reality to cope with, too. He had never before had a concussion, so Waxy wasn't quite sure what was happening to him.

"ALLLLLLL-BERRRRRRRRRT!" Waxy bayed. He coughed and spat blood. "Oh, Albert, this just isn't our day. I want to go home now, Albert. I want to go back to Ohio."

Albert did not answer.

"Albert, tell Jimmi to cut it out. PLLLEEEAAASSSEEE! This isn't fun anymore."

But Jimmi the Pilot was dead.

High Street

The blue bus is calling us...

Albert and Waxy woke one Thursday morning to the guttural gurgling of diesel engines. Albert's blue Ford panel van was parked between a North American moving van and a Monsanto chemical tanker—a portentous sign, they both later concurred—at an Indiana rest stop just across the border from Ohio on Interstate 70. Waxy and Albert emerged from the van with a vacuity of will and comprehension so common to those suffering a hangover.

"Where the hell are we?" asked Albert.

Waxy squinted his eyes and sniffed the air. "Indiana? Maybe?"

"Oh God, I knew it. We've died and gone straight to hell."

"It could be worse."

"How in the hell is that?" Albert scowled and stared hard at Waxy.

"I don't know." Waxy shook his head. "I miss it."

"Miss what?"

"Home."

"AAAAIIIIRRRRRGGGGHHHH! GO DIRECTLY TO CLEVELAND! DO NOT PASS GO! DO NOT COLLECT $200!"

"You know what I mean."

"For Christ's sake, we're not even two hundred miles from Columbus. We haven't even been gone twelve hours, yet," Albert exclaimed in disbelief. "Besides, it's Ohio. *O-Hi-O,* Waxy. Remember? That four letter word with three syllables."

"Huh?"

"Ohio, boy, Ohio. The Buckeye State, where that veritable Imperial Wizard of the Big Ten, Woody Hayes, reigns supreme. Home of the Rubber Capital of the world and the Pro Football Hall of Fame—the one hundred forty-seventh and two hundred sixty-third wonders of the world, respectively. Give me a break already, will you? Don't tell me you want to go back-back-*back there!* Don't tell me that you really, really want to be known as one of the only two human beings on the planet to legitimately flunk out of *The* Ohio State University. Have you forgotten about garfing that God damned midterm in Kragies' Torment of the Soul 101 yesterday? She'll crucify us, Waxy—nail our asses to the God damned cross. We won't be able to get jobs pumping gas at a piss-ant Sohio station by the time she's finished her Inquisition with us. As Immanuel Kant would say, *'get real already.'* Face it, we're screwed."

"Well, yeah, but-but I sure don't want to stay in Indiana."

"Go west, young man, go west," Albert whispered seductively.

"Is Alaska west? Or North? Or northwest?"

"Details, Waxy, don't bother me with details. Get a focus on *The Big Picture.*"

"Oh, yeah. I keep forgetting."

Waxy wasn't very good at all at focusing in on *The Big Picture.* Albert was the idea man and that suited Waxy—and Albert, too—just fine.

The Big Picture came to be defined in ever broader, ever more artistically abstract strokes as Albert and Waxy made their way down High Street hitting every bar across from the OSU campus

Somethin' for Nothin'

that was open at 10:30 in the morning from the *North Berg* to the *South Berg* immediately after "garfing" their Introduction to Philosophy midterm examination. *The Big Picture* had its genesis in shots of Yukon Jack bourbon, which Albert and Waxy washed down liberally with Moosehead Lager beers.

"Look at that label! Look at that God damned label, Waxy! Have you ever in your life ever seen anything as ugly as that moose?!" Albert pointed to the label of his beer bottle. His voice had the timbre and decibel rating of a Pratt and Whitney jet engine roaring at take-off power in Waxy's ear. "They've got to have Paul Bunyan-sized balls to put something that hideous on a beer bottle and still expect people to drink it! Yup! Genuine Paul Bunyan-sized testicles with sperm cells as big as rainbow trout! Waxy, my man, that's where we belong! In the land of the *ug-ug-ugliest* member of the deer family and brew masters with the biggest balls in this quadrant of the Milky Way! It's gotta be! It's Jack London's call of the fucking wild! It's just gotta be! Look at that son-of-a-bitching Bullwinkle bastard! Look at him and tell me we don't belong! We'll be sucking down caribou milk and snarfing eagle eggs over easy with a side of reindeer back bacon for breakfast! Put hair on a hairless ass! Look at this! Look! When have you ever seen an uglier hunk of shag carpeting? Look at him. *Am I right or am I right or am I right?*"

"No man of reason can dispute this," Waxy slurred as he squinted hard at his own bottle of Moosehead Beer.

The main ingredients of *The Big Picture* included collecting obscenely excessive amounts of money, Arctic springs welling up with honey-sweetened sour mash whiskey straight from the center of the earth, and clutches of Scandinavian-looking Eskimo women named Annika, Inge, Karena and Rika clawing at Albert and Waxy's naked bodies. The more he drank, the more animated and enthusiastic Albert became, albeit the more Salvador Dali-like his vision of getting rich working on the construction of the Trans-Alaska Pipeline became.

Waxy, being of like mind and intoxication, measured Albert's skewed vision of reality, riches and adventure against his own mundane high school existence in Delaware, Ohio; the abrasion of a liberal arts course of study at Ohio State University on his pragmatic, agrarian sensibilities; and the prospects of going to work on the second shift in the local luggage factory back home when his utter failure to comprehend the Humanities was verified in his hastily scribbled blue book by Professor Kragies. He came to the one and only conclusion a man who had sucked boiler makers for six hours straight possibly could: "Who cares if the mule is blind, let's load up the wagon."

"Huh?" asked a perplexed Albert.

"Why the hell not!"

"Now you're talking."

Their Manifest Destiny came to be symbolized in the soft, almost whispered *a cappella* chant, "The blue bus is calling us…"—a line from Albert's favorite song off of his favorite album by his favorite rock band, "The End" by *The Doors.*

On the way to the bank to close out their accounts:

The blue bus is calling us…

On the way to the package store to buy provisions for their long, cross-continental pilgrimage:

The blue bus is calling us…

Somethin' for Nothin'

Back to their dorm room to gather only their most essential belongings, including swim suits, Cheryl Tiegs and Farrah Fawcett posters, as well as cassette tapes of *Lynyrd Skynyrd, The Rolling Stones* and, of course, *The Doors:*

The blue bus is calling us…

Watching their text books, piled along the banks of the Olentangy River, doused with gasoline and burning brightly:

The blue bus is calling us…

All the way to Indiana:

The blue bus is calling us…

Thursday morning at the rest stop, after squinting silently into the sun for what seemed like hours, Albert began chanting their mantra:

The blue bus is calling us…

Calm immediately crossed their troubled countenances. Peace reclaimed their souls. Their thoughts became focused on *The Big Picture* and the mission they shared. Their lives came to have purpose and meaning again.

Albert and Waxy got back into Albert's blue Ford panel van and merged onto Interstate 70, westbound.

~~~

Gateway to the West

"Oh, he'll kill me, of course," Albert answered Waxy as they crossed the mighty Mississippi through the shadow of the giant stainless steel arch built in St. Louis to represent the "Gateway to the West." With four weeks until the statement closing date on his father's Visa account—a plastic passkey to which waited on DEFCON 2 red alert in Albert's wallet like a Minuteman intercontinental ballistic missile snug in its silo—plus ten working days allowed for bank processing and U.S. Postal Service delivery of the bill to the Stiles abode in suburban Akron-Canton, Waxy and Albert allotted five weeks to take "The Scenic Route" via Salt Lake City, Las Vegas, Los Angeles and San Francisco, on their way to Alaska. "But, then again, what are fathers for?"

"Pa's gonna beat me like a red-headed step child," Waxy moaned, weaving into the passing lane without signaling.

"I'm telling you, we'll make it up to them in spades. Five C-notes a day. Three grand a week. One hundred fifty-six big bazangas a year! Not bad for a couple of dudes bounced out of *The* Buckeye Whatsamatta U., eh? And we're not even twenty-one yet. Who needs that Nazi Nietzsche any who?"

"I wouldn't go filling out no 1040 forms in ink just yet, if I were you."

"I'm gonna buy him that cherry red '57 *T-Bird* he pines away for in his heart. Have I ever told you that my old man has the largest private collection of used Ford *Pintos* this side of the Iron Curtain?"

"Only about every thirteen miles."

"It is truly amazing that the family homestead was never consumed in a spontaneous eruption of flames. Of course, what did he expect with eight horny little Catholics running around primed to live adolescence to the fullest—*'give us puberty or give us death'*—was our battle cry. He should have thought of that before he popped off on Mom all those times."

"Treat every firearm as if they was loaded with live ammunition. That's what Pa always told me."

"You know, I'll bet the Pope's got a piece of the action in the used car market for himself. Who else but the Vatican could possibly be behind all those bad salesmen in bad rugs making excruciatingly bad used car ads on late night TV? It is positively diabolical. Get me *60 Minutes* on the phone. Hello Mike? How's it hanging, babe? Have I got a hot scoop for you."

"What does your dad do, anyway?"

"The Field Marshal—as we affectionately refer to him—is the Steel Belted Radial Czar of Akron. Loyal disciples come from the far flung corners of the world to pay him homage and, yea verily, to kiss his tread."

"How come you call him the Field Marshal?"

"Cause he drives his tank of a Mercedes sedan like he's Rommel storming across North Africa."

"And you're sure he can afford to foot the bill for this?"

"*Waxy, Waxy, Waxy*—it's irrelevant at best. You have got to understand that we have an obligation—nay, a sacred duty to do this very deed we so selflessly set out to do. No one will deny that success is a son's Holy Grail to seek—*eventually*. In the mean

Somethin' for Nothin'

time, though, we have to help our fathers out by giving them the cannon fodder for their war stories. I don't care whether it's at the Goodyear Annual Interplanetary Tire Salesman Convention or at the Acme Feed and Grain Store of greater Delaware County, when business is put to bed and scotch is flowing freely, the conversation inevitably turns to who has the most frightening juvenile horror story. You know, 'Jesus Christ, you'll never believe what that crazy-ass son of mine, Albert, did this time: he set the God damned cat on fire trying to play lion tamer and that son-of-a-bitching feline raced through the house setting the living room curtains ablaze and scorching the sofa before we could catch it.' And then, of course, Mort from Accounting will try to top that one with a tall tale about the uninhibited antics of his own son. Fat chance of that, though. I'm pretty tough to top."

"Did that cat thing really happen?"

"I was young and quite immature at the time. But no matter. The question before us now, though, is what are we supposed to do, here? Send our fathers out to do battle with, 'that crazy-ass Waxy, he garfed a midterm on Aristotle's *Poetics,* can you imagine that?' Oh, I'll bet that'll just split the sides of the boys at *The Stag Bar* in downtown Delaware right open and spill their spindly intestines all over creation when your old man tosses it out for them to chaw on."

"Nobody in my family ever even got to go to college before. I'll be slopping hogs till the day I die."

"Are you kidding me? We'll be thirty-five and hearing this story with a glazed look in their eyes and a hunk of pride caught in the back of their throats. Then it'll be, 'why, son, when I was your age, I did a crazy thing or two myself...' That's when we find out the real story. Don't you get it? Fathers have to be respectable and upstanding citizens. It's their role in society to be healthy, wealthy and wise—spiffy, nifty and thrifty. They have to attend meetings of the Kiwanis, the Rotary Club and the International Order of Odd Fellows. IIIEEESSSHHH! Can you imagine? Just the thought sends a chill through my spine. They can't do shit like this anymore, so we have to do it for them. That's what sons are for, Waxy. That's our mission in life, until we get to be dads and have sons of our own to piss and moan about ourselves."

"He's gonna beat me like a red-headed step child."

"It's the final frontier. It's the only chance we'll ever get to let our American pioneer spirit out of this gilded cage called the Twentieth Century to soar untethered across the horizon—like prospecting during the California Gold Rush—like taming the Wild, Wild West—like laying the transcontinental railway—like digging the Panama Canal." Albert sighed mightily. "It is our duty as sons, as citizens, as men, to embark on this bold journey to the far fringes of the wilderness of this great land of ours to seek our fortunes."

"I really didn't think I'd need my galoshes till we got there."

"Whatever else happens, it's going to be one hell of an adventure, Waxy."

Waxy thought for a moment. "Yeah. It is, isn't it."

"We'll have our kids and grand kids bored to tears every time we tell them about it. It'll be great. I seriously cannot wait."

Waxy recalled his own hours of merciless boredom at the hands of elder relatives. "You are a work of art, you know that? King of the hill of bullshit if ever there was one."

"Trust me. Have I ever been wrong yet?"

Somethin' for Nothin'

"Only about Philosophy 101."

"Yeah, well, everybody has an off day every now and then."

Albert would have another "off day" shortly after they arrived in Anchorage, when *The Big Picture* suffered a catastrophic tent-pole failure.

~~~

The Lucky Wishbone Diner

They sat a long while, parked on the side of Highway 1 coming out of the Chugach Mountains, staring through the windshield at the lights of Anchorage, a glittering pool of civilization spilt like milk beside Cook's Inlet in the foggy dusk, an oasis to slake their thirst of loneliness after two thousand miles of travel through desolate Canadian wilderness.

Albert reached between the seats for the last, nearly empty bottle of Yukon Jack. He held it up in toast, "It is the call of the wild, my friend. The call of the fucking wild."

Albert took a pull and passed the bottle to Waxy. "No man of reason can dispute this."

When they had finished off the bottle, Waxy put the blue Ford panel van into gear and Albert tossed the empty Yukon Jack bottle out the window to shatter on the shoulder of the road.

They drove around downtown Anchorage, gulping down the uniquely municipal manifestation of humanity's presence which seemed so foreign to them now after a near terminally long absence since leaving Seattle. After circling back past the *Lucky Wishbone Diner* for what seemed to be at least the ninth or tenth time, they pulled in and grabbed a booth across from the counter.

"Tomorrow, man, tomorrow we strike it rich," said Albert.

Waxy paid no attention, having tuned out his partner's three day monologue marathon a mere two hundred miles into British Columbia. He was mesmerized by the young waitress in their section, scurrying between tables.

"Welcome to the *Bone*. My name is Emma and I'll be your server tonight," she said, delivering two glasses of water and menus. Waxy grabbed his glass and began gulping. He ogled Emma's jet black hair and broad smile spread across her pretty Native American face. She eyed them suspiciously, having easily pegged them as new arrivals from the lower forty-eight with the help of Waxy's Ohio State ball cap and Albert's Cleveland *Indians* sweat shirt. "Our chef's specials today are Salisbury Steak, Meatloaf and Chopped Sirloin Wellington."

"What's the difference?" asked Albert.

"You're right. We're all going to die one day, so what is the difference?"

"No. I mean between the specials."

"Gravy. No gravy. Crust."

"I'll go gravy," blurted out Waxy. "With a large whole milk and pie. Blueberry. And more water, please."

"Right." Emma wrote down Waxy's order then pointed her pen at Albert. "And you?"

"Jesus, look at these prices," Albert said as he flipped through the menu. "I don't see a highway nearby, but I'm sure I'm being robbed."

"Welcome to the final frontier, slick."

"How about eagle eggs over easy, reindeer back bacon and caribou milk," Albert shot back, confirming her suspicions.

"Right. Now, seriously."

"Don't you have anything like an Arctic Omelet? You know like a Denver Omelet only, like, from Alaska?"

Somethin' for Nothin'

"A Denver Omelet?"

"No, an Arctic Omelet?"

"What's that?"

"Oh, never mind. How about Flapjacks?"

"Can do."

"And back bacon?"

Emma cocked her head and telegraphed her impatience with a smirk.

"Okay. Regular bacon—extra crispy."

"Can do." Emma turned, rolled her eyes back and headed towards the kitchen to put in their order.

Waxy watched her girlish figure move seductively beneath the baggy waitress dress as she walked away.

Albert watched Waxy watch Emma and shook his head. He surveyed the sparse crowd in the *Lucky Wishbone Diner*. His eye was drawn to an Hispanic man in a booth across the dining room, dressed as if he had just received a delivery from L.L. Bean and had not even taken the tags off the clothes. A lanky man in a leather aviator's jacket and Boston *Red Sox* baseball cap came in and sat down at the booth with the L.L. Bean customer. Albert turned back to his companion and watched Waxy follow Emma around the dining room. Waxy squirmed uncomfortably when she greeted the lanky man with a friendly hand on his shoulder, betraying a coveted familiarity.

"Put a sock on it already, Pablo. Do ten pushups."

"Hey, I never met a real, live Eskimo before," Waxy whined sheepishly. "She's pretty."

"Nanootchka of the North."

Emma returned to deliver Waxy's milk.

"So, where do we go to get the pipeline jobs?" Albert asked her.

"Down at the west end of Sixth. There's a trailer," Emma said, looking deliberately from Albert to Waxy. "Just make sure you get there early, boys."

"How come?"

Emma just smiled knowingly and turned to fetch their dinners.

"What?" Waxy blurted out in the same confused surprise as when he let Albert talk him into registering for the Introduction to Philosophy class. He looked at Albert.

"Come on, she's just yanking us. That's what townies do."

"But—"

"Trust me."

They ate their dinners and drove to the end of Sixth Avenue to find the Alaska State Employment office and the mobile home trailer right where Emma said it would be. They then found an out of the way parking spot up near the train yard to try to catch some shuteye between the yard signals and Rule 14L crossing blasts from the locomotive horns.

When they got to the State Unemployment offices by mid-morning the next day, a long line had already formed outside the trailer, much to their dismay, so they joined the tail end.

"No problem," Albert said, sizing up the competition in line ahead of them. "Hear me? No problem. Look at these losers. No prob."

"How long you think this is gonna take?" Waxy asked. "I'm kind of hungry."

"We'll be picking permafrost out of our hair by lunch."

As they shuffled their way to the door, Albert preached the gospel of *The Big Picture* to an apostle filled with doubt.

Once the line got inside, they were assaulted with a cacophony of clerical chatter and clatter from Alaska state

Somethin' for Nothin'

employees parked at folding tables crammed into the single large room taking up the entire trailer's inside space, interviewing pipeline worker wannabes squirming in folding chairs and officiously pushing paper hither and yon. When Waxy and Albert reached the front of the line, a large matronly clerk motioned one of them over and Albert nudged Waxy forward. A younger, prettier blonde clerk then motioned Albert over, who winked at Waxy as he passed by.

"Name?" the matronly clerk queried curtly as Waxy sat down across the table from her.

"Wesley Aaron Biederby. They call me Waxy."

"Residency papers."

"Huh? You mean like my Ohio driver's license?"

"When did you move to Alaska?" she asked with a heavy sigh.

"Um, what's today? Tuesday?"

"Well, then, son, you are only three hundred and sixty-three days short of the one year state residency requirement for placement eligibility in a pipeline position."

"Huh?"

"Fill out this form to establish your D-list priority date," she said shuffling official state paperwork across the table to Waxy.

"D-list?"

"And fill this one out to register with the State Unemployment Services Bureau, but I have to warn you that there are far more individuals registered than there are jobs available. And, of course, without any earnings within the state of Alaska during the past twelve months, you will not be eligible for state unemployment benefits or food stamps."

"But, Albert said, you know, *The Big Picture...*"

"Son, we don't have an Albert that works here." She slammed a rubber stamp against yet more paperwork with an aggression that belied a rage simmering beneath the surface like a volcanic lava dome. She passed the government consecrated forms across the table, then summarily dismissed Waxy with a loud bark, *"NEXT!"*

As Waxy walked towards the exit in a daze, feeling like a pork shoulder being processed into sausage in a meat packing plant, he noticed Albert making time with the pretty blonde clerk, laughing and carrying on like it was a party. He went outside and waited for Albert, watching from across the street the line that never seemed to end or shrink leading into the government meat grinder.

Considering the quick and ruthless dispatching of Waxy's hopes for gainful employment, he could not imagine what was taking Albert so long inside the trailer. He paced restlessly up and down the block across the street from the mobile home trailer, yearningly watching the exit door like Old Yeller, until Albert bounded out with a spring in his step and jaywalked across K Street. Halfway down the block to Waxy, Albert was accosted by an unshaved, raggedly dressed man from deep within a doorway.

"Hey, kid. Yeah. Yeah, you."

Albert stopped short and looked curiously at the man.

"Yeah. You. You want a job, don't you? I got one for you." The man wiped his arm beneath his nose. "I got a B-List slot. Top job. Top dollar. You can have it for the right price."

"Who do I look like? Monte Hall?"

"Or you can starve to death in the cold, asshole."

Somethin' for Nothin'

Albert waved his hand across his nose. "Seriously. Soap. Water. Try it sometime."

The man stared Albert down.

"Yeah, well, what have you got?"

Waxy watched the exchange from down the block, wondering what they were talking about.

"Ten grand gets you working tomorrow," said the man.

"Get out of town."

"It's a B-List card. Top job. Top dollar. Come on, college boy. What else are you gonna do? Figure it out. You got no union card. I'm figuring you got no trade. Got no time in country—you probably never worked a day in your life. Huh?"

"Ten grand is stiff."

"Sell your car. You won't need it in camp. Besides you'll make it back in a few weeks."

"Sell the Blue Bus?"

"What else are you gonna do, college boy?"

"Fuck off, old man. How good could it be if you're getting your mail delivered to a lamp post?" Albert started to walk away.

The man stepped out from the doorway and grabbed Albert's shoulder with his left hand.

"Hey, dude," Albert said, turning to confront him,

"It was a hell of good living until a cable snapped." The man raised his right hand to Albert's face, showing him a palm and thumb, but no fingers.

Albert shook the other hand off his shoulder and silently backed away.

"What do you think? It's all just a big game? Eh, college boy?"

Albert turned away and hurried down the block towards Waxy.

"What did that guy want?"

"Him?" Albert looked back over his shoulder at the man. "Nothing. Spare change, you know."

"What took you so long?"

"Hey, Anna's lonely. Her husband's been up at Prudhoe Bay for the past couple of months and I think she's getting frisky."

"Great. How, exactly, does that help us?"

"I know. I know. I know. She also said that we can buy our way onto the C-List, just like her husband did. They're from Minnesota and they've only been here seven months"

"Seven months? If this ain't lightnin' striking the outhouse, I don't know what is," Waxy exclaimed. "How are we going to survive for seven months?"

Albert looked back at the man in the doorway.

The man waved back at Albert with his mangled hand.

"You hungry?" Albert asked turning back to Waxy.

"I'm starved."

"Well, my friend, if we're going to starve to death, it might as well be on a full stomach."

"You think the Field Marshall's Visa card is still good?"

"Well, I say we find out. What do you think? Caribou burgers—medium rare—and a couple chocolate mooseshakes."

Waxy and Albert walked up K Street and turned down Fourth Avenue, looking for a place to eat.

~~~

Fenway Park West

"Hey, I think this might be the place," Albert said, stopping in front of a bar called *Beantown Bob's Fenway Park West*. He pressed his face against the window to peer inside. "I think providence may have delivered us."

"Where East Meets West," Waxy read the flashing neon sign and shrugged his shoulders. "What the hell. I'm getting cold."

"Stop whining already," Albert said, pushing into the bar.

Waxy followed and immediately noted the stale smell of spilled beer that brought back dreaded memories of the campus bars on High Street in Columbus, where their adventure began. "I'm getting an ugly sense of *déjà vu.*"

"Yes, sir. This is it. This is it." Albert inhaled deeply. "Note the delicate bouquet of Schlitz with just a hint of Miller High Life and a quite pleasant Pabst Blue Ribbon after taste. Any bar that captures the aromatic essence of downtown Milwaukee has got to rate four stars in the *Mobile Travel Guide.*"

Albert let his eyes adjust to the dim lighting inside and led Waxy to a middle booth against the front window facing the bar under the watchful eyes of the few patrons scattered haphazardly about, mostly men on the downhill side of life, hunched over their afternoon boilermakers.

They sat down in the booth and silently absorbed the ambiance of *Fenway Park West,* carefully surveying the decor which included pictures of Ted Williams, Carlton Fisk, Luis Tiant, Carl Yastrzemski, along with a fair amount of sports memorabilia—bats, balls, hats, helmets and jerseys—nested amidst a hodgepodge of road signs from across Alaska and Canada, a weird assortment of airplane, bus and automobile parts that might well have been collected at accident sites, and a zoo's worth of taxidermy. There appeared to be much to recommend about this watering hole on first glance, including but not limited to a whole back room fully equipped with nearly every pinball and arcade machine known to man, a stage for a band and a multi-colored, lighted disco dance floor—and yet Beantown Bob had still been able to maintain a certain frontier charm in his establishment.

"WARNING: MOTORISTS FREEZE BEFORE BRIDGES," Albert read out loud the yellow highway warning sign hung over the bar. "We have arrived my friend. We have definitely arrived."

Waxy was fascinated by the eight-and-a-half foot specimen of genuine Kodiak bear enshrined upright on his back legs in attack stance by a skillful taxidermist and strategically placed in a corner adjacent to the juke box. His eyes were then drawn to an impassive Eskimo sitting alone at the end of the bar by the door to the kitchen, who, Waxy decided, might well have been taken for being stuffed himself were it not for the regular movement of his hands to and from his mouth—the right with a cigarette and the left with a tumbler of straight whiskey that did not even induce a facial grimace like it always did to Waxy. Waxy reflexively began a mental dialog with himself, debating whether the apron hung from the Eskimo's neck, across his chest and over the front of his black and white

Somethin' for Nothin'

checked trousers that were two-and-a-half sizes too big meant that the Alaskan native before his eyes was the cook or the dishwasher.

Albert's gaze gravitated to the only female in the bar, a young, Madonna-faced beauty with long reddish-brown hair who sat at a table near the stage with a skinny male about his own age, who absently twirled a drum stick in his left hand. The pair passed a pad of paper back and forth, pointing, commenting, scribbling, scratching out previous scribblings and scribbling some more. Dylan Roberts and his sister CiCi were negotiating the set list of songs they would perform that evening with their band, *Torchlight*.

CiCi wrote, then pushed the pad to Dylan. She planted her chin in her palm and looked away from her brother, scanning the bar until she noticed Albert staring at her.

Albert smiled at CiCi.

CiCi motioned her head towards Dylan and rolled her eyes.

Dylan pushed the pad back and pointed to a song on the list.

CiCi smiled and looked away from Albert.

"What do you guys need?" asked Eddie the bartender who startled both Waxy and Albert from their people watching when he suddenly appeared at their table.

"Need?" Waxy asked.

"Caribou steaks—this thick," Albert spread his thumb and index finger two inches apart.

"How do you want those steaks cooked?"

"You really have caribou steaks?" asked Waxy.

"Could you tell the difference?"

"I don't know. Do they taste like venison?"

"No. More like Holsteins."

"Excellent. Excellent," said Albert, rubbing his hands together. "Medium rare for me."

"Medium well," said Waxy. "I like my game meat cooked."

"Got it," said Eddie

"And, good sir, two Moosehead lagers and Yukon Jack shooters for my esteemed colleague and I." As Eddie returned to the bar, Albert looked back over at Dylan and CiCi, just in time to see her look away from his direction. He smiled.

"What are we going to do?" whined Waxy.

"Huh?"

"A one-year residency requirement? What are we going to do?"

"Who knew? Come on, it's not like we missed that particular class lecture," said Albert. "I suspect that Kragies must have read our blue books and scrambled out the door in a flurry of philosophy midterms to get word out on the wire to the FBI, the CIA, Interpol and the ASPCA. That shriveled up prune has black balled us, Waxy. If only she could cannibalize her own body and shit herself into oblivion the world would be a better place and we'd have our pipeline jobs by now."

Waxy just shook his head.

"If someone—*anyone* could just take five minutes and explain to me what some crazy-assed Greek geek named Heraclitus has to do with putting a four foot glorified sewer pipe across the Alaskan wilderness, I'd...I'd...I'd..."

"You'd what?"

"I might read the son-of-a-bitch, for Christ sake."

"Pull yourself together. This is no time to get hysterical,"

Somethin' for Nothin'

Waxy said with a hint of malevolence in his voice. "I don't want to have to slap you around—not too much, anyway."

For a moment, Albert wasn't quite sure whether Waxy was kidding or not. "Am I going to be hounded to my grave by the furies of unfinished homework for this one little, stupid mistake?"

"I reckon the connection between ancient Greece and our particular situation here is that you can't step in the same shit twice," Waxy offered. "Least ways, I hope not."

"Very funny, Waxy. A regular Bob *FUCKING* Hope you are."

"Okay, Hope and Crosby, here are your drinks," said Eddie the bartender, returning with their shots and beers. "How do you want to take care of this?"

"Just run a tab for us," said Albert, handing Eddie the Field Marshall's Visa card.

The steaks were thick and delicious, though not caribou. As they ate and drank, and drank some more, *Fenway Park West* slowly filled with working types from the businesses and offices in Anchorage, older than Albert and Waxy, but younger than the ghostly, middle-aged men who had been there when they first arrived and who now hungrily ogled the thirty-something women, who nursed their first drinks, which they bought themselves, waiting for the band, the flirting and the dancing to begin.

By the time *Torchlight* took the stage there was a respectable crowd that was audibly absorbed by their loudly amplified covers of southern California country-rock style favorites from Linda Ronstadt, *The Eagles, Little Feat,* Bonnie Raitt, Jackson Browne and others. The energy level in the bar rose and Albert hopped up from the booth to fetch another round of drinks, stopping along the way, to and fro, to talk to small klatches of women.

On his third trip for drinks, he detoured to the dance floor with a blonde that he had culled from her friends. They stayed on the lighted disco dance floor for a second slow dance, when CiCi, spotting Albert who had deliberately worked his partner up to the front of the stage, sang Karla Bonoff's "Someone to Lay Down Beside Me." Waxy watched from the booth like a solitary *Red Sox* fan in the bleachers. When the song ended, Albert spoke to CiCi, who had to lean down close to hear him, carefully cradling her Martin D-18 guitar in her arms. She laughed, shook her head as she stood back up straight again and watched Albert lead his dance partner back to the bar, glancing repeatedly back over his shoulder at the stage.

Albert bought the band a round and towed Misty, his dance partner, and her two friends over to the booth with fresh drinks in their hands. Up close the women appeared a bit more weathered than they had from afar.

"This, girls, is my legal advisor, Laslo," Albert said as he was sandwiched in between Misty and Eileen, while Karen sat down on the other side of the booth, pushing Waxy over towards the window with her hips. "And as an attorney, he rarely exhibits a positive attitude towards any activity that may entail a possible legal entanglement, potential liability, litigation or adverse risk exposure. Laslo, do you have the release forms for them to sign?"

"Huh?" asked Misty.

"Don't mind him. He's just being his usual sour puss self."

"Pleased to meet you, Laslo," said Karen in a husky voice, leaning in against his body.

Somethin' for Nothin'

"Ah, I'm, uh, Waxy,"

"Are you guys brothers?" Eileen asked pointing back and forth from Albert-to-Waxy-to-Albert, "Because you don't look like brothers."

"No, ma'am. We are—were roommates at Ohio State," answered Waxy, while Albert whispered something in Misty's ear.

"The Ohio State University," corrected Albert.

"The College? In Ohio?" asked Karen. "I was near Ohio once."

"I was near it once, too," said Waxy. "But now, I'm not."

"Hey, Waxy, I asked, but the band doesn't know 'North to Alaska'," explained Albert.

"The Johnny Horton song?" asked Misty.

"Yeah. Oddly enough, we found a cassette of it in Oakley, Kansas—home of the world's largest prairie dog and a five-legged goat—the sixteen thousand two hundred seventy-seventh and seventy-eighth wonders of the world, respectively—while we were having the water pump on the Blue Bus replaced."

"World's largest prairie dog?"

"Shhhh…it's not real."

"Yeah, it's just a stupid statue," explained Waxy.

"But it's like ten feet tall—Paul Bunyan-sized," exclaimed Albert.

"That's funny," chortled Eileen.

Albert pulled Eileen to the dance floor where he divided his attention between her and CiCi for a couple of songs before returning to the booth with another round of drinks.

The evening slowly dissolved into a foggy swirl of drinking, dancing, conversing and carousing, until closing time, when Eddie approached the booth with their tab.

"Hey, sport," Eddie said, tossing the Field Marshall's Visa card onto the table. "Declined."

Misty, Eileen and Karen excused themselves quickly and stumbled toward the exit. Waxy and Albert were the last patrons left. CiCi watched from the stage as she put her guitar away in the case.

"You ever seen *White Heat?*" Albert asked Eddie. "With Jimmy Cagney?"

"Nope."

"Top of the world, Pa," Albert called out and gulped down the last of his last Moosehead lager. "Top of the world...*literally.*"

Dylan and CiCi walked towards the door. Albert followed them, until CiCi looked over and met his gaze with a sympathetic smile before leaving Waxy and Albert alone with Eddie in the bar.

"And you were afraid we wouldn't get jobs in Alaska," Albert chided Waxy just a half hour later. "I have to admit, though, that I am not entirely pleased with Beantown Bob's sartorial selection for his employees."

Waxy and Albert were dressed in the same over-sized black and white checked pants and stiffly starched white aprons and shirts as the Eskimo they had seen earlier at the bar. Moe the Eskimo, as Albert referred to him because of his haircut's resemblance to the more aggressive of the Three Stooges, was the cook.

"Did you have to buy drinks for everybody in the place?" Waxy asked as he sorted silverware at the clean side of the dishwasher in the kitchen.

"I'll have to admit that Bob does do a far better trade in his *Fenway Park* as the evening wears on than I thought he might,

Somethin' for Nothin'

but buying a round of drinks for our new found friends seemed the appropriate thing to do."

"Three times?"

As Waxy washed dishes, Albert stood at his side and soliloquized on the virtues of manual labor. Later, he argued passionately, eloquently, yet unsuccessfully with Moe the Eskimo, that to mop the floors would jeopardize Beantown Bob's four-star rating in the *Mobile Travel Guide*.

Their mopping was interrupted by sounds from above: Step-step-THUMP! Step-step-THUMP! Step-step-THUMP!

Beantown Bob had lost three toes off his right foot to frostbite working on the North Slope Haul Road from Fairbanks to Deadhorse in preparation for the building of the Trans Alaska Pipeline System, but that short stint of manual labor, a disability settlement and the syndicated series of articles he wrote about that experience bankrolled his beloved *Fenway Park West*, so he figured he came out about even on the deal. He grew up in the bleachers of the real Fenway Park and had come to Alaska fresh out of college to be the sports writer for the *Anchorage Daily News*. He used every bit of his creative writing skills to provide on-the-scene coverage of major sporting events live from the UP and AP wire service machines in the dreary newsroom until the glamour of the newspaper game began to fade, the spigot of petrodollars opened up, and he could finally afford to buy the bar he had haunted religiously with tall tales of sluggers, stuffers and stickers to escape the grind at the *Daily News*.

The inside of *Fenway Park West* opened clear through to the second floor with offices over the kitchen and the pinball room facing out over the back alley. On the catwalk that ran

along the front of the offices and looked down over the bar
and the multi-colored, lighted disco dance floor, Albert and
Waxy heard Beantown Bob punctuate his steps with the
business end of a 'Ted Williams' Louisville Slugger, a prized
souvenir of his childhood, that he used as a makeshift
Shillelagh: step-step-THUMP! Step-step-THUMP!

Albert and Waxy quickly mopped themselves into
inconspicuous corners of the bar: Albert into the doorway of
the pinball room and Waxy into the shadow of the eight-and-
a-half foot Kodiak bear by the juke box. They watched as
Beantown Bob step-step-THUMPed over to the bar and
wordlessly put every molecule of his six foot, three inch, two
hundred sixty pound frame behind a picture perfect swing for
the fences that connected with a rack of glasses Waxy had just
finished washing, drying and stacking on the bar.

"You've been in the pie, you fucker," Beantown Bob poked
Eddie in the chest with the business end of the Louisville
Slugger. "Haven't you?"

"Come on, Bob. You—"

"I told you about your fingers in the pie—in *my pie*.
Didn't I?"

"But Bob—"

From the tenor of the twenty-minute tirade of abuse
Beantown Bob heaped upon Eddie, it seemed that there was
more to his transgressions than skimming cash register
receipts or pouring free drinks. While Albert and Waxy were
content to watch with rapt attention from the bleachers, Moe
the Eskimo came out of the kitchen and got a box seat at the
bar to spectate behind a haze of blue cigarette smoke and a
tumbler of whiskey. A hairline crack of a smile parted his lips.

Somethin' for Nothin'

"Either of you two numb nuts ever tend bar?" Beantown Bob bellowed out into the dark reaches where Albert and Waxy had sought refuge. They both slowly stepped back out into the open.

Albert, of course, spoke up immediately, "Well, I—"

"Great. You're hired. Start tomorrow." Beantown Bob went behind the bar and emptied the cash register drawer. As he walked past Albert by the door to the pinball room on his way upstairs again, he looked down, nearly nose-to-nose into his face. "But if I ever catch you with your fingers in my pie, I'm going to stick your head into an empty whiskey bottle just like a fucking Tom and Jerry cartoon. Got it?"

"Got it," Albert echoed faintly.

"If you and your buddy need a place to stay, there's an apartment soon to be for rent upstairs. Eddie will be out tomorrow. Five hundred a month."

"Great."

Beantown Bob yelled back at Eddie, "Didn't I tell you to get the fuck out of here?"

Albert and Waxy listened to the step-step-THUMP! step-step-THUMP! as Beantown Bob went upstairs to the office to count the night's receipts.

Eddie yanked off his apron and scowled at Albert. "I saw you man."

"Huh? What? Who me?" Albert feigned innocence. "What do you mean?"

"CiCi. She's Bob's." Eddie put on his coat and headed towards the door. "You didn't think he was talking about apple pie, did you? She's trouble. You'll see."

When Eddie left and the door to Beantown Bob's office above slammed shut, Waxy dropped his mop and ran over to Albert and whispered, "Are you nuts? Are you out of your ever lovin' tree?"

"Out of my tree? Are you kidding me? I haven't even finished out my first shift here at *Fenway Park* and I got myself a promotion."

"You don't know a dang thing about being a bartender."

"What's to know? You don't have to be Louie Pasteur to figure out which end of a beer can to open up. Lighten up already; nobody ever got nominated for a Nobel Prize for tending bar. Plus now we don't have to sleep in the Blue Bus any more. Did I tell you things would work out or what?"

Moe the Eskimo shook his head as his right arm pumped a cigarette and his left arm pumped the tumbler of whiskey to and from his mouth.

~~~

Jimmi the Pilot

"B.B.! *My man!*" a tall, lanky young man called out in a severe Texas drawl as he was ushered into *Fenway Park West* by a gust of cold evening air.

While Albert watched himself push his dinner aimlessly around on his plate, Waxy and Moe the Eskimo looked up from the gourmet, open-faced, barbecue baloney sandwiches they were eating at the end of the bar by the kitchen to take note of Jimmi the Pilot's entrance.

Beantown Bob groaned and wrung his hands around an imaginary baseball like a pitcher with the bases loaded desperately trying to get his fastball hopping. Jimmi the Pilot was a week late. For the past six nights, Beantown Bob had been tormented by recurring nightmares about his half-share of $50,000 worth of cocaine (wholesale) dusting a forest somewhere or sinking into the bottom of some body of water along the route or vaporizing in a giant, aviation-fueled, free-basing explosion at ten thousand feet.

Jimmi the Pilot was only twenty-eight, but, like most who had weathered several Alaskan winters, he looked much older. Even Beantown Bob himself, who was only twenty-nine, looked thirty-seven—at least he did to Albert and Waxy. Jimmi's ears hung out like a Cessna's full flaps on final approach and he wore a grin flash frozen on his face as if he had heard the best joke of his life staring straight into a one hundred twenty below zero wind chill. He was dressed in a leather Naval Aviator jacket, a souvenir—along with a gimp left leg—of his brief, but colorful, military service career flying an A-4 *Skyhawk* off the USS *Forrestal* in the South China Sea until a North Vietnamese surface-to-air missile caused a catastrophic deviation from his flight plan. Pushed back jauntily on top of his head full of reddish-brown hair was a Boston *Red Sox* baseball cap, a gift from a dear friend. He limped over and parked himself on the bar stool next to that dear friend and illicit business associate. He watched the waves of concern at high tide beat against the beach of Beantown Bob's brow. With a quick wink and a nod, he calmed those troubled waters and initiated their almost religiously ritualistic greeting ceremony. "How's Lucille been treating you good buddy?"

"The thrill is gone," Beantown Bob replied in the best gravelly, Mississippi Delta, blues man voice he could muster. In spite of the mass oral infusions of bourbon Jimmi the Pilot had administered while playing records by B.B. King, Albert King, Freddie King, Earl Hooker, Muddy Waters, Mississippi Freddie McDowell, Howlin' Wolf, *et al*, at maximum sound pressure levels, Beantown Bob still sounded more like John F. Kennedy than John Lee Hooker. "You gots to pay your dues if-en you wants to sing dem blueses."

"Ask not what the Blues can do for you, but what you can do for the Blues."

"Boogie 'til you barf."

"You know, B.B., if the river was whiskey, I'd be a diving duck."

Somethin' for Nothin'

In unison, they wailed an off-key blues riff: *"I'd dive to the bottom and drink my way back up."*

"Stiles! Get this floppy-eared, shit-eating, son-of-a-bitching Texan a boilermaker."

"Got yourself a couple of fresh D-Listers, I see," Jimmi the Pilot said, watching Albert drag himself away from his dinner and trudge behind the bar to pour a shot and pop the top off a long neck bottle of Budweiser. "They just never learn that you don't come to the Great White North unless you already got yourself a job, do they."

"Nah. They just keep coming and coming like God damn lemmings into the God damn sea. Course, I'd be wicked shit out of luck for kitchen help without them."

"So, what happened to Eddie? He get a job with Uncle Al," Jimmi the Pilot asked, referring to the Alyeska Oil Company, which was building the Trans Alaska Pipeline.

"He got a little too greedy. I can only overlook so much, you know. And besides, I didn't like the way he was giving CiCi the eye."

"That'll be five-fifty," Albert said with obvious impatience and, perhaps, a touch of malice in his voice, as if he had not been gagging on the Oscar Mayer baloney slices swimming in tepid barbecue sauce that Moe the Eskimo had prepared for dinner.

"Shit damn, B.B., I ain't been gone that long, have I?"

"Stiles, you moron, this is my personal envoy to Latin America. He has spared no expense or risk to return immediately with news of delicate, top level, foreign trade negotiations initiated at my behest." Albert watched with disdain as Beantown Bob and Jimmi the Pilot poked one another in the ribs with their elbows and cackled at their own inside joke. "He drinks for free."

"Jimmi's my name. Glad to meet you, Stiles good buddy." Jimmi stood up and held out his hand. It got heavy as Albert let it just hang in mid air over the bar. Jimmi slowly sat back down. "Jesus H., where do you find these guys, B.B., Akron, Ohio?"

"As a matter of fact, I am from Akron."

More cackles, chuckles and rib poking on the customer side of the bar.

"Yeah, his father is the steel belted radial czar of the free world or some damn thing—ain't that right, Stiles," Beantown Bob said between guffaws.

"And what do you have against Akron?"

"Nothin' boy. 'Ceptin' it just seems like a good place to be from—if you catch my drift."

"Yeah, I catch your drift. And which one of them stinking Texas feed lots with an illiterate excuse for a mayor do *you all* hail from cowpoke? Bootlick, Texas, home of the Barbed Wire Fence Museum and the Rodeo Tabernacle Choir—the four hundred ninety-fifth and seven hundred twenty-third wonders of the world respectively?"

"Son, I don't think I think much of your attitude towards the Lone Star State." Jimmi the Pilot stopped laughing.

"Aw, when it comes to thinking, you Aggies are all alike. If you get your heads turned just right the wind whistles 'The Yellow Rose of Texas' right through your ears."

Beantown Bob tried unsuccessfully to whistle "The Yellow Rose of Texas" between his increasing gusts of laughter.

Waxy couldn't believe what he was hearing. He glanced sideways over at Moe the Eskimo who slurped up the last of

Somethin' for Nothin'

his barbecued baloney with the help of a folded-over slice of week old Wonder Bread, his eyes fixed firmly on Albert and Jimmi the Pilot.

Jimmi the Pilot downed his shot. He stood up. Poking Albert in the solar plexus with his index finger, he said, "How 'bout I just hit you so hard that I make change for every bill in your wallet?"

Albert stared back across the bar and up into Jimmi the Pilot's menacingly grinning face.

Beantown Bob rested his chin on his palm and watched with amusement dancing at the ends of his mouth and sparkling in his eyes, thinking how it would serve Albert right to get pounded seriously for his smart-ass mouth. It would also serve Jimmi the Pilot right for being a week late. He couldn't lose either way. As always, his Louisville Slugger was close at hand, just in case things got totally out of control.

Waxy fidgeted nervously on the bar stool.

Moe the Eskimo sat with his eyes glued to the scene like a polar bear watching a seal's blow hole in the ice.

Jimmi the Pilot began clenching and unclenching his fists.

"Shit, Bob, your friend's got no sense of humor whatsoever—as flat as the spare on the Blue Bus," Albert said with a dramatic change in the tone of his voice. He became instantaneously sunny in his disposition. He poured another shot. Slapping Jimmi the Pilot's cheek lightly, he told him,

"It's a joke. J-O-K-E. Ain't you ever had your dank yanked, cowpoke? Sit down and cool your spurs. Fuck 'em, Bob, if they can't take a joke. Just fuck 'em."

Albert walked back to the end of the bar shaking his head and muttering unintelligible insults about Aggies under his breath, occasionally saying loud enough for Jimmi the Pilot and Beantown Bob to hear, "Fuck 'em. Fuck 'em all."

"I reckon it's gonna take a large economy-sized can of Black Flag to kill that bug you got stuck up your ass," Waxy said to Albert. "It's got to be the size of a Buick *Electra Deuce and a Quarter.*"

"You know, Waxy, I'm getting real tired of this fucking job. Lousy pay. Lousy hours. No God damn respect."

"Albert, what are you talking about? We've only been here four days. It's a sweet deal with meals and an apartment to boot. All in all, not a bad way to clock time till we get our residency cards and at least get on the union's C-List. You are just too dad-blamed impatient sometimes."

"I didn't come to Alaska to clock time. I could have done that easy enough in Columbus—where the women don't look like walruses. Look, we've been here four days, right? Well, Waxy, my friend, that's twenty-five hundred bucks we've lost out on. Instead, we get to beat off idiot customers and cockroaches the size of Soviet weight lifters with baseball bats and eat slop like this for dinner." Albert exchanged a hostile look with Moe the Eskimo. "No offense, Moe, but Bob doesn't exactly give you much to work with."

Moe the Eskimo grunted, indecipherable as either agreement or dissent.

Albert picked up his dinner plate and went into the kitchen.

At the other end of the bar, Jimmi the Pilot still stood perplexed, blankly watching Albert and Waxy talk out of earshot. He relaxed, unclenched his fists, and slowly sat back down on his bar stool.

Somethin' for Nothin'

"You know what that little shit told me I should do?" Beantown Bob said, pointing at the door to the kitchen. "He said I should paint that wall there behind us green, just like the left field fence at Fenway, and put a yellow foul line in the corner and paint the distance from home plate on it in big white numbers, three hundred thirty feet."

Jimmi the Pilot pondered for a moment. He downed his second shot. Turning to Beantown Bob, he said, "He's right, you know. Damn near outright fraud to call this place *Fenway Park* without a Green Monster."

"Yeah-yeah-yeah. I know. I know. I should have thought of it myself, though. The kid's from Akron—they don't even have a ball club. And his father's a steel belted radial czar, for Christ's sake."

"You're slipping, B.B."

"And God damn that kid can talk. He's got more bullshit than a Kansas City stockyard. By closing time, this place looks like Pamplona after the bulls have run."

"Stands his ground, too. I like a man who stands his ground. I like that boy. Got a sense of humor, too. Did you hear that crack about the Rodeo Tabernacle Choir? I nearly busted a gut trying to keep from laughing myself. Yes, sir, I like him, B.B. You got a keeper there."

"I'll probably have to give him a raise to keep him, God damn it. He's only been here a week. Won't take him long to figure a way to buy himself off the D-List."

"What about that one," Jimmi the Pilot asked, pointing at Waxy. "He the kid's Tonto?"

"Uh-huh. A package deal. Doesn't talk much, but he seems to get along with Nanuk of the North." Beantown Bob nodded at Moe the Eskimo. Even he did not know the native Alaskan cook's real name. Moe the Eskimo had been inherited from the previous owner of the bar that became *Fenway Park West*.

"That's a big plus. Maybe you won't find the boy hog-tied and hanging naked from a meat hook in the walk-in fridge, like Freddie O." Jimmi the Pilot stood up. "What do you say we make like the little train that could, go upstairs and sniff ourselves a few rails, then run a few errands."

"I think I can—sniff-sniff. I think I can—snort-snort." Beantown Bob stood up and grabbed his Louisville Slugger. The errands he and Jimmi the Pilot ran inevitably involved mass quantities of sex, drugs, rock-'n'-roll and pinball machines and usually took days to complete. "Mr. Ambassador, won't you step into my office? And pray tell, how is Bogota this time of year?"

Just as Beantown Bob and Jimmi the Pilot walked by Waxy and Moe the Eskimo on their way upstairs, the sound of Albert's plate of barbecued Oscar Mayer baloney impacting the wall at warp speed came out of the kitchen. They simultaneously stopped and pivoted their heads towards Waxy.

Waxy cleared his throat as he stood up. "Albert's been a tad cranky lately. He ain't been laid since Vegas."

Waxy stood for a moment, expecting further interrogation.

No questions came, so he turned and went into the kitchen.

~~~

Las Vegas

"Well, it's about God damn time, " Albert said as the Blue Bus crested a hump in the desert on Interstate 15 and the glowing lights of Las Vegas splayed out before them like a puddle of spilt neon on the desert floor.

"Fear and loathing in La-La-Land," Waxy said, mesmerized by the electronic mirage of rubies, emeralds and diamonds there in the sand for the picking. "Just look at that. Red-lining it at two AM."

Albert grunted, indecipherable as either assent or dissent.

"As your attorney, I must advise you to begin drinking heavily," Waxy said.

Another primordial, precognitive grunt from Albert.

"Lighten up already. The worst of it is behind us."

"Thank God for that." Albert had been railing mercilessly against the state of Utah for the past three hundred and fifty miles. Although Waxy was fascinated by the presentation in Salt Lake City of how the early Mormon settlers had been saved by the Romanesque gluttony of sea gulls, which repeatedly binged and purged on swarms of crickets threatening to destroy their crops, thereby earning the distinction of being named the official state bird of land-locked Utah, Albert was manifestly ill-at-ease in a place with so much salt and so little tequila. The "highlight" of their passage through Utah was a repulsive stroll through maroonish clouds of brine shrimp in the Great Salt Lake—hardly the stuff epic journeys are made of, as Albert noted rather bitterly with each and every passing highway mile marker on their way out of town, because certainly theirs was supposed to be an epic American journey.

Meanwhile, Waxy silently imagined himself hurtling through the "vast darkness of space" that was the canyon lands of Utah leading into the Great Basin and, in his mind, the Blue Bus temporarily became Apollo XI. Touchdown in Vegas came not a moment too soon.

"Ah, Houston *****CCCCCKKKKK***** Tranquility Base here. The *Eagle* has landed *****CCCCCKKKKK***** say again, the *Eagle* has landed," Waxy said, trying to humor Albert as he parked the Blue Bus in the lot at Circus-Circus Casino. "That's one small ante for man, one giant wager for the Buckeye state."

Albert turned the engine off and glared at Waxy.

"Gosh dang it all, Albert, what is chawin' at your ass?"

"Nothing, God damn it. Not a thing."

"Well, you just about wore a pair of button holes in that seat all across Utah."

"Let's hoof it." Albert bolted out of the Blue bus and headed for the strip with Waxy in trail.

Before the sun came up that morning, Albert had consumed over half a bottle of Johnny Walker Red Label; had won seven hundred forty-six dollars playing black jack; and had disappeared with the tall, lanky cocktail waitress whose curly blonde hair, high cheek bones and broad, toothy smile detracted from her otherwise not unpretty plainness—Waxy

Somethin' for Nothin'

certainly would not have booted her out of the sack, but he had regularly observed Albert do much better—leaving Waxy to arm wrestle unsuccessfully with nickel slot machines and grimace at the taste of scotch at six o'clock in the morning. Waxy did not really mind being abandoned in Sin City by Albert with too little cash for a hotel room and no keys to the Blue Bus. It had happened innumerable times when they cruised the strip of bars on High Street across from the Ohio State campus. After becoming separated, Waxy would all too often return to their dorm room only to find the trademark Holiday Inn 'DO NOT DISTURB' sign hung on the door. Besides, Waxy could only conclude that in the two and a half weeks since they left Ohio, Albert's testosterone levels had surely reached near toxic levels in his system. Allowances had to be made, especially if they were going to survive two more weeks or so on the road to Alaska.

Whenever Waxy took stock of Albert, as he did for the forty-seven hours and thirty-six minutes he spent wandering aimlessly up and down the Las Vegas strip—and, to be sure, Albert gave Waxy ample and frequent cause for reflection—he always emerged from the inventory with his friendship and loyalty intact to the young man Waxy's mother vehemently swore possessed the very soul of Satan. Of course, her opinion stemmed from a rather unfortunate and precipitous bit of timing, which had, certainly to date, been the watershed event of Waxy's young life.

The very first time roommate met computer-matched roommate, Waxy arrived at their assigned dormitory room at three-thirty in the afternoon to find Albert had already claimed a bed and was in it. The obvious rustling beneath the blankets, though, was not Albert's bony knees. It was his girl friend from Akron, Donna, who chose that very moment to poke her head out from between Albert's legs and from underneath the covers licking her lips, much to the mortal embarrassment of Waxy's God-fearing parents, who had officially escorted their eldest son to his very first day at a noble institute of higher education. Not only was Albert caught enjoying a sexual act that Waxy's mother believed absolutely-positively was illegal in at least forty-seven of the fifty states—including Ohio—Donna was a glossy brunette vision straight out of the six-page magazine spreads that had fertilized Waxy's hormonal imaginings all through high school. Both Waxy and his father were mercilessly reprimanded for impolitely staring as his mother frantically herded them out of the room, but any lingering doubts still troubling Waxy about going away to college thoroughly vaporized.

Not only was there Donna from Akron, there was also Jill from Canton and Kate from Cleveland and Denise from Denison and Mary from Athens and an apparently endless string of *ad hoc* conquests during the fall term, each proclaimed by the dreaded Holiday Inn 'DO NOT DISTURB' sign hanging from the door knob. Even granting the obvious—that the Field Marshal was rich and supplied Albert with abundant cash and credit cards; that Albert had his own set of wheels; and that Albert looked somewhat like the dark-haired, green-eyed male models in Sears and J.C. Penney catalogs—Albert's success with women was beyond Waxy's ability to provide any reasonable explanation or even put forth a plausible hypothesis. Nevertheless, Waxy was bound and determined to hitch himself to this playboy heir to a steel belted radial empire and get himself one hell of a ride.

Somethin' for Nothin'

Second only to Waxy's annoying—to Albert anyway—streak of honesty was his tenacity. Once he put his mind to task or goal, he was a veritable runaway freight train charging down the tracks he laid for himself with no stopping and no turning back. In this case, he ran head-on into Albert's long-standing aversion to any sort of *pro bono* activity. Whether Albert bowed to the inevitable or, perhaps, viewed vanquishing Waxy's virginity as a veritable Mt. Everest of a challenge, worthy of a Sir Edmund Hillary of Sex such as himself, the two became inseparable companions and, eventually, even close friends, as Albert valiantly, yet vainly, attempted to school Waxy in the ways and wiles of love.

"So, the first thing you do when you get back to her dorm room or apartment is go to the bathroom and check out her toothpaste to see if the tube is nice and smooth or if it's all mangled up, so you know what you're in store for."

"I don't get it." Waxy scratched his head.

"Think about it, Waxy!" Albert slapped his forehead. "Think hard!"

The furrows in Waxy's brow slowly smoothed like a plowed field filling with wind-whipped snow. A smile crested and ebbed across his face like a sine wave across an oscilloscope. In dismay, he exclaimed, "But what if I get that far and she up and gets all cross-legged on me?"

"The Stiles Sexual Secret Weapon, developed after years and years of dedicated and diligent lab research and field testing: promise her a Technicolor orgasm."

"Huh?"

"A Technicolor orgasm. Come on, remember Psych 101? And the big debate about whether a person dreams in black-and-white or in color?"

"Uh-huh…" Waxy still didn't have the scent of Albert's trail of thought.

"Same thing. You just sort of get around to asking her whether or not she climaxes in color or in black-and-white."

Waxy nodded his head, but his eyes squinted nearly shut in his desperate effort to comprehend.

"It doesn't even matter if you don't know what you're talking about. She won't know either, but she won't be able to resist the opportunity. Trust me, Waxy. I know what I'm talking about. Just trust me. It works."

"Yeah, but you got the gift of gab. You could talk the Pope into prophylactics."

"You know," Albert said with a sigh of resignation, "the best secret of all is to just listen."

"Listen?"

"Yup. Sure, keep your mouth shut, nod every now and again, grunt or moan, ask a question three or four times an hour—look, every other swinging dick is out there trying to smooth talk a babe into the sack when all she really wants is a little understanding. She wants someone to hear about her problems, to share her hopes and fears and to care whether she feels good or bad. And all you have to do is keep your lips zipped. If girls want to hear speeches, they go to work for McGovern. If they want to fornicate, first they communicate."

"Wow, really?"

"It's a small price to pay."

"Just listen, eh? It sounds too easy."

And Albert nodded his head. But when all his tutoring had come to naught, on the way out of Vegas, Albert used the Field Marshall's Visa card to procure the services of a hooker for Waxy.

Somethin' for Nothin'

"Yes, my friend, Disneyland is, indeed, a blast and a half, but always, always bear in mind that you cannot get a blow job in the Magic Kingdom—even with a three day passport."

~~~

Waxy

Waxy didn't really like washing dishes, *per se,* but there was something about it that appealed to him, especially now that Albert was out front tending bar instead of standing next to him relentlessly lecturing on some arcane aspect of manual labor—always from the spectator's point-of-view, never from a participant's point-of-view. Albert was the ultimate Monday morning quarterback in all matters other than sex. Although most times he made some sense, it did become a bit Kragies-like to listen to after a while. Whether spouted from Socrates or Albert, philosophy was philosophy, which was a subject that didn't really resonate in Waxy and aurally flowed past his ears like water running off of a duck's back.

The thing that Waxy liked best about dish washing was, ironically enough, a bit metaphysical, which was probably why he could not put his finger on what exactly about it appealed to him. The bus tubs came in a mess—a dirty, disorganized jumble of used glassware, utensils and crockery—and went out transformed into the clean, organized raw materials of diner place settings. With his own bare hands, Waxy took hold of chaos and wrestled it into order. Scraping and spraying food bits from plates, corralling glasses, diving deep for errant silverware lost in the depths of garbage at the bottom of the tubs, he blazingly put them all in place on the plastic coated rack and pushed them into the dishwasher's washing chamber, pushing out a clean rack on the other side. Slamming down the door and pressing the button for the wash cycle to begin, Waxy side stepped to the other side to unload the rack of clean dishes, organizing the knives into piles, spoons into platoons, forks into formation, towering up stacks of dishes, cups and saucers. Once the rack was cleared, it was out to the bar to clear tables to feed the ever hungry dishwasher.

The chattering of food on the grill, the rush of water flowing in the dishwasher, the clatter and clapping of dishes and bowls, moved Waxy mysteriously through each day almost before he knew it. Both he and Moe the Eskimo were in sync with the natural beats and rhythms at the very heart of the food service industry. Though he would never say so, Moe the Eskimo, son of the Tundra, felt a kindred brotherhood with Waxy, son of fertile central Ohio farmland. With the tension in the air gone once Albert was out front, these two "country" boys fell into the ebb and flow of kitchen work. Nothing was spoken. It was all understood as only sons of the earth can understand those things which a by-product of suburbia like Albert could not or would not ever comprehend.

Waxy worked hard. The day ran from four in the afternoon to nearly two in the morning. At the end of the day, though, he never felt exhausted. Closing always came before he expected it; and with it time to get the last bus tubs, scrub the pots and pans from Moe the Eskimo and, once the kitchen was squared away, fill the mop bucket to clean out front. Waxy was so thorough and conscientious that Beantown Bob's four-star rating in the *Mobile Travel Guide* initially awarded by Albert upon first entering *Fenway Park West* was in serious jeopardy. This, of

Somethin' for Nothin'

course, pleased not only Moe the Eskimo, but Beantown Bob as well, though he never let on that he noticed one wit that Waxy was doing a better job than anyone expected or anyone had ever done before, except to curse at him for whistling while he worked. When Waxy finished mopping, he and Moe the Eskimo would sit silently at the bar in a nightly ritual of having one last drink after their daily labors, before he would walk up the outside stairs to the second floor apartment he now shared with Albert courtesy of their employer.

Waxy finished his beer and nodded towards his kitchen co-worker. One short, sharp nod from Moe the Eskimo sent Waxy on his way upstairs. He paused out back in the alley to look at the lane of stars visible above his head. His breath no longer puffed up like a factory smoke stack. Slowly, but surely, the days were getting longer. He wondered what it would be like when he and Albert finally experienced the full wrath of an Arctic winter season. But that was many, many months off and such thoughts slowly evaporated from his mind until he was left only feeling great—greatly tired to be sure, but, paradoxically, drained, yet fulfilled—as in the Sartre truism that being is nothingness, which Waxy might have learned had he finished the Philosophy 101 class. Waxy had given his all in the kitchen of *Fenway Park West* and was much the better for it. But of course, Waxy wasn't one to be philosophical about things. He was grounded in the grunt and sweat of reality, of things seen, not things unseen. He savored the warm, good feeling coursing in his blood until he mounted up the stairs and saw hung on the door knob to the apartment the infamous Holiday Inn 'DO NOT DISTURB' sign.

He should have known the sign would make an appearance before too long, and, suddenly, he was overcome by weariness.

Usually he was asleep before such realizations forced their way into his consciousness. Now it hit him full like a cold blast of winter wind.

"Oh well, what the heck," Waxy muttered to himself as he turned on the landing to go back downstairs. He would sleep in the booth next to the juke box, under the watchful eye of the stuffed Kodiak bear in the corner. At least, he hoped, Albert might get his mind right by getting laid so he might be a little more bearable to live with. With that in mind, he started whistling to himself.

Waxy fell asleep within moments.

In the morning, Waxy walked down to the *Lucky Wishbone Diner* for breakfast in Emma's section.

"Good for you," said Emma, setting down a slice of cherry pie and a large milk in front of Waxy. "Not easy getting work in this town."

"It's okay. I am definitely glad to have a job—don't know what we'd have done otherwise," said Waxy. "Albert's a tad impatient."

"His type always is."

"He's a good guy."

"I don't know what you see in him."

Waxy took a bite of pie and remembered first meeting his roommate—and his girlfriend Donna—in their dorm room, then his last night in Las Vegas with the prostitute. "He's an okay guy. Really. He's taught me a lot."

"Yeah? 'Bout what?"

"Oh, stuff." Waxy smiled. "You know."

"Any of it worth a damn?"

Waxy pondered for a moment. "And, I have to admit, it has

been a heck of an adventure ever since we left Columbus." Waxy took a gulp of milk and looked sheepishly up at Emma.

"Right."

After breakfast, Waxy walked over to Merrill Field to watch the airplanes take off and land.

Hope might have taken wing and fled as well, if he had known that it was not Anna from the Employment Services trailer behind the 'DO NOT DISTURB' sign with Albert, but CiCi, Beantown Bob's girlfriend.

Prowling

When Waxy got back to the apartment from Merrill Field, the 'DO NOT DISTURB' sign as well as the Blue Bus were gone, so he went upstairs and collapsed into bed to get some restful sleep before his next shift at *Fenway Park West.*

Albert turned north on K Street and slowed the blue Ford panel van to a crawl as he peered into the depths of passing doorways and alleys. When he got to Third Avenue he circled the block around the library and turned south again on K Street.

He turned left into the alleyway between K and I Streets. He suddenly stopped halfway down. Putting the van into park, he hopped out and slowly approached a man sleeping against the back of one of the buildings, stalking him like a predator. Snoring loudly, the man did not stir when Albert gently raised his right arm by the sleeve. He let it drop when he saw the hand had five fingers. The man snorted and rolled away without waking. Albert returned to the Blue Bus and continued to prowl the neighborhood.

Albert always knew his time working at *Fenway Park West* would be short, but now, securing a pipeline job took on a certain desperate urgency after spending the night with CiCi. Anna from the Employment Services trailer had explained how her husband bought his way into a pipeline construction job. She promised to help every time Albert came to visit at her apartment in the middle of the night after his shift behind the bar to make hot monkey love with her, but she had not come through with any leads yet and Albert concluded that her loneliness and horniness had gotten the better of her good intentions and promises—to him and her partner in marriage—at least until her husband got back from the North Slope. So, he cruised the west end of town looking for the fingerless man with the 'B' list union card.

He abandoned his search and drove to Elderberry Park to ponder his situation. He wandered out and aimlessly gazed out over Knik Arm, dreading crossing paths with Beantown Bob at work. An Alaska Rail Road locomotive intruded on the view, muscling by, dragging a long line of assorted freight cars. After the train passed, Albert reluctantly went back to *Fenway Park West*.

"You're late," said Waxy, as he tore up bread loaf butts to feed magpies on the back steps of the bar.

"Whatever."

Moe the Eskimo stood behind Waxy, smoking as he closely watched Albert pass by. The two men eyed each other warily.

"Something bothering you?" Albert asked the silent cook.

Moe the Eskimo cracked a slender, knowing smile, then exhaled a cloud of blue smoke, which seemed to chase Albert inside.

"I wish he wouldn't be late."

Moe the Eskimo just took another drag off his cigarette.

~~

CiCi

CiCi sat alone in a booth at *Fenway Park West* next to the picture window facing Fourth Avenue. A cup of coffee and a pad of paper with scribbled lyrics and angry doodles sat in front of her, but she gazed out the window focused on nothing in particular, her pen resting on the pad of paper and the coffee easing its way to tepid.

Albert watched her from behind the bar, aching to go sit beside her, but fearful of Beantown Bob's imminent return from his alcoholic escapade with Jimmi the Pilot. They had been M.I.A. for four days now. Almost against his will, Albert's thoughts drifted back to the night before and the melting together of his and CiCi's sweaty bodies again and again.

Dylan came in from the back entrance. He allowed his eyes to adjust to the dim and smoky interior lighting then scanned the bar for his sister. Spotting her, he went over and slid into the seat across from CiCi. He began absently drumming on the table top with his fingertips.

CiCi tried to ignore him, until the tapping became unbearable, then turned to give him an impatient stare.

Albert saw an opportunity. He grabbed the pot of coffee and a cup for Dylan, then went over to the booth. When he got to their side, CiCi transferred her cold glare to Albert.

"Hey, thanks, man," said Dylan as Albert set down the cup and poured.

He silently offered to warm up CiCi's cup, but she shook her head. A slender smile melted the hard edges of her icy demeanor ever so slightly. "So, Dylan, do you dream in color or in black-and-white?"

"Huh? What do you mean?" her brother responded before taking a sip of coffee.

"Albert has some interesting theories about color—*Technicolor*, in particular." Her smile broadened as she teased Albert. "Tell him."

Albert slowly smiled back at CiCi. "Oh, it's just something that *came* to me in a psychology class once...*or twice.*"

Dylan frowned as CiCi covered her mouth with her hand to hide a smile. He glanced up at Albert, then back to his sister.

"But I think he may be on to something." CiCi winked at Albert, then quickly turned away to look back out the window.

Dylan gave Albert a quizzical look.

Albert shrugged his shoulders, but smiled knowingly.

Dylan shook his head as if his sister was crazy.

Albert turned and went back to the bar without another word. He watched CiCi hungrily from afar, thinking hard about the freedom he was convinced the fingerless man with the 'B' Card could provide.

CiCi sighed as she mindlessly watched the passing traffic on Fourth Avenue, second guessing her decision to come to Alaska yet again, as she did each time Beantown Bob vanished into the night with Jimmi the Pilot.

CiCi met Beantown Bob at the Seattle bookstore where she worked during the day to make ends meet while struggling to earn a living playing music at night. He had flown down

Somethin' for Nothin'

from Anchorage to meet his literary agent and had charmed her while waiting for the agent to keep their appointment to sign the publishing contract for his first novel. Later that night, Beantown Bob showed up at the sleazy bar where *Torchlight* played to a meager crowd. He bought the band several rounds of drinks and later took CiCi out for a late night snack at IHOP. Beantown Bob made good on his promise that she and the band could pocket some "good coin" at the bar he was buying in Anchorage with his advance check as a down payment. She had never seen a check for that much money. He came up wanting, though, as the Hemingway she romanticized him into being in her mind. Sure, he had been a reporter of some kind at a newspaper, had published articles in a few magazines and he even had the book deal from Hemingway's publisher, but his first novel sat in the middle right hand drawer of his desk upstairs in his office above the bar, stalled on page sixty-three for the past seven-and-a-half months. She doubted his writer's block would melt with the coming spring thaw and started to think that Jimmi the Pilot was a convenient escape from confronting looming literary and fiscal failure, as the advance from Charles Scribner's Sons was long gone and the contract's submission deadline loomed.

CiCi was just glad that she had resisted Beantown Bob's nearly constant entreaties to move into his cabin with him. Instead, she, Dylan and the rest of *Torchlight* rented half a duplex for a band house, so she had a measure of privacy as the only female in the band house and, perhaps, a bit more leash than Beantown Bob preferred, which allowed her to stray first with Eddie and now Albert. She had to be careful, though, about exercising too much freedom. While she did not have to come home every single night to Beantown Bob, he was still the sole source of her income, by *Torchlight* playing three nights a week at *Fenway Park West*—at least until they got the tracks together for their album and could head out on tour back in the real part of the United States.

"Almost time, sis," Dylan said, taking a last gulp of coffee and sliding out of the booth. "I'm going to get set up."

CiCi looked at the clock over the bar: twenty-to-nine—bar time, anyway; it was twenty minutes fast. Over on stage, Graham tuned his guitar and Nordo, the bass player, set mics into the stands and plugged them in. "I'll be right up."

CiCi didn't know how Beantown Bob found out about Eddie. The jerk probably shot off his big mouth around the bar in front of Jimmi the Pilot or the inscrutable Eskimo in the kitchen or one of his regular bar flies, any of whom, no doubt, would have tattled on her at the first whiff of her improprieties. She looked over at Albert behind the bar. She hoped Eddie's replacement would be more discrete for his own sake, but more importantly for hers. Beantown Bob's temper was becoming as unstable as nitroglycerin. Their eyes met. Eddie got fired, but she was the one that paid a physical price for the affair. CiCi cocked her head to the side and gave Albert a subtle, yet encouraging smile. Albert was entertaining enough for her—for the time being, at least—but certainly not worth risking all for—but then again, what was a girl to do? Alone and stuck so far away up in Alaska with all this time on her hands? How close could she stand to the flame? How much heat could she absorb before she flinched or burned?

CiCi gathered her lyrics and doodles, then slowly ambled over to the stage with a little extra motion in her hips for

Somethin' for Nothin'

Albert's benefit. The Yukon adventure was definitely beginning to wear thin like Beantown Bob's regular disappearing act, as well as his increasingly abrupt and sometimes bruising sexual romps. CiCi was definitely not interested in spending another Arctic winter in Anchorage.

Watching CiCi, Albert made up his mind to get that 'B' card one way or another.

Waxy came out of the kitchen with a rack of glasses for the bar. He followed Albert's stare locked on CiCi's ass and felt a knot slowly pull tight in his gut. He slammed the rack of glasses down on the bar in front of Albert, shaking him out of his reverie.

Albert looked at Waxy and smiled. They both looked back towards the stage. CiCi waved at Albert, then put her Martin over her shoulder and adjusted her microphone.

Waxy shook his head and went back to the kitchen, where he stewed for about twenty minutes, remembering how Beantown Bob had dealt with Eddie, before settling back into the mindless nirvana of his shift.

Torchlight finished their last set just as the bar clock showed one AM and Albert announced last call. By that time on a Thursday night the crowd was usually pretty well thinned out and they could make a quick escape, not like Fridays or Saturdays, when the good citizens of Anchorage cured their cabin fever by crowding *Fenway Park West* until closing time at two.

"I'm beat," CiCi said as she leaned her guitar case against the end of the bar.

Albert wiped his way down to her. "Calling it?"

"I think so."

He looked upstairs towards the apartment he and Waxy shared.

She shook her head. "Too tired."

Albert shrugged his shoulders and continued wiping the bar.

"Come on. Let's get out of here," Dylan called out impatiently. He was drunk again, like he always was at the end of their gigs.

CiCi shrugged back at Albert, grabbed her guitar and headed out the back way behind Dylan, Graham and Nordo.

Albert watched her leave and sighed heavily.

"What the fuck are you doing?" Beantown Bob said as he pushed through the front door.

Albert looked back over his shoulder, thinking, *I have got to get that B Card as soon as possible.*

"I saw you."

"Saw me what?"

The two men stared each other down.

"Stop standing around with your thumb up your ass and get back to work—and get me a fucking burger while you're at it."

"I think the kitchen's closed—"

Albert was interrupted by Moe the Eskimo coming out of the kitchen carrying a plate with a burger and fries. Moe the Eskimo set the plate down in front of Beantown Bob, smirked at Albert, then went back into the kitchen.

"I could use a beer," Beantown Bob sneered at Albert.

Albert retrieved a Budweiser long neck and set it in front of Beantown Bob, who hungrily attacked his meal.

"And tell that half-wit farm boy to..." Beantown Bob stood up on the rungs of his bar stool and raised his voice to a yell to be heard in the kitchen, *"STOP THAT GOD DAMNED WHISTLING!"*

Waxy's happy tune ceased.

Albert started putting glasses away behind the bar. "So, Bob, how was it, working on the pipeline?"

"I worked the haul road. Why?"

"You were out there, right? So, what was it like?"

"Lots of sweet rolls and porn."

"Huh?"

"Not much to do when you're not working, so they try to keep you fat and happy—you're already dumb enough for being there."

"How's that?"

"Hard work. It's serious construction in tough places. Why?"

"Just wondering."

"Yeah. Right." Beantown Bob took another bite of burger and said around the mouthful, "You wouldn't last a week."

"Why's that?"

"Weren't you listening? It's hard fucking work. A lot harder than pouring drinks and making time with horny tellers from the bank."

The two men stared at one another.

"I lost three toes to frostbite," Beantown Bob finally said. "It ain't no picnic, trust me."

"Was it worth it?"

"What? The toes? They're fucking toes," said Beantown Bob. "It was good coin. I got a series published based on my time there, which scored me a book deal, which got me this place."

"So, was it worth it?"

"Yeah. For me. You won't last a week, though."

Albert watched Beantown Bob finish off his Budweiser.

"Get me another beer, huh?"

"Sure, Bob," Albert said reaching into the cooler for another long neck bottle. "So, where's Jimmi?"

"Trying to get laid, I suspect. He's gotta hunt for it. I don't."

Albert winced and decided to go looking again for the man with no fingers first thing in the afternoon when he got up.

Jimmi the Pilot's Beaver

Jimmi the Pilot pushed into the *Lucky Wishbone Diner* and saw Waxy at the counter talking to Emma. He went over and planted himself on the stool next to Waxy, interrupting their conversation.

"Hey, Em."

"Hi, Jimmi."

"The usual?"

"Two sugars. Two creams. Shaken, not stirred."

Emma already had a to-go cup in her hand. She turned to pour it full of coffee.

"So…" Jimmi the Pilot turned and pointed his finger at Waxy like a pistol. "Waxy, right?"

"Yes, sir."

"Don't call me 'sir.' Bad memories from 'Nam. Just call me Jimmi."

"Okay, ah, Jimmi," Waxy said suspiciously.

"So…what are you up to?"

"Just pie and milk."

"You know, I see you at the airport fence a lot when I go to work."

"I like to watch the planes."

"Ever been in one?"

"Once. To go to my cousin's funeral."

"Yeah, but that was an airliner, right?"

Waxy nodded.

Emma set the to-go cup in front of Jimmi.

"What do ya'll got going on the rest of the day?"

"Nothing."

"Well, then, come on, kid, let's go flying. It'll be fun." And when Waxy hesitated, Jimmi the Pilot added, "You can help me out—there's fifty bucks in it for you."

Waxy's eyes lit up, and he looked over at Emma. She cocked her head and smiled. He looked back at Jimmi the Pilot, shrugged his shoulders and answered hesitantly, "Sure, I guess."

"Let's hoof it, then." Jimmi the Pilot slapped a ten dollar bill down on the counter and winked at Emma. "I'll pick up the kid's tab and keep the change."

Emma smiled broadly. "Thanks, Jimmi."

Waxy followed Jimmi the Pilot out of the *Lucky Wishbone Diner*, waving good-bye to Emma.

They drove over to Merrill Field in Jimmi the Pilot's weathered GMC pickup, belching smoke and announcing their presence with the hole rotted in the muffler. They parked on the public side of a hangar and Jimmi the Pilot got a duffel bag out of the back bed. He opened a gate on the chain link fence and motioned Waxy through, then followed, closing the gate behind him.

"Are we going to be gone overnight?"

"Huh?"

Waxy pointed at the duffel bag.

"Nah. We'll be back by dinner time."

As they started walking down the flight line, Waxy noticed Jimmi the Pilot's slight limp.

Somethin' for Nothin'

"How'd you get hurt?"

"Just an off day at work," Jimmi the Pilot answered, but Waxy's eyes didn't accept his mechanically bland explanation. "I, um, had a most unfortunate meet up with a Russian SA-2—that's a surface-to-air missile—over Haiphong Harbor, which caused a significant deviation from my flight plan. Fortunately for me, I got feet wet before I had to punch out of my A-4 and one of the helos fished me out of the Gulf. That rocket ride on the ejection seat ended up making me an inch or so shorter than when I went into the Navy, not to mention the hunk or two of shrapnel in my leg that gives me this hitch in my get along. Hey, but now I've got an uncanny knack of knowing when it's gonna rain."

"Oh," Waxy answered, nodding, but not understanding most of the details of Jimmi the Pilot's story of his last combat mission in Vietnam as a Naval Aviator. They stopped at a red, white and black de Havilland *Beaver* parked outside the hangar. Waxy stood back and watched Jimmi the Pilot toss the duffel bag into the cabin and start to walk slowly and deliberately around the hulking high-wing, single-engine plane to pre-flight it.

Jimmi the Pilot climbed into the cabin, rustled around the cockpit, then emerged to sit down on the tire to wait and sip his coffee. Before long a fuel truck pulled up. After a brief conversation with Jimmi the Pilot, the driver pumped avgas into the fuel tanks and left. Jimmi the Pilot sat back down on the tire and stared blankly across the tarmac until a flat bed truck pulled up. After a brief conversation with the driver, he got up to supervise the loading of boxes, crates, mail sacks and oil drums into the back of the plane. A brief flurry of paperwork passed between the two men and the flat bed truck pulled away. Jimmi the Pilot went to the front of the plane, handed his coffee to Waxy and proceeded to push the propeller through with his shoulder five or six times.

"Shall we?" Jimmi the Pilot motioned for Waxy to board the plane.

Waxy climbed in the side door and was shocked at how the spartan interior was crammed tight with cargo.

Jimmi the Pilot climbed up behind him and pulled the door shut. He motioned for Waxy to sit in the right hand seat in the cockpit and slid effortlessly into the seat on the left.

"Now whatever you do, do not touch that cap," Jimmi the Pilot said, pointing to the oil tank filler cap next to Waxy's left knee, "or you'll get black gold all over the place."

Waxy nodded, put his hands into his lap and watched Jimmi the Pilot go through the mysterious ritual of starting the engine. Once the big radial fired up in a noisy cloud of smoke, Jimmi the Pilot pulled out the *Anchorage Daily News* and read the news of the day while he finished his coffee. Fifteen minutes later—the engine of the de Havilland *Beaver* having fully warmed up—they taxied out to the end of Runway 24 and soon began their take-off roll in an incredible roar and clatter. They broke ground and slowly climbed west. Waxy saw them pass over the *Lucky Wishbone Diner* and thought of Emma, fleetingly wondering if she had served him his last piece of pie ever that morning. They circled Fire Island in a broad sweeping left hand turn to gain altitude, then Jimmi the Pilot turned north. When he got to the Alaska Mountain Range, he turned right to follow them to the pipeline route, where they would turn north again to cross Isabel Pass on

Somethin' for Nothin'

their way to the construction site that would be Pump Station #10 on the Trans Alaska Pipeline.

Waxy pulled himself forward in the seat to get a better view of the peaks and glaciers, which glistened in the morning sun.

"Told ya," said Jimmi the Pilot. "Great, ain't it?"

"No man of reason can dispute this."

"Huh?"

"Unbelievable."

"Yeah. A bit different than flying the friendly skies of United. Personally, I much prefer this to driving a desk disguised as an airplane."

Waxy scanned across the horizon from north to south—from the jagged mountain peaks to the forested valley floors below. "Tuuluuwag talks a lot about this country."

"Who?"

"Tuuluuwag. You know, Moe the Eskimo at *Fenway Park*. That's his real name. He's got a million and one amazing stories about his clan and their adventures. I don't know how much of it you can believe, but it's pretty cool to hear him talk about growing up in the village and stuff." Waxy looked over at Jimmi the Pilot. "You ever see the plane wreck he talks about?"

"He never talks to me about anything." Jimmi the Pilot sighed and looked to his left at the mountain crags, then ahead at the deceptive calm and softness of a standing lenticular cloud. "The mountains and valleys are filled with plane wrecks from FNG bush pilots trying to do what they can't do and old timers who should have already known better than to try."

"FNGs?"

"Fucking New Guys."

"Oh. Anyway, he said it was some kind of big Air Force plane or something."

"Big Air Force babies—always complaining about this and that. You try landing a jet on a boat, then complain about the bumps in your ten thousand foot runway or losing one of your eight engines."

"Moe said that there's a big payroll that they were supposed to be flying over to Japan for soldiers in the Korean War."

"Payroll?"

"He said it's trapped up on some glacier where they crashed. Millions, he said."

"Hmmm."

"Ever see it?"

"So, where did Moe say his village was?"

"I don't know. Somewhere up by the mountains up north."

"You believe him? About the plane wreck?"

"I dunno. Why would he lie?"

"Hmmm."

They flew on, not speaking, listening to the throaty drone of the Pratt & Whitney *Wasp Junior* radial engine. Soon they approached a scar in the wilderness cut out by bulldozers and flattened by road graders and trucks. Jimmi the Pilot turned north and followed the intended route of the Trans Alaska Pipeline. They crossed Isabel Pass and began descending until landing at a two thousand foot gravel runway at the construction site for Pump Station #10. Once the de Havilland *Beaver's* engine shut down, a yellow Alyeska pickup truck pulled up along the plane. Three burley men jumped down from the back bed and two more stepped down from the cab.

"About fucking time," the driver hollered at Jimmi the Pilot in the cockpit.

"Time to go to work," Jimmi the Pilot turned and said to Waxy. "I don't let these gorillas get inside the plane, so we gotta move the stuff to the door for them. Just do what I say and be careful, so nothing gets damaged, and we don't get ourselves blown to smithereens."

"What?"

"Yeah, that's dynamite in those crates and cooking oil in the drums."

"What the hell?"

Jimmi the Pilot laughed and led Waxy into the back cabin to start carefully unloading the supplies. They took on mail bags, document pouches and two Alyeska employee passengers. Waxy watched the obligatory ritual of signing and countersigning paperwork. After what appeared to be a final off-the-books transaction as Jimmi the Pilot traded his duffel bag to the truck driver for a thick envelope, they boarded the plane, strapped themselves into the cockpit and quickly took off from the improvised gravel airstrip. After climbing to cross Isabel Pass again, Jimmi the Pilot pointed the *Beaver* west.

"So, do you think Moe is right about that payroll plane?" Jimmi the Pilot asked Waxy. "I mean, how would he know?"

Waxy thought for a moment, then nodded his head. "Well, he said it snowed twenty and hundred dollar bills down on his village the night that the plane crashed."

They flew back to Anchorage in silence. Jimmi the Pilot steered a course a little further north, a little closer to the mountains and strained to scan every valley, gorge and glacier for signs of a plane wreck.

Beantown Bob's Story

Beantown Bob sat at the desk in his office above *Fenway Park West* staring at the empty sheet of paper rolled into his IBM Selectric typewriter staring back and taunting him with its severe white blankness. He felt like a musher lost in an Iditarod white-out—hopelessly lost, but still racing to get there.

He looked over at the half-empty bottle of Bushmills Irish Whiskey sitting just behind a steaming cup of coffee. He resisted the urge to fortify the last of his morning coffee and looked back at the blank page. A dull anger began to percolate in his chest and splash against the inside of his skull. Not unlike real life, the fictional characters he depended upon had let him down and he began to resent them for it.

It seemed like it should have been so easy—a no-brainer. But it wasn't. After sixty-some pages, Beantown Bob's inspiration petered out and the fetus of the novel he had contractually promised to deliver to Charles Scribner's Sons lay stillborn in a pathologically neat stack next to the typewriter. He never faced this dilemma as a sportswriter for the *Anchorage Daily News,* because a steady, unending flow of characters, scenes, events, dramas and neat, definitive denouements came his way each and every day, courtesy of a plethora of different sports leagues and associations. All he had to do was prune and edit the action from the fields, courts, rinks and courses to fit into the needed number of 11 pica wide column inches expected that day by Walter, his editor, to satisfy the paper's advertisers to keep the printing presses rolling and to insure the whole unholy enterprise of journalism did not collapse like a house of cards.

Of course, in their own minds, everyone in the newsroom was really a yet undiscovered novelist hidden in the daily grind of being a reporter *ala* Hemingway. Beantown Bob was one of the extremely rare ones who actually landed a publishing deal and now he studiously avoided confronting the disturbing fact that his long sheltered and carefully nurtured self-image of himself as a great American novelist was a mere mirage, incapable of providing the financial thirst-quenching required to sustain human life on the planet—particularly in Alaska—in the late Twentieth Century. Oh, how he now missed those regular paychecks from the *Daily News*, which is why—against his better judgment—he had been forced to supplement the cash flow from *Fenway Park West* as a silent partner in Jimmi the Pilot's drug smuggling operation. It was a decision he regretted from the start and one which, along with the looming Scribner's deadline, caused him many a sleepless night.

Beantown Bob's losing battle against the nothingness on the page in the typewriter raged on through lunchtime, until a phone call from Jimmi the Pilot broke through the siege of his inspiration and rescued him from the artillery-like pounding his ego endured. Beantown Bob listened in gratitude to Jimmi the Pilot's story recounting Waxy's story about Moe the Eskimo's story about the payroll plane crash.

Somethin' for Nothin'

"Let me call down to the *Daily Snooze* and check it out," he answered Jimmi the Pilot and hung up, then picked up the receiver again.

Beantown Bob checked the time and figured it was safe—Walter and Vince, the Managing Editor, would be pounding down Jack Daniels and Cokes at lunch—so he dialed. He was *persona non grata* in the newsroom ever since the day he cashed his advance check from Charles Scribner's Sons—not because of the intense jealousy of rival reporters, but because his notice of resignation involved solidly connecting his knuckles with Walter's W.C. Fields-like bulbous red nose with enough force to spew blood all over that day's copy—fulfilling not only every reporter's dream of landing publishing deal, but their simmering desire to stand up to the petty editorial tyrants who ruled their lives. Needless to say, Beantown Bob's resignation was accepted without the customary two weeks notice, though he secured the undying respect and admiration of his fellow journalistic word-slaves at the *Daily News*.

"ADN archives," the weary female voice on the other end of the line answered.

"And how is Mrs. Archives today," Beantown Bob asked.

"Well, well, well—as I live and breathe: A real live writer calling little old me."

"I've missed you, Adele."

"Tell me a story—and make it a good one this time. I'm bored out of my mind. Things have been like that since you left."

"Once upon a time, there was a snowstorm, an Air Force cargo plane and a sleeping princess."

"I think I've heard this one."

"You have?"

"Are there dwarfs and magic apples involved?"

"Busted again. I can't fool you."

"And when was this magical snow storm?"

"Late Forties to mid Fifties. My source tells me it was probably a 'C' Fifty-four *Skymaster* or a 'C' One-Nineteen *Flying Box Car* out of Elmendorf headed for Japan or Korea."

"I take it they didn't make it to where they were going."

"And they were never seen ever again. It's not one of those happily ever after tales."

"What the hell. I'm just sitting here clipping my little heart out and waiting for my prince to come."

"You're a doll."

"How's the novel coming?"

Beantown Bob winced. "I can't wait for you to read it."

"I'll stop by on the way home from work and you can buy me a drink."

"Deal."

Beantown Bob hung up the phone. He glanced at, then quickly looked away from, the still empty page in the typewriter, as if it were a horribly deformed cripple he had caught himself impolitely staring at on the street. He poured Bushmills into his empty coffee cup and pondered the positive fiscal possibilities of a huge military transport plane filled with cash buried out there somewhere in the snow, just waiting to be found.

~~~

The 'B' List Card

Albert suddenly had a thought and retrieved the empty Yukon Jack bottle he had tossed into the trash before Waxy could take the garbage out to the dumpster in the back alley at the end of the night. He washed it out and carefully refilled it three-quarters full with iced tea so he would know which one it was. He then liberated a new, unopened bottle from the store room and sneaked out of *Fenway Park West* while Waxy was still mopping behind the bar, figuring that his roommate would assume that he had gone to meet up with a female patron.

Both Yukon Jack bottles now sat in a brown paper bag on the front passenger seat of the blue Ford panel van as Albert headed towards the west end of downtown at three in the morning. He noticed a patrol car passing in the opposite direction one block over and realized that he would be conspicuous cruising the empty streets of Anchorage in the early morning hours, so Albert turned south, then west up the alley off K Street and slid the van into a parking spot behind the Captain Cook Hotel. Albert had gotten quite familiar with this section of downtown on his repeated hunting safaris.

He sat in the van thinking as he cut up a newspaper into two-and-a-half inch by six inch rectangles. It was quiet, except for the occasional locomotive signals from the rail yard to the north. He was way early, but he wanted to be in place well in advance of the morning hour when the city woke up. Albert looked over at the bag containing the two bottles. It wasn't so much a plan as an impulse that struck him as he poured boilermakers for the old timers who closed the bar on the usually slow Tuesday nights. He watched as the whiskey fogged their minds, slurred their speech and skewed the time-space continuum continuity of their memories. He didn't want to wait any longer. He didn't want to have to confront Beantown Bob over his affair with CiCi. His impatience had gotten the better of him and this seemed like the best course of action.

Albert sat and stared and pondered for the better part of an hour until he dozed off, leaning against the door of the van, awakening with a start as Anchorage just began to stir for the business day.

He grabbed the grocery bag with the Yukon Jack bottles and headed to the first of the three places he thought he would find his quarry.

Albert wondered why the homeless would be up so early, since they didn't have jobs or responsibilities, but it was something he had observed over the past few weeks.

He made his way west towards the Alaska Department of Labor trailers where he had first met Anna and the man with no fingers on his right hand with the 'B' List union card. He watched the hopeful slowly collect in the parking lot, waiting for the offices to open, first in clots, then as more came, they naturally organized themselves into a line like the well-indoctrinated products of public schools they were, pointed toward the trailer entrance door, where the bureaucracy would allow them in for processing at the properly appointed hour.

Somethin' for Nothin'

He saw the men follow the state employees hungrily with their eyes as they arrived for work, passing them by as if they did not exist to enter the trailers, punch in and take their places at desks and tables to begin the day's pushing of government paper.

Albert reflexively pressed himself back into a building doorway when he noticed Anna walking up the street towards him. He had not been with her since her husband had come home from Prudhoe Bay for a two week break from work on the pipeline. She joined up with a couple of her fellow workers and walked past the desperate men who came to her for help. She had not helped Albert and he doubted she ever would.

He scanned up and down the buildings across the street, looking for the human residue that collected there like some kind of grit discarded in the daily grind of commerce that stained the corners, cracks and creases of the city. Albert waited and watched, much more patiently than his nature normally allowed, until the homeless began to ooze out of the seams between the buildings and started to gather in small groups, as if they were workers gathering at the coffee maker in the morning to compare notes about their bowling league games won and lost, dinner with the in-laws or a television show watched the night before. He could not understand why they collected there, of all places, as if the prospects of panhandling a scraggly line of unemployed men were at all good.

Feeling conspicuous, Albert walked away from the trailers and around the block opposite them, all the while alert for the fingerless man with the 'B' card. He hugged the brown paper bag with the two bottles and the stacks of rubber banded newspaper cut into dollar-sized rectangles, book ended with the government issued portraits of Abraham Lincoln and Alexander Hamilton to be used as legal tender, scanning the faces gathering on the sidewalk in front of the government that the desperate ones hoped would help them and the defeated ones knew would not.

"Well, well. If it ain't the college boy," the voice sneered from behind.

Albert turned on his heels and saw the man with no fingers on his hand leaning against the corner of building at the edge of the alleyway. *Perfect,* he thought.

"Whatcha got in the bag college boy? Groceries for your mama?"

Albert stood and looked back at the man with disdain, but held his tongue, knowing that he had what Albert needed and that the negotiation had begun. He looked down at the bag and slowly uncurled the top. He made a show of looking inside, then reached in to pull up one of the bottles, just high enough that the fingerless man could see the label, the shape of the whiskey bottle and the amber liquid inside.

The man pawed his chin with the knuckles of his fingerless hand like a hungry but wary feral cat as he watched the bottle disappear back into the bag.

"You still got that 'B' card?" Albert asked, mentally editing his sentences to the bare bones necessary to keep from spooking his prey.

The man smiled a craggy grin. "I might."

"Or you might not?"

"Why? You thinking you could handle a real man's job, college boy—gonna get your hands dirty for once in your life?"

Somethin' for Nothin'

Albert smiled and shrugged his shoulders.

The man licked his lips, thinking of the contents of the bottle, imagining its taste and already feeling the warm glow in every swallow. "And if I might?"

"Well, I might be interested."

"Take more than drink to get it in your hands."

Albert looked into the bag again. He reached in and pulled out the stack of banded newspaper with a ten dollar bill on the top and showed the man Alexander Hamilton.

"You sell your vehicle?"

Albert dropped the thick stack of paper worth exactly twenty dollars back into the bag. He shrugged his shoulders. "Somebody told me I didn't need my van up at camp."

"Sage advice, for sure." The man pushed himself away from the building and started to take a step towards Albert.

"Uh-uh." Albert shook his head. "Not so fast. I showed you mine."

The man stopped and reached behind with his left hand to fish a wallet out of the back pocket of his grimy khakis. Pressing the wallet against his chest with his right hand, he slipped a Laborers International Union card halfway out, then slipped it back in again and quickly returned his wallet to his back pocket. "Well?"

"Then I might be interested."

The man took a step towards Albert.

"Not here," Albert said in a hushed tone looking up and down the street.

"Step into my office, then." The fingerless hand gestured towards the alley.

Albert took a step towards him. He pulled the new, full Yukon Jack bottle out of the bag and offered it to the man, who took it, but kept his eyes locked on the bag with the money. Albert pulled out the three-quarters full bottle and rolled the bag closed around the stacks of newspaper inside and tucked it under his left arm.

"Shall we do some business, then?" Albert said motioning towards the alley.

The fingerless member of Laborers Local 942 out of Fairbanks smiled and opened the Yukon Jack. He took a long pull as he walked into the alley, keeping a wary eye on Albert over his shoulder.

Albert let him get a few steps ahead and followed. When he got into the alley, he opened his bottle, lifted it in a toast to their deal and took a sip of iced tea, feigning a grimace as he recapped the bottle. He looked back over his shoulder, then down to the other end of the alley. They were alone.

"College boys." The laborer shook his head and smiled. He lifted his bottle and started a long three-swallow gulp, as if to show Albert how a real man drank whiskey, not noticing that Albert had flipped the Yukon Jack bottle in his hand to hold it by the neck and had quickly closed the gap between them.

Between the second and third swallow, Albert clocked the laborer in the side of the head with his bottle as hard as he could and the fingerless man crumpled first to his knees, as if in prayer, releasing the whiskey bottle from over his head, before he fell over on his side.

The crash of the bottle on the pavement startled Albert. He looked up and down the alley again, then, ignoring the stench of the unwashed corpse, retrieved the union card from the laborer's wallet. He hesitated, wondering about leaving the wallet, then put it into the brown paper bag with his bottle. He quickly headed down the alley hugging the sides of buildings and looking back over his shoulder until he got to a parking lot that let out on Sixth Avenue.

Albert serpentined around the blocks of downtown Anchorage back to the parking lot at the Captain Cook Hotel. He got into the blue Ford panel van and rested his forehead on the steering wheel, panting and feeling the adrenaline in his bloodstream slowly dissipate.

He drove out of the city until he was surrounded by forest in the Chugach Mountains, where he pulled off the road and parked. He opened the brown paper bag, retrieved the wallet and looked inside.

He had it. He had his ticket—the 'B' list union card.

Albert sighed in relief and allowed himself to doze off, dreaming of being with CiCi.

~~~

Carlos and Tony

Carlos and Tony did not want to be there. They missed Los Angeles and hated the cold. They knew they looked stupid in the outfits they had bought from L.L. Bean, but it didn't matter—they needed the layers to stay warm. It was sunny and eighty degrees back in Southern California. The Alaska spring was mostly dark and still freezing cold. The cartel had sent them up to check out Jimmi the Pilot and his operation. To them, Anchorage was a shit hole—a very cold shit hole—but business was business.

Jimmi the Pilot had been a fairly reliable, though small change connection into the Arctic drug trade, but with all the activity surrounding the construction of the Trans Alaska Pipeline, his volume had grown to the point where it attracted the attention of the cartel's upper management, which sent them up north to evaluate whether it was time to cut Jimmi the Pilot out of the deal and take over the territory and its profits directly.

Carlos and Tony hated that they seemed to attract attention wherever they went. At the airport. At the diner. Almost anywhere they went downtown.

Now they found themselves in a booth at some shit hole bar on Fourth Avenue, listening to a band playing insipid rock ballads that dominated the clubs and airways back in LA. Not their kind of music, but they weren't there for the entertainment. Somebody at Merrill Field told them to check the bar out, because Jimmi the Pilot was known to hang out there.

Beantown Bob came in through the front door, carrying an envelope bulging with microfiche machine printouts collected by Adele. He had just come from the *Anchorage Daily News* building. He was definitely glad to be free of the newsroom. It stank like fear and frustration. He hated going there and always worried that he would have an unpleasant run-in with Walter.

As he came in, Beantown Bob heard Carlos and Tony talking in Spanish and it caught his ear. He detoured towards the bar and motioned Albert over.

"Hey," Beantown Bob said, leaning over the bar. Then he noticed Albert's pallor and was brought up short.

"Hey, what?" Albert asked back.

"What's with you? You just seen a ghost or something?"

"Nah. Just a late night."

"They're all late nights, pal," Beantown Bob said looking suspiciously at Albert.

"You rang?"

"Anyway, what's with the Spanish Inquisition?" Beantown Bob pointed back over his shoulder at the booth where Tony and Carlos had stopped talking and started watching Beantown Bob and Albert.

"I dunno. Came in and asked about Jimmi. Been drinking coffee ever since."

"Great. Fuck. Great."

Beantown Bob turned and went upstairs to his office. He tossed the fat envelope on top of his manuscript and reached

Somethin' for Nothin'

for the phone to call the hangar at Merrill to warn Jimmi the Pilot that his business partners were in town. Cindy at the Fixed Base Operator answered and said Jimmi the Pilot was still en route back from a delivery, so he left a message to call before he came over, because his cousins from the lower forty-eight had come to town for a surprise visit.

"Fuck. Great. Fuck," Beantown Bob said as he angrily hung up the phone. He had been very clear with Jimmi the Pilot from the start. He absolutely did not want their drug business in *Fenway Park West.* "I knew it. I just knew it."

Then he spied the envelope, picked it up and opened it. Inside was a sloppy stack of fifty or, maybe, a hundred pages of slick thermal paper printouts of *Anchorage Daily News* stories from the Fifties, reporting on plane crashes. It might have seemed like a lot to an Outsider, but Beantown Bob figured it went with the territory, 'cause placed end-to-end, all the runways in Alaska probably equaled the length of paved roads in the state. He quickly went to work sorting the stories into piles based on a quick scan of the headlines and lead paragraphs, separating them first by civilian versus military aircraft involved. By the time he had weeded through all of the articles, the civilian pile was twice as thick as the military pile.

He set aside the stack of articles about civilian plane crashes and started reading deeper into the articles of the military incidents reported, sorting those stories into two piles, one about cargo planes, the other about fighter planes and helicopters. By the time he had winnowed the pile down, he had eight articles that he put in order by date and started to read through carefully.

"God damn," he said when he got to the fifth story about a C-124 *Globemaster* that took off in 1952 from Elmendorf Air

Force Base headed for Japan. It had made a stopover in Anchorage to refuel and disappeared without a trace, having taken off, ill-advisedly, directly into the teeth of an Arctic Clipper storm. Though the Air Force searched for months and months—through the spring, summer and into the fall of that year—they could find no trace of it. No mention was made of the cargo lost.

"God damn. He's right."

Beantown Bob got up and went outside his office to the catwalk to check: Tony and Carlos were still in the booth sipping coffee.

He went back into his office and left another message for Jimmi the Pilot that he had found some information on his missing brothers-in-arms, but not to come to *Fenway Park West* until later.

Beantown Bob went back into his office, poured a shot of Bushmills into his coffee mug and contemplated what the future held in store for him with the drug cartel camped out in his bar and the prospect of millions of dollars of cold hard cash locked in a glacier somewhere near Moe the Eskimo's boyhood village. He eyed his stunted and deformed manuscript, then suddenly grabbed it and hid it away back in the right-hand middle desk drawer. Out of sight, out of mind.

Flying High

"It was great. I mean, wow, just amazing," Waxy gushed to Emma at the counter between bites of Dutch apple pie. "And I made fifty bucks."

Emma smiled at Waxy's child-like excitement over his first Alaska bush flight.

Waxy took a big gulp of milk and asked, "So, you know Jimmi. Has he ever taken you up?"

Emma shook her head and ran her finger across her upper lip.

Waxy smiled and wiped the milk mustache away. "I mean, how great is it that he can fly a plane like that?"

"I like my feet on the ground, thank you very much," said Emma.

"No, really. You should come with us sometime. You'll really like it."

Emma gave Waxy a skeptical look. "With Jimmi?"

"Yeah, he's a real good pilot. He flew jets off a boat in the Navy. Is that crazy or what? He actually got shot down in Vietnam and had to parachute out of his plane into the ocean. He's got a picture of himself on the aircraft carrier with his jet. Boy, I wonder if he could teach me to fly."

"I'm sure you could do anything you put your mind to." Emma winked at Waxy.

"Really?"

"Yeah. Really."

Waxy gazed dreamily at Emma and found himself wondering what the toothpaste tube in her bathroom looked like. He shook that thought from his head to enjoy the blossoming smile on her face, like the flowers in his mother's gardens scattered about the farmhouse, little oases of frivolous vegetative beauty in a Delaware County plot of land dedicated to the agricultural industry.

Moe the Eskimo

It was early still, before the happy hour crowd would start filtering in after work, leading to the dinner rush, then to the slow steady trickle of alcohol dispensed to the residue of regulars left at the end of a Tuesday night. The prep work was done, so Waxy and Moe the Eskimo sat out on the back steps of *Fenway Park West*. Waxy broke up slices of stale bread and tossed them to a small gaggle of magpies which fluttered, squawked and fought at each of his offerings. Moe the Eskimo smoked a cigarette and watched the mini-feeding frenzy.

"Have you ever been up in a plane?" Waxy asked.

"Sure."

"Do you like it?"

"Sometimes it's the only way to get from here to there. You do it. Liking doesn't matter."

"I liked it."

Moe the Eskimo grunted, neither assenting nor dissenting.

"Jimmi asked a lot of questions about you."

Moe the Eskimo raised an eyebrow.

"I mean about the plane crash you told me about," Waxy paused and tossed another scrap to the magpies. "Was it true?"

Moe the Eskimo squinted at Waxy.

"I'm just askin'."

Moe the Eskimo stared straight ahead and took a pull off of his Camel cigarette.

"Tell him," said Beantown Bob, who had come up behind Waxy and Moe the Eskimo without being noticed. In his hand was the *Anchorage Daily News* story about the C-124 plane crash in 1952. "Go ahead. Tell us—*Is it true?*"

Moe the Eskimo looked back over his shoulder and up at Beantown Bob, leaning on his Louisville Slugger. He flicked the Camel cigarette butt into the alley. It hit the pavement in a burst of orange embers, scattering the magpies.

"So?" asked Beantown Bob.

"It was night. It was snowing." Moe the Eskimo spoke slowly, evenly, his voice was a monotone. He looked at neither Waxy nor at Beantown Bob, instead staring into the space the magpies once occupied. "The wind howled down off the mountain like a rabid wolf chasing demon hares through the village, crashing into the doors and windows and shaking the walls with his fury."

Waxy looked back up at Beantown Bob, but his boss did not acknowledge him.

"Go on," said Beantown Bob, burning a hole into Moe the Eskimo's brain with his eyes.

Moe the Eskimo turned his head ninety degrees. He rolled his eyes to look behind, but Beantown Bob had moved closer and stood directly behind him, just out of his field of view. He looked back to the where a trio of magpies regathered in front of Waxy, squawking and hopping for more pieces of bread.

"Go on."

"We all heard the airplane overhead. Low. Too low. We knew. Too low."

Waxy looked at Moe the Eskimo intently as he listened.

"And?"

Somethin' for Nothin'

"In the morning, after the storm had passed, a trail of money spilled down from the mountains." Moe the Eskimo reached into the front pocket of his clean, stiffly starched, industrial white shirt and took out his pack of Camels. He slowly went through the ritual of pulling out a cigarette and lighting it.

"And?"

"The storm had passed. The sky was blue and the sun bright. The wreckage sparkled in the sunrise, like a diamond."

"Is it still there?"

Moe the Eskimo shrugged and smoked. "It made some of the villagers a little mad."

"Mad?" Waxy asked. "Like angry mad?"

Moe the Eskimo shook his head. "No. Crazy mad."

"Is it still there?" Beantown Bob asked again, reining back his impatience.

"Rabid, like the howling wolf wind," Moe the Eskimo turned and said directly to Waxy, ignoring Beantown Bob. "It wasn't enough for some to spend day after day gathering the ten, twenty and even hundred dollar bills scattered across the valley—even though it was more money than any of them ever made or ever had. More than all the village ever had, probably. They could not stop, even when there was no more to be found. Just the thought of that diamond sparkle taunted them every morning and every evening, even when the clouds hung low over the valley blocking the sun. They knew it was there even when they could no longer see it wink at them. And they knew—or thought they knew what was there if they could just get it. It became the village secret and no one spoke to outsiders of hearing the crash in the night, or the money in the valley or the taunting wink from the glacier. And it drove them mad."

Moe the Eskimo was the first to look down the alley and notice Jimmi the Pilot walking towards them, hugging close to the back of the buildings, following along a crooked line around stairways, dumpsters and parked pickup trucks and cars.

Waxy, Moe the Eskimo and Beantown Bob silently watched Jimmi the Pilot approach. He stopped in the alleyway at the bottom of the steps leading up to *Fenway Park West* and looked from face to face.

"Is it still there?" Beantown Bob asked again, punctuating his question with a rap of the Louisville Slugger on the landing.

"It haunted the village. Taunting from the glacier, many followed the trail of money up the valley to the foot of the mountain. Some gave up there and came back. Some climbed on and died up on the glacier. More tried, but none ever reached it and returned to tell." Moe the Eskimo turned around and looked up at Beantown Bob. "Yes. It is still there. Eventually, it was swallowed by the snows and glittered no more. I left. And my village died. Gone, all gone now."

Moe the Eskimo turned back from Beantown Bob and crushed out his cigarette. He stared at the magpies, who regarded him with curiosity.

Jimmi the Pilot looked at Beantown Bob and broke the silence. "It's true then?"

"Evidently," said Beantown Bob. He handed Jimmi the Pilot the news article about the C-124 plane crash.

"Wow," whispered Waxy.

Somethin' for Nothin'

"I'll bet I can get us there," said Jimmi the Pilot.

"Where?"

"The glacier."

"How?"

"Land there."

Moe the Eskimo just shook his head and took out another Camel cigarette to smoke. It was madness.

~~~

Dylan

Dylan heard the clattering of dishes, pots and pans from the kitchen and rolled over in bed, pulling the covers over his head to try to hibernate for a few more minutes. Ironically, a lull in the noise caught his attention—it was hard to concentrate on ignoring nothing—and when the clanking started up again even louder, he pinched his eyes shut and groaned, acknowledging that his sister was in one of her moods. He dreaded arising, but knew he could not stay in bed any longer.

He sat up and saw Nordo, the bass player, still cocooned in sleep in the twin bed against the other wall. Dylan pulled on a pair of jeans and a T-shirt, then patted around on the nightstand for his pack of cigarettes. He lit one up and listened to his sister's cookware percussion solo. He glanced at the clock: almost three in the afternoon. Nearly eight hours of sleep—a minor victory, anyway. He hoped against hope the noise from the kitchen meant that CiCi was fixing something to eat, but knew in his heart of hearts he'd have to fend for himself, as always. Oh, well, he consoled himself, she wasn't that great of a cook anyway. When he was done, he smashed his cigarette butt into a nearly full ashtray and padded quietly out of the front bedroom, closing the door behind him, so Nordo could slumber on in peace.

The living room of the band house was haphazardly furnished with a mismatched sofa and love seat angled around an empty wooden cable reel that served as a coffee table. Red cream soda bottles, beer cans, pizza boxes and ashtrays littered the floor and table tops. Dylan padded through the living room and into the dining room filled with music equipment, where they practiced and worked on their original songs. Stepping over the speaker cables and guitar chords, around the amplifiers and under the microphone boom stands, he stopped just around the corner to the kitchen and listened to his sister. He sniffed the air hoping for at least the aroma of coffee, but came up empty-nosed. With a heavy sigh, he rounded the corner and went into the kitchen.

"Coffee?" Dylan asked futilely.

"You know where it is," CiCi answered sharply without turning to look at him. She scrubbed furiously at a frying pan in the sink.

Dylan walked over to the cabinets and reached around her for a can of Folgers coffee out of the cupboard. He slid behind her, grabbed the Mr. Coffee carafe and waited for a break in the scrubbing action to fill it. CiCi stepped back from the sink and paused impatiently. Dylan filled the carafe and made the coffee. He listened to the water percolate and the black fluid drip. CiCi went back to her scrubbing.

"This place is a pig sty," CiCi said.

"Yes, mother."

"Don't you dare."

"Why are you doing dishes?"

"Because I can't stand to look at a sink full of dirty dishes."

"But, that's why we have three place settings for four people—so that if somebody wants to eat, they have to wash what they need and nothing ever gets to the stage of being a moldy science experiment."

CiCi looked over her shoulder and frowned at her brother.

Dylan closed his eyes to pray silently for a fleet brewing process. He opened the refrigerator to survey his options for a meal.

"There's nothing in there—*again.*"

"At least it means there's nothing to go bad."

CiCi rinsed the frying pan and dropped it loudly into the draining rack. The Mr. Coffee erupted in a brief finale of gurgling. Dylan gave thanks, took a coffee cup from the rack and poured.

"You know, this is a pretty sweet deal for us. A lot better than things were back in Seattle."

"*Really?*"

"Yeah. *Really.* Or did you like working all the time at the bookstore? At least here, we can live off what we're making playing."

"Is this what you want? Jumping on a string for a coke head, just because he owns a bar?"

"Hey, that coke head pays us pretty good. No washing dishes. No waiting tables. No more killing your back stocking book shelves. I don't know about you, but I hated bussing tables at *Denny's*. And then, after I got fired and had to work at the old folks' home—that was the pits."

CiCi grabbed another pot and started to scrub.

"It's a pretty sweet deal. Plus we get food and drinks for free."

"But it's not— "

"Yeah, yeah, I know. It's not where we want to be, but it's

closer—closer than what we were back home. They'll be done with the pipeline in another year or so and by that time— "

"Another year?

"And by that time, we'll have our songs recorded. Then, we can cash out and go back to the lower forty-eight and get hooked up with a record company to get out on tour."

"Another year?"

"Maybe not that long, but, hey, we gotta pay our dues. And better on stage here than behind a cash register ringing up Dr. Seuss epics, slopping food off dirty dishes or mopping up piss and puke, wishing we were doing exactly what we're doing now: gigging full time."

CiCi scrubbed.

"Come on, don't screw this up. *Please,*" Dylan begged. "Honest, we'll be out of here before you know it."

"I don't know if I can wait. He's getting worse and worse."

"Bob?"

"Of course, Bob. Who else?"

Dylan knew about Eddie and, now, Albert. Dylan's greatest fear was that his sister would piss off Beantown Bob beyond repair. Dylan didn't like the guy either, but he also did not want to get fired and have to return to Seattle to make more money on the very bottom rung of either the food service or healthcare industries than he could gigging. Of course, he was smart enough never to say anything about pimping out his sister in an outside voice, so he just shrugged his shoulders.

"Maybe it wouldn't be so bad except for that Jimmi pal of his. He brings out the worst in him."

Dylan sighed and drained the last of the coffee in his cup. Personally, he liked Jimmi the Pilot and his amazing stories about

Somethin' for Nothin'

sex, drugs and war in Southeast Asia, not to mention his seemingly endless supply of dope. He filled his cup again from the Mr. Coffee. "You want me to go get something to eat from the store?"

CiCi shook her head. "We might as well cash in one of our free meals."

Dylan nodded. He went to shower and get dressed, trying to think of a way to talk his sister back off the ledge—again. It was tough being related to a *prima donna.*

By the time they got to *Fenway Park West,* Beantown Bob, Waxy and Moe the Eskimo were seated around a table in the dining area with an aviation sectional chart spread out in front of them. Jimmi the Pilot stood at Moe the Eskimo's side asking him questions.

Dylan took a seat at the bar. CiCi sighed and meandered over to the table. "What's going on?"

They all looked up at her, then Waxy and Jimmi the Pilot looked back over at Beantown Bob.

"We're having a little meeting here, babe," Beantown Bob said patronizingly. An uncomfortable silence hung in the air between them. "Is there something...you...um...need...?"

CiCi looked at the map, then at Beantown Bob again. She shook her head, turned and ambled towards the bar to sit next to Dylan. She glanced over her shoulder at the table, turned back and sighed heavily before parking herself on a barstool.

Just then, Albert came out of the kitchen, tying an apron around his waist. He was brought up short by the sight of CiCi, then slowly walked to the end of the bar where she sat with Dylan. He noticed Waxy at the table with Beantown Bob and Moe the Eskimo.

"So, what's the big pow-wow all about?" asked Albert, nodding towards the table.

"Don't know," CiCi said, pouting and shrugging her shoulders. "Don't care."

"Any coffee?" asked Dylan.

"No, but I'll make some," answered Albert. He asked CiCi, "Can I get you anything?"

"Water," she said wearily.

Albert filled and started the coffee maker. He brought CiCi back a glass of water and set it in front of her. He hesitated, then announced quietly, "I got a card—one good for a 'B' job."

"Really? Sweet. Congratulations, man." Dylan smiled broadly, relieved that the biggest threat to CiCi and Beantown Bob's relationship would soon be gone and the *status quo* would be secure again.

CiCi looked up at Albert, knowing the 'B' card meant he would soon be leaving for one of the construction camps along the pipeline.

Albert met her eyes and held her gaze, immediately feeling doubts well up in his gut over his recent good fortune and his hand in the fingerless man's misfortune. "Called the union and got a job, too. At Camp Delta, south of Fairbanks. I guess that's not too far away—not like I'll be way up on the North Slope."

"Oh…" CiCi suddenly realized that she might actually miss Albert, unlike the other lovers taken to distract her and to annoy Beantown Bob.

"I told you. I can't read this fucking map," Moe the Eskimo blurted out loudly.

CiCi, Albert and Dylan put their conversation on pause and all looked over at the meeting in the middle of the dining area.

"You don't have to," Jimmi the Pilot drawled back angrily, losing his patience. "Just tell me where the damn village is."

Somethin' for Nothin'

Albert frowned at Cici.

CiCi shrugged her shoulders in apathy.

Albert poured Dylan a cup of coffee, then grabbed three coffee mugs and the pot. He came out from around the bar and headed towards the table, which had flash-frozen in a moment of silent frustration.

"Jimmi—*Jimmi*, sit down," Beantown Bob coaxed softly.

"He is impossible," said the Texan. "Fucking impossible."

Waxy watched Moe the Eskimo take out yet another cigarette and begin to smoke it, drawing hard and blowing out the blue-gray smoke with noisy exhales.

"Got some joe," said Albert putting down the three mugs and making an offering of the Bunn coffee pot. Beantown Bob, Jimmi the Pilot and Moe the Eskimo all nodded, relieved at the break in their wrangling. Albert surveyed the crinkled aviation map, then the *Anchorage Daily News* article headline in front of Beantown Bob. "*God damn*—God damn it, it's true isn't it?"

No one at the table spoke. They all stared into the center of the table, looking at the map, but, really, focusing on nothing in particular to avoid Albert's accusatory tone.

"Waxy?"

Waxy looked up at Albert and nodded his head.

"And you all are seriously going to go after it?"

Waxy shrugged his shoulders. "We've got to find it first."

"*God damn*. And I just got me a TAPS ticket."

Albert's revelation got everyone's attention.

"What the fuck?" asked Beantown Bob.

"Albert?" asked Waxy.

Jimmi the Pilot and Moe the Eskimo waited for Albert's answer.

"Yeah—I report to Fairbanks next week."

"But—Bu —" Waxy stammered.

"You son-of-a-bitch. You're quitting on me?" bellowed Beantown Bob angrily. "I ought to kick your ass all the way from here to Deadhorse."

Beantown Bob's outburst got the attention of CiCi and Dylan. They turned around and became an audience of two for the sudden twist in the meeting as the conspirators turned on each other.

"Hang on there, Bob. Hang on," Jimmi the Pilot tried to calm his friend down. "This could actually work out for us."

"Yeah? And how's that?"

"Well, if the work don't kill him outright at least it will get him out of our hair once and for all—"

"Hey—" blurted out Albert.

Jimmi the Pilot looked up at Albert and cut him off, cautioning, "You better cowboy up there pard. It ain't no Sunday picnic out on the line. It's hard work."

"So I keep hearing," sneered Albert.

"They work those guys like dogs," Jimmi the Pilot warned.

"God damn it, get that coffee the hell out of here and bring me the Bushmills," Beantown Bob barked at Albert.

"And bring me a Budweiser," said Jimmi the Pilot.

Albert backed away from the table a couple of steps and took the coffee pot back to the urn.

"The mouth doesn't know what he's getting himself into," Jimmi the Pilot said.

"It'll kill him for sure," growled Beantown Bob as he eyeballed Albert and CiCi talking at the bar.

Waxy silently looked at Beantown Bob, then at Jimmi the Pilot.

Somethin' for Nothin'

"Now, can we get serious about figuring out where the hell this plane wreck is?" Jimmi the Pilot turned and glared at Moe the Eskimo.

Beantown Bob and Waxy looked at Moe the Eskimo, too.

"I ain't getting in that damned plane," said Moe the Eskimo. "I won't do it."

"It's not that bad," Waxy said quietly. "It's kind of fun."

"Bullshit. Not to land on a god damned mountain—not that mountain. You guys are crazy. I won't do it." Moe the Eskimo stood up abruptly, grabbed his pack of Camel cigarettes and stormed off to the kitchen.

Beantown Bob and Jimmi the Pilot watched Moe the Eskimo go, then they both looked over at Waxy.

"And *your* fucking job is to keep our native friend on the reservation," Beantown Bob said to Waxy, "If you know what I mean."

From the look on Waxy's face, he obviously did not know what Beantown Bob meant.

"He's the key to this enterprise. He knows where the wreck is," explained Jimmi the Pilot. "You got to work him, keep him all happy-smiley face and keep him on board with the plan or we may never find it out there. And once we find it, we'll need his native know-how."

Waxy nodded.

Beantown Bob noticed a group of men gathered at the front door of *Fenway Park West* and peering in through the front windows. "Go unlock the God damned door. I still have an establishment to run—and get back in that kitchen and talk to that crazy Eskimo."

Waxy pushed back from the table and went to unlock the front door. He exchanged a questioning glance with Albert who was bringing a Budweiser and Bushmills back to the table. He set them down and started to say something, but Beantown Bob cut him off.

"Don't say a fucking word to me right now." Beantown Bob took a sip of Irish whiskey.

Albert went back behind the bar.

"What was that all about?" CiCi asked.

Albert ignored her and watched Waxy walk, head down, from the front door back to the kitchen. Dylan followed Waxy closely with his eyes, too, grateful that he was no longer employed in the food service industry.

"Now, explain to me what the fuck those wetbacks were doing hanging out at my bar," Beantown Bob said to Jimmi the Pilot.

"It's just business, Bob. No doubt a little field trip north to check in on their business interests. You know, market research and all. I've been pushing them hard for more product to keep up with demand and for some reason they haven't been too forthcoming."

"God damn it."

"The *Beaver's* engine is nearly T-B-Oed. No plane, no toot for the roustabouts—no toot for the roustabouts, no moola to pay the Mexicans—no moola for the Mexicans, no product for the roustabouts *and* no obscene profit margins for you and yours truly."

"God damn it, I told you when we got into it that I didn't want this business in the bar. Too risky."

"Yeah, I know," Jimmi the Pilot said wearily. "Truth be told, I'm getting a might tired of dealing with those banditos, myself—not the most trustworthy souls in the world."

Somethin' for Nothin'

"I don't want it in the *Park*. Get it out and keep it out."

"Finding this payroll plane can make things right again for you and me. Make us whole. Get the banks off our backs and get the cartel out of our lives—and pronto-quick. I bet, we'd be set for life."

'God damn it."

"This can work, B.B. This can work."

"It God damn better work."

Jimmi the Pilot took a swig of Budweiser, nodded and muttered to himself, "Yeah, it better or we could end up dead."

$$***\sim\sim\sim***$$

The Wolf Out There

Saturday night, at the end of their last set, CiCi cased up her Martin quickly. She bounded off the stage and over to the bar. Dylan watched from behind his drum kit as she and Albert talked briefly, then his sister headed out the back door and, no doubt, up the outside stairway to Albert and Waxy's apartment. Dylan looked up at the door to Beantown Bob's office, behind which he was counting the night's receipts. He shook his head and spun the wing nuts counter-clockwise to take his cymbals off their stands. Albert hurried through the closing tasks for the last time and was soon out the door and up the stairway, too. The next day he would be leaving for Fairbanks, then on to construction camp Delta for orientation and his work crew assignment on the Trans Alaska Pipeline, courtesy of the fingerless man's union card.

When Waxy came out of the kitchen with a rack of drink glasses, Dylan, Nordo and Graham had packed up and left, too, leaving *Fenway Park West* empty and uncharacteristically quiet. He saw the bar was unmanned and knew Albert had bugged out for one last night with CiCi. With a weary sigh, he put away the glasses and finished the half-ass cleaning that Albert had done behind the bar. At least by tomorrow, the imminent danger of Beantown Bob coming after him and Albert with his Louisville Slugger, like he went after Eddie, will have passed. Waxy was in no hurry, as he assumed the Holiday Inn 'DO NOT DISTURB' sign already hung from the apartment door and he'd be sleeping there in the booth beneath the stuffed grizzly bear yet again. He went back into the kitchen for the bucket and mop. When Waxy was finally done with the floors, he wearily joined Moe the Eskimo at the end of the bar, after pulling a beer for himself from the cooler.

Moe sipped his whiskey and smoked.

Waxy stared hard at the label of his Moosehead lager.

Moe the Eskimo lit another cigarette from the butt of the nearly expired Camel.

They sat in silence.

"It is stupid," Moe the Eskimo finally verbalized in an exhaust cloud of blue-gray tobacco smoke.

Waxy was not really in the mood to have the conversation, as he was preoccupied with the fact that Albert was leaving him behind in the morning, but with Moe the Eskimo, communication was like hunting: you took your shots when you could. Waxy looked over. He took a long pull off his beer bottle and squinted at Moe the Eskimo.

"Stupid."

"Yeah, well, stupid drunk got me here in the first place."

"But it didn't get you dead."

"Not yet anyways."

Moe the Eskimo grunted and took a sip of whiskey. "There's still time."

Above them, the door to Beantown Bob's office opened and closed. Waxy and Moe the Eskimo heard the key turn in the deadbolt lock and felt Beantown Bob staring down on them from

Somethin' for Nothin'

the catwalk. Waxy looked up over his shoulder. Beantown Bob scowled down at him and pointed at Moe the Eskimo's back. Waxy's shoulders slumped visibly and he turned back to study the label on his beer bottle some more.

"So, who died?" Waxy asked finally, after listening to Beantown Bob clunk down the stairs using his Louisville Slugger as a cane, then leave through the back entrance.

Moe the Eskimo peered through the swirling cigarette smoke that hung about him like clouds about Denali.

Waxy sighed softly and waited.

"It turned them. And killed some outright. Like a hungry wolf. Others died inside."

"Trying to get the payroll."

"Thinking about it all the time." Moe the Eskimo sighed. "It is a hard life. No one can make it alone. No one."

Waxy nodded.

"Why have a village otherwise?"

"Is the village still there?"

Moe the Eskimo shook his head.

"I knew it would die, too. So I left as soon as I could."

"But who got killed?"

"A few. Too many. They all knew better, but died anyway. They couldn't help themselves." Moe stubbed out his Camel cigarette with a long, last exhale of smoke. "My older brother and his best friend."

"How?"

Moe the Eskimo grunted and took a sip of whiskey.

"Did they know where the plane wreck was? Did they actually find it?"

"Don't know. They all thought they knew where to go. But no one ever knew for sure, except that it was up in the mountains above the village. People, they talked and they looked up at the mountains and they talked. They pointed and argued among themselves. And soon they stopped talking. But they still looked up, away from the village. Away from each other. And soon everyone was turned away from being a village."

"How did they die?"

"Some froze and just never came back, I guess. My brother fell, climbing the mountain while everyone in the village just stared and argued."

Waxy took a long, thoughtful drink of Moosehead lager. "Do you think it's still up there?"

Moe the Eskimo nodded.

"How come?"

Moe the Eskimo shrugged his shoulders. "It is there. I just know. Like I know the wolf is out there."

"But you don't think we can get it?"

Moe the Eskimo shrugged his shoulders and lit another Camel. He sipped his whiskey and stared back into the past.

"You need to do this, don't you?"

Moe the Eskimo sipped again and smoked.

"You need to kill the wolf."

"And if we did?"

"I don't know. I guess it depends upon what we find when we get there."

"If we don't die trying."

~~~

True Love

Albert lay on his back staring at the ceiling above the bed. Cici's head rested on his shoulder and her naked body pressed against him as she doodled aimlessly on his chest with her finger. They lay like that, silent, for a long while. Both of them had been taken aback at the mysterious infiltration of passion into what had been, until then, purely physical and hunger-driven sexual encounters. CiCi and Albert lay together, each trying to make sense of new and unfamiliar feelings.

All night long, Albert watched CiCi on stage ever more closely from behind the bar, listening as if for the first time to the lyrics of the lonely ballads she crooned, the plaintive blues she wailed and the driving rock songs she belted out. He worked his last night at *Fenway Park West* caught in a purgatory of desire, wanting one AM to come quickly so they could be together, but also wishing time would stay frozen, so he could listen to her sing forever. In the post coital twilight of the first time he and CiCi had actually made love to one another, he stared at the ceiling and contemplated *The Big Picture*. More just an instinctive talker than a particularly deep thinker—one of the main reasons he had abandoned Professor Kragies' Philosophy 101 class at *The* Ohio State University— Albert pondered the imminent fulfillment of that original High Street vision quest to trek north in search of wealth working on the Trans Alaska Pipeline.

It probably would be hard work, like Jimmi the Pilot kept harping on and on and on about, but that taunt barely registered among Albert's worries. And maybe it would be dangerous, but even if he lost a finger or a toe, the occasional thought of carrying such a war wound and battle scars back to Akron to show the Field Marshal made him smile at the childish thoughts of vengeance over his father for cutting off the money pipeline of his VISA card. Even the hard grip of conscience on his gut in those first days after he had acquired the Laborers 942 card relaxed a little more with every edition of the *Anchorage Daily News* he scoured carefully which failed to report or mention any crime against a homeless man near the Alaska state employment trailers at the west end of town, until, like a long-healed muscle pull, his guilt was all memory and no ache.

What had been gnawing at Albert was the chilling effect of *The Big Picture* being overshadowed by an even bigger picture and an even greater adventure: Waxy's big treasure hunt with Beantown Bob, Jimmi the Pilot, and Moe the Eskimo. Albert chided himself for not paying closer attention to his roommate's mindless prattling on about his kitchen talk with Moe the Eskimo. Now, the prospect of making tens or even hundreds of thousands of dollars working on the pipeline faded in comparison to the payroll riches sure to be found in a crashed Air Force cargo plane somewhere out there in the Alaskan wilderness. He marveled and silently cursed that his farm-boy friend would be part of such an adventure, while he was not—*not yet, at least*. Thoughts of finding a way to finagle himself into their scheme began to consume his waking hours, until he was struck by the realization just then that he was in love with CiCi.

Somethin' for Nothin'

Love was a new and unfamiliar complication in what had been a pretty uncomplicated and enjoyable relationship Albert always had with women. He had never mourned the loss of a lover, always confident a new conquest would appear just over the horizon or, more likely, just down the street in the next High Street bar to satisfy his hungers. He glanced at CiCi's Madonna-like face framed by her soft auburn hair that waterfalled about her shoulders. CiCi was certainly as beautiful as any woman Albert had ever been with, possibly *the* most beautiful. Echoes of her strong, sensual voice singing songs about love, loss and regret rang in his ears and haunted him.

Albert did not want to leave, but, now realizing he was in love with CiCi, also knew absolutely he could not stay without incurring a potentially fatal train wreck with Beantown Bob and his Louisville Slugger. It would pain him intolerably to stay away too long and it would take an intolerably long time to pile up enough cash for him to rescue CiCi from Beantown Bob's clutches, even with the ridiculous wages he would be earning working on the pipeline. Albert became convinced that the hull of a wrecked Air Force cargo plane held the solution to his dilemma and the key to a future with CiCi. Albert lovingly studied CiCi. A dreamy smile curled the ends of her lips. Her eyes were locked in a soft, distant focus. As he wondered what she might be thinking, a new *Big Picture* began to form in his mind.

CiCi was happily confused and annoyed. She was so used to getting her way, especially when it came to men, that not knowing exactly what she was feeling and what she wanted was as disconcerting as it was exhilarating. Albert had always been a much better lover than any of the other clumsy boys and impatient men she had been manipulating all of her life, including Robert the Assistant Manager at the book store in Seattle, Eddie the bartender, and Beantown Bob. But that night there was something different, something more, something new in the way Albert had touched her, caressed her breasts, fondled her womanhood—had kissed her, entered her and drove her slowly, steadily and relentless towards ecstasy that had completely unmoored her from herself, her thoughts, her wants, her needs and her desires—had driven her into an unexplored frontier of orgasmic madness, like no other man had. A medley of Bonnie Raitt, Linda Ronstadt and Emmylou Harris songs she sang floated foggily through her head, fragmented lyrics fitting together like jigsaw puzzle pieces in her mind to make sense on a deeper emotional level than they ever had before. She desperately did not want Albert to leave in the morning. The desire to be free of Beantown Bob and out of Alaska—only now together with Albert—flared with an intense heat. CiCi smiled dreamily, knowing for the first time the pain men surely felt at the thought of losing her, and cursed her own heart's helplessness.

Of course, Beantown Bob steadfastly refused to share any information about his plans with Jimmi the Pilot to recover the payroll from the Air Force plane, gruffly deflecting her discreetly innocent inquiries like the abusive father-figure that he was. But CiCi was well-practiced at feigning disinterest to nonchalantly eavesdrop on his conversations and phone calls with Jimmi the Pilot. And, of course, he had to sleep, shower and shit sometime, which gave her ample opportunities to peruse the manila file folder filled with the clippings from the *Anchorage Daily News* about plane crashes and Jimmi the Pilot's marked up flying maps. CiCi had no doubt she would never see a dime of payroll money, if it was ever actually found. She also knew that she would quickly be granted her freedom from Beantown Bob, but not on anything near the terms she wanted. She looked at Albert, who stared with a lightly furrowed brow and squinted eyes at the ceiling. Somehow, she knew exactly what he was thinking.

CiCi cleared her throat softly.

Albert looked over at her, tucked her hair behind her ear and gently stroked her cheek.

CiCi closed her eyes and smiled.

Albert kissed her forehead.

"Do you think it's all for real?" CiCi finally asked. "Or just some pipe dream?"

"Pipe dream?"

"Huh?" CiCi opened her eyes.

"*Pipe* dream."

"Oh, yeah. I didn't think of that," she whispered. She began humming softly. It was a song by Karla Bonoff, "Lose Again."

Albert listened, then asked, "Do I think what is real?"

"You know, the payroll."

Albert looked back up at the ceiling. After a few moments, he answered, "Waxy does. Bob does. Jimmi really does."

"Do you?"

"If Waxy says Moe is telling the truth, I believe him. He's got a funny sense about people. I don't know why, but I trust it."

"So, it *is* true."

Albert slowly nodded, then looked CiCi in the eye. "I think so."

"What if they actually got it?" CiCi climbed on top of Albert and straddled him at the hips. "How much do you think is there?"

"I dunno." Albert looked up into her heavenly face and saw something not so angelic. "I suppose it could be a whole lot."

"Millions?" CiCi's eyes danced.

"It's the government. It could easily be millions."

"Hmmm."

Albert eyed CiCi warily for a moment, then smiled.

CiCi smiled back. "What would you do with a million dollars?"

"I don't know."

"But isn't that why you came? To strike it rich?"

Albert nodded. "What would you do?"

"Oh, wouldn't it be great? We could get out of here to somewhere warm again just for starters."

"*We?*"

CiCi smiled seductively.

"Like where?"

"I don't know, anywhere—far away from here." She looked slyly at Albert. "Far away from Bob."

"You would leave?"

CiCi smiled warmly at the prospect. "Yeah. In a heartbeat. So, are you going to help them?"

Albert searched her face. Somehow, he knew exactly what CiCi was thinking. "I'll find a way."

CiCi bent down to gently suck Albert's lower lip. She consciously brushed her nipples back and forth across his chest. She felt his arousal beneath her hips. "Mmmm—that seemed to get a rise out of you…or is it the millions?"

Somethin' for Nothin'

Albert set aside scheming and pondering upon the new *Big Picture* for the moment. He entered her and they made love again and again until dawn.

~~~

First Love

Waxy sat at the counter in the *Lucky Wishbone Diner*, staring down into the empty six-inch round plate that just recently held a piece of blackberry pie. He pushed around a hunk of crust with his fork, studiously avoiding the messy jumble of thoughts, worries and forebodings that collected in his mind like a dirty bus tray filled with the chaos of soiled dishes, glasses and silverware.

Emma watched Waxy from the kitchen and wondered what was troubling him. He was strangely quiet and unsmiling. She went and got another piece of pie and a fresh glass of milk and took it to him.

"On the house," Emma said, sliding the pie across the counter and picking up the empty plate. She put it into a nearly full bus tub under the counter.

"Thanks," Waxy said without looking up.

"How's work going?"

"Okay."

Emma stared at the top of Waxy's head. "So…have you been up flying with Jimmi lately?"

"Yeah," Waxy sighed without his usual enthusiasm for aviation.

Emma felt something in her heart, as if it had lost a beat. "Where to?"

"You know, just deliveries to the construction camps," Waxy answered with another heavy sigh, but thought about Jimmi the Pilot's long northerly deviations towards the mountains to search for where Moe the Eskimo's village had once been, hoping to find nearby a plane wreck with the government payroll hidden inside—a treasure that beckoned so loudly to Beantown Bob and Jimmi the Pilot with an urgency that Waxy simply did not comprehend. "I have to go meet up with him in a little bit for a run."

Emma bent down in front of Waxy, putting her elbows on the counter and her chin in her palms, so she was eye-to-eye with him.

He looked up at her.

She could see the hurt in his eyes.

Her beauty pained him.

"What's going on? Come on, you can tell me," Emma said softly.

"Albert left this morning for his new job on the pipeline."

"Mmmm…"

"I just dropped him off at the airport."

"Think he'll make it? It's no picnic. That's for sure."

Waxy shrugged his shoulders. "Sometimes he surprises you. Sometimes, not."

"And?"

"I dunno." Waxy poked at the new piece of pie with his fork. "I dunno."

Emma felt a wave of sympathy for Waxy. She gently patted, then softly rubbed his forearm.

Waxy looked down at Emma's hand on his arm. A simple touch he so often yearned for, it sent a tingle through his body.

Somethin' for Nothin'

"He didn't even tell me. He didn't tell me about getting his card, about getting the job or—" Waxy caught himself before he blurted out 'about making it with CiCi' and revealed a secret that would surely bring the wrath of Beantown Bob and his Louisville Slugger down upon him. "—or anything. Why wouldn't he at least tell me?"

Emma was curious about that, too, but had no answer to offer. "So, now what happens?"

That very question pounded relentlessly in Waxy's mind, until his head ached. He paused for a moment, contemplating the long ago plane crash, the payroll and the secret scheme that was simmering in the minds of Beantown Bob and Jimmi the Pilot. The entire enterprise had been haunting his subconscious ever since the two confronted Moe the Eskimo with the aeronautical chart and pressed him with their questions. Waxy was at once intrigued and wary. He read the second thoughts on Albert's face about leaving to work on the pipeline after he learned about the treasure hunt and started to doubt whether he really wanted to join him in the hard labors that lay ahead for his friend. As Waxy washed, sorted and stacked dishes in the kitchen of *Fenway Park West,* he caught himself fantasizing on how his life might change with a windfall of wealth far greater than what he and Albert had used as a carrot to lure themselves north to Alaska in the first place—and even dared to allow himself to contemplate how it might change his prospects for the better with Emma. He was convinced it would take far more than a dishwashing job to win her heart. Waxy slowly began to have a *Big Picture* of his own to chase.

But pleasant thoughts of a life together with Emma were chilled by the cold shadow of death from the stories Moe the

Eskimo told of the hard, clawed grip the unreachable treasure held over his village and the tragedies their greed for it spawned. The empty hours of his dish washing shift had been filled with these thoughts, which left him more exhausted than the actual physical labors of the job. He was tired of thinking. He was scared of what might happen if they actually found the plane wreck. He stood at a precipice, frozen in doubt, not knowing what to do. Stay and join Beantown Bob and Jimmi the Pilot in their crazy scheme? Be patient and eventually join Albert at Camp Delta? Use the money he had secretly saved from washing dishes to buy a plane ticket back to Ohio, back to his father's farm and the surrender to failure it would mean—especially the failure of his own *Big Picture* to ever possibly come true.

But what if they were right about the treasure? Could it make him rich? Then again, what if they found it, but the hungry wolf of Moe the Eskimo's past came back again—this time *for them?* Waxy tired of thinking. He was just plain worn down and worn out with worry and unanswered wonderings.

Waxy shrugged.

"You going to stick around?"

He felt the weight of the question bear down on him. Waxy shrugged again.

"I'd miss you, if you left." It surprised Emma that saying it out loud seemed to crystallize the vague feelings that swirled in and out of her consciousness like a thick, ghostly fog oozing between the downtown buildings off Cook's Inlet into something real and tangible. By the time the words had been said, she realized that she really meant them.

Waxy looked up at Emma and furrowed his brow at her unexpected confession.

Somethin' for Nothin'

She smiled vulnerably.
At that moment, Waxy knew he was in on the plan.

~~~

Brotherly Love

Jimmi the Pilot sat on the wheel of his de Havilland *Beaver* waiting for the fuel truck, absently turning a folded up sectional chart around and around in his hands. He saw Waxy and Emma talking at the counter when he stopped by the *Lucky Wishbone Diner* for coffee. He paused at the front door and watched her lean down to look Waxy in the eye and touch his arm—a look and a touch he had so often yearned for himself, but knew would never come his way. At least Emma had not been a total bitch about it and they remained friends. It wasn't what he wanted, but it was better than nothing—and who knew? He harbored a small secret hope that maybe someday...*maybe*...

Jimmi the Pilot left and went over to Merrill Field without going in for his usual morning coffee to go. It was a good thing that he was genuinely fond of Waxy, like a little brother he never had.

Days were getting longer. The cold was not quite so biting and the frosty clouds of his exhales were not quite as dense. Good, he thought. He could use all the daylight he could get to find the crash site as soon as possible. Once he did, there was simply no telling how much time it would take to recover the payroll from the wreckage. Though he could feel spring's approach, Jimmi the Pilot knew that next winter was not as far off as it might seem for what they needed to get done. With any luck at all, Alaska would be fading in life's rearview mirror and he would find himself some place much, much warmer by the time old man winter rolled back around. He rubbed his leg to work out some of the stiffness the cold induced around the shrapnel still buried in his flesh.

As his hand massaged his thigh, his mind tried to massage the hopelessness of his situation out of his mind. As much as he regretted the deal he had made with the cartel, he could not take it back, ignore it or, as he slowly came to realize, ever pay his way out of it. He had lied to Beantown Bob: the Mexicans had already saved his ass by fronting him the cash for the new engine on the *Beaver* when it timed out. It had all seemed so simple, straight forward and logical. They kept him flying and he'd pay them back out of the profits from dealing weed and coke to the construction camps on the pipeline. But Jimmi the Pilot could never keep up with the vig and now—at least in their eyes—the cartel owned his beloved *Beaver* and his soul. He had even brought Beantown Bob into the deal to try to increase the volume of product he was able to move in a desperate attempt to claw his way out of debt. It hadn't worked and the Mexicans were squeezing him hard, forcing him to take more and more product at lower and lower profit margins until he was caught in a graveyard spiral. Beantown Bob didn't know it, yet, but it wasn't just a treasure hunt. It was survival.

Jimmi the Pilot opened the sectional chart and tried to figure out where the hell that Air Force cargo plane might have gone down.

~~

Skinny City

Albert stared out the bus window at the rugged country south of Fairbanks passing by as he rode to his first day of labors on the pipeline. A hunger began to gnaw at him the moment the plane lifted off from Anchorage to take him to Fairbanks and continued to grow in his gut day-by-day, during his orientation at Fort Wainwright and his assignment to Camp Delta. He had not known what to say to Waxy at the end, when he had to exit the concourse at the final boarding call for his flight. They awkwardly shook hands, but Waxy couldn't look Albert in the eye, so he left without a word. Albert hadn't given it much thought, but there on the bus, he realized a part of the gnawing in his gut was missing his friend. After traveling together so long and far across the continent, they had parted ways and Albert reluctantly admitted to himself that he felt an unfamiliar loneliness.

Of course, the bigger part of his hunger was for CiCi. In the early morning darkness, they had parted wordlessly, too, but not without a long, wet kiss and a last embrace that bore witness to their new found passions and their resolve to escape Alaska with a share of riches from an aviation disaster that happened before either of them had been born. While Albert sometimes thought about Waxy, he often dreamed of CiCi.

The slowly blooming Alaska spring brought a spawning stream of workers back to the pipeline. When he got to

Fairbanks, the employment process took Albert back to the previous fall, reminding him of freshman orientation at *The Ohio State University*. Communal camp life with its twenty-three rules and cafeteria food was a lot like dormitory life, though the crunch of gravel everywhere underfoot seemed like a taunting whisper in his ear that he would soon wish he were back in Professor Kragies' Philosophy 101 class, where life was easy. The gathering welders, drivers, operators and laborers were every bit as motley, albeit quite a bit more hardened and rough-edged, as the schooling youth in the campus tidal pool north of downtown Columbus. The workers naturally congealed into blobs by union affiliation: Pipeliners, Teamsters, Operators, Steamfitters, Electrical Workers and Laborers. Of course, the union groups separated further into wide-eyed, overwhelmed "freshmen" and smirking, experienced "upper classmen" returning for another semester of construction.

Albert couldn't help but notice similarities between the veteran workers and Beantown Bob's regulars who planted themselves at the bar every afternoon and drank themselves into a stupor: craggy, weathered visages; stiff, hard-calloused hands; and loud, hoarse voices. It wasn't hard to connect the dots between the coarse, rough-and-tumble pipeline workers there with him on the bus and those painfully-hunched, bone-weary men who had been taken into the crushing, hydraulic jaws of hard labors in a tough land, chewed up and spit back out, broken in both body and spirit, to quietly seek liquid relief at *Fenway Park West*. Albert shuddered at the thought of ever becoming one of those lonely men. Revulsion for such a future brought visions of Roy Walsh to mind, wiping his mangled, fingerless paw across his craggy, sneering smile in an

Somethin' for Nothin'

Anchorage alleyway. Of course, now, as far as Laborers Local 942 and Perini Arctic Associates, his employer on section two of the pipeline, were concerned, Albert *was* Roy Walsh, thanks to the union card he had stolen.

"Be careful what you wish for..." Albert said softly to himself, feeling as if he was about to start serving his punishment on a chain gain for assault and battery on Roy Walsh with the Yukon Jack bottle. He tried to tune out the banter of Roy's fellow Laborers on the bus and searched the passing Alaska wilderness for an escape path from his guilt. Soon, though, he would have no time for such idle thoughts, as the bus turned off the Richardson Highway and down a side road to the Trans Alaska Pipeline right-of-way. As it squealed to a halt next to the scar that cut through the wilderness, the din of conversations quieted. Veterans knew what the work day would bring. Albert and the other rookies searched their faces for some clue, but in the end quietly stood and joined them, shuffling one-by-one down the center aisle of the bus and out into the chaotic activity of the construction site.

"Come on, *Buckeye Boy*. Over here," Mac called out as he gathered his crew together. "Grab a shovel. You know the drill."

Albert waved and trotted over, holding his hard hat down on his head. Diesel exhaust fumes filled the air as it seemed like a whole herd of trucks, bulldozers, power shovels and sidebooms had gathered there like huge, prehistoric beasts at a watering hole. Some idled, others groaned under the weight of their labors pushing, scraping and drilling the earth; lifting and stacking huge sections of four-foot diameter pipe; or shoveling gravel into dump trucks to carry and drop somewhere further north or south along the pipeline's path. Albert grabbed a shovel and climbed up into the back of a yellow Alyeska pickup truck. Before he sat down, Mac pounded on the cab and the truck took off heading north to some anonymous spot between the clearing crews and the welders, where Mac's crew was assigned to help erect Vertical Support Members, the giant H-shaped towers that would hold the pipeline high up off the valley floor to keep the hot flowing oil from melting the permafrost as it zig-zagged its way south from Prudhoe Bay. Although diesel-powered machines did the heavy lifting, there were literally millions of shovelfuls of dirt, gravel and debris that had to be dug, moved and replaced by the member muscles of Laborers Local 942. Albert stared down into the pan of his shovel, no longer thinking of CiCi and Waxy. He mindlessly watched his breath meet the cold spring air in clouds that appeared and vanished in slugs like a steam engine smoke stack, until the truck stopped. In front of them, augers on the backs of bulldozers drilled twenty-four inch holes in the earth. Sidebooms lifted the vertical supports of the VSMs up and into the holes, holding them in place as crews aligned them and water trucks filled the holes, while Mac's crew shoveled sand and gravel into the water in the hole, which, once the water froze, would hold the VSM in place like concrete.

"Slow down, man," Wil said as he elbowed Albert. "Take it easy and pace yourself. We don't have to finish this bitch in one day."

Albert nodded and let himself fall into sync with the steady rhythm of Wil, Sully and Jack as they filled hole after hole after hole. It wasn't until after their lunch break that he began to doubt seriously whether he would be able to make it through the rest of the shift, as his muscles began to ache and his bones themselves seemed to groan with every shovelful of sand and gravel he scooped. Albert's mind became as dense as a stone and just as incapable of thought through the long afternoon of work that seemed to have no end in sight, but eventually Mac called it a day and they climbed back into the yellow pickup truck to take them back to the bus, to take them back to Camp Delta. Albert could only think of collapsing from exhaustion into his bunk, until he dozed off on the ride back to camp. Fortunately, Wil, Sully and Jack dragged him to the cafeteria to fuel his body up first. He chewed and swallowed his food without tasting. He heard the banter of his coworkers without listening. After dinner, he let the hot shower water beat down on his back long after he had scrubbed the grit from his body, then went right to his bed and fell quickly into a stone hard sleep so deep that it allowed no dreaming—not even of CiCi.

In the morning, Albert wrestled unfamiliar muscle aches and body stiffnesses to get up and do it again, holding on hard to memories of CiCi, until the bus ride north ended and the work day began, turning his mind to stone again.

He got up the next day and the next and the next, eventually gaining strength and falling into the numbing routine of the pipeline construction. He soon lost all connection with the outside world and was absorbed into the living organism that was the Trans Alaska Pipeline project.

~~

Moe's Minder

Waxy had never been in Beantown Bob's office up on the second floor. There were two windows: one looking outside over the back alley and another looking inside down over the bar area. As he sat across the massive desk from Beantown Bob, waiting for him to finish a phone call with Jimmi the Pilot, Waxy surveyed the slow-motion avalanche of junk that was, like a glacier, ever so slowly bearing down on its owner from every corner. There were book shelves lined with volumes, which, from the cakes of dust, had not been pulled down in years. On top of the books were stacked newspapers, magazines and manuscript pages. Spilling off the shelves devoid of books was an eclectic collection of taxidermy, trinkets and tools of the sports trade, including baseballs, fielder's and catcher's mitts, bats, mud-caked spiked shoes, a hockey puck and stick, speed skates, a lacrosse stick, a football helmet, a mouth guard, a kick-off tee, a race car driver's helmet, motocross knee pads, a curling broom and stone, horseshoes, a jai alai pelota and cesta, a cricket bat and wicket, a croquet mallet and balls, a putter, sand wedge, niblick, and a pin flag from the Masters. Waxy would have been hard pressed to identify half of the items Beantown Bob had collected. On the walls were framed sports jerseys and newspaper sports pages chronicling triumphs and tragedies, mostly of the Boston *Red Sox*, though some commemorated lead stories in the *Anchorage Daily News* which carried Beantown Bob's by-line. In short, the office decor was a concentrated replica of the bar downstairs, crammed into a crowded twelve-by-fifteen foot space.

Beantown Bob cradled the phone between his shoulder and his ear and leaned back nearly prone in his squeaky office chair, tossing a baseball up over his head and catching it again in a well-worn catcher's mitt. After every third or fourth toss, he closed his eyes in a grimace and rubbed the baseball into the pocket of the mitt. Once or twice, after a heavy sigh, he squinted a sideways glare at Waxy, which made him squirm a bit in a chair that was already uncomfortable.

On the desk next to the IBM Selectric, loaded and ready on the typing wing with a blank page in its roller, Waxy noticed the neatly stacked manuscript that was arrested in its development at just under an inch tall. Splaying out from the fiction frozen in time were pencils, pens, drug paraphernalia, a Bushmills bottle and several shot glasses stacked in a replica of the Leaning Tower of Pisa. On the other side of the green banker's lamp in the center of the desk was a haphazard heap of invoices, notices and official letters regarding the on-going enterprise activities of *Fenway Park West*.

"Yeah, yeah, yeah—Right, right, right. I'll talk to him," Beantown Bob said to Jimmi the Pilot over the phone. "He's sitting right here. *I said, I'll talk to him.*"

Beantown Bob hung up the phone. He tossed and caught the baseball a dozen more times. When he finally sat upright and turned towards Waxy, he ground the ball into the pocket and stared at the agrarianly blank look on his face, thinking that he'd hate to sit down in a poker game with a bunch of farmers and try to read their hands from their visages.

Somethin' for Nothin'

Waxy didn't know why he was there in Beantown Bob's office, but figured he'd find out soon enough. While he felt some anxiety about this sudden meeting with his boss, his thoughts kept getting tugged back to the *Lucky Wishbone Diner,* Emma's smile and her confession that she would miss him if he went back to Ohio.

"How's that chowder head pal of yours making out actually having to work a day in his life for a change?" Beantown Bob finally asked Waxy.

Waxy shrugged his shoulders. "I dunno. I haven't heard from him. Albert's more of a talker than a writer. Anyways, I don't imagine there are postcards where he's at."

Beantown Bob chuckled. "No. I can tell you for sure, that they don't have postcards in the camps."

Waxy nodded.

"Your friend—*My employee*—Mr. Moe is giving Jimmi a hard time."

"Why's that?"

"Why? I don't know; but Jimmi's feelings seem to be hurt that they aren't getting along and playing nice-nice together like elementary school chums. He prides himself on being a friendly sort."

Waxy frowned trying to comprehend.

"Look, I didn't hire the guy for his gift of gab, but it is a waste of everybody's time and mostly *my* money for Jimmi to be burning up gasoline joy riding over the mountains looking for that damn wreck without any help from the one guy who might actually have some idea of where it is."

Waxy nodded.

Beantown Bob sighed wearily at Waxy's silence, empathizing for the moment with Jimmi the Pilot. "Well?"

"Well, what?"

"Well, if you want to be in on this caper, you need to pull your weight. You need to work Moe to get him to be a little more talkative, so we can find the crash site before next winter hits." Beantown Bob threw the ball hard into the mitt. "You've got a pretty sweet deal here, what with an apartment all to yourself now and everything. I need you to start pulling your weight and pronto. We've only got a short window of time where the weather will cooperate, so we need to get moving—or you can drag your ass back to the Buckeye State for all I care."

At Beantown Bob's suggestion of exile from Alaska and Emma, Waxy got the message. "I'll talk to him."

"You'll do more than talk to him. You'll get that taciturn tundra head spilling the beans on what he knows."

Waxy nodded.

"*Son...*"

"I'll take care of it."

"I don't care if you have to sit beside him and hold his dick in your hand in the back of Jimmi's plane."

Waxy nodded.

Beantown Bob nodded and noted, again, the blank expression on Waxy's face and thought of sitting across from the boy in a poker game. "Well?"

"Well?"

"Don't you have pots to scrub or something?"

Waxy stood up to go.

"Get your ass in that plane with Jimmi and Moe the next time they go up."

Waxy nodded. "Sure thing, Bob. Sure thing."

Somethin' for Nothin'

Waxy left and went downstairs to the kitchen, worried about losing Emma.

Beantown Bob leaned back in his chair to toss the baseball up over his head and catch it again in the well-worn catcher's mitt, ignoring his stalled manuscript and the blank page in his typewriter.

~~~

Hot Flashes

CiCi skated a slice of zucchini around the plate with her fork, watching Beantown Bob across from her in the booth attack and slash his sirloin steak with more than the usual portion of repressed rage. The meal had been a silent one, though the thoughts that danced furiously like whirling Arctic dervishes about the curves in their gray matter shared a common obsession: the flight manifest of a long ago downed cargo plane. He fretted that with the growing pile of receipts for aviation fuel it would never be found. She worried that it would, but would forever remain beyond her reach.

She sighed and gazed out the front window of *Fenway Park West* at the passers by on Fourth Avenue. CiCi was not upset at Beantown Bob's recent preoccupations. This and other quiet meals allowed space for her to contemplate life, specifically her own regarding how and, now, precisely when she would be able to return to a real life in the lower Forty-Eight. 'When' had never before been a subject for much serious thought, as *"immediately, if not sooner"* was typically the default answer, but the how, though yet unseen, was now as real as the bite of winter wind and when seemed tantalizingly near. Beantown Bob's preoccupations also served to distract him from coming to her to satisfy his physical needs, which was okay, except that with Albert gone to work on the pipeline, her own yearnings had been nipping at her heels for attention. Nine weeks did not seem like a long time at first. Two and a half weeks later, though, Albert's R&R seemed to be an eternity away, especially when the ecstasies of their last night together came to mind uninvited at most inopportune times—like just then. As CiCi's thoughts drifted hazily off, she felt a warm rush of blood flush her face. She quickly excused herself from the booth and by the time Beantown Bob looked up from his sirloin, he saw only her backside heading towards the ladies room. He pushed a forkful of beef into his mouth and admired her ass as he chewed.

CiCi passed by the ladies room and slipped out the back door leading to the alley to cool her simmering passions. She tried to delude herself by forcing the thought into her mind that the labored breathing was due to scurrying away from Beantown Bob's presence, but she knew better and cracked a Mona Lisa smile as she watched her exhales cloud in the cool evening air. At least Albert was as ready to leave Alaska as she was, though it irked her a little that even the vaguest of notions that there might be some kind of future together came to her. It was an unfamiliar weakness and if it weren't for the pleasant warmth Albert's memory lately brought over her, she might be more upset with herself.

But that future was perilously still beyond reach. She and Albert were on the outside and needed to get in on Beantown Bob's plan somehow. She frowned at a lingering, gnawing doubt that the treasure might not even be there after all.

A throat cleared itself deliberately and from below a question arose, "Are you okay?"

Startled, CiCi looked down and saw Waxy sitting on the steps at her feet, looking up in a glow of reverence at her.

Somethin' for Nothin'

"Mmmm...Just a hot flash."

Waxy furrowed his brow.

"It's a woman thing, you know." CiCi smiled at Waxy's vulnerability. An idea came to her. "Can I sit down for a moment?"

"Uh, yeah. Um, sure." Waxy scooted his butt over to make room.

"Thanks." CiCi sat down next to Waxy, close enough that their thighs touched, insuring the intended hormonal meltdown of his male willpower. She smiled as Waxy's respiration rate increased noticeably.

Waxy looked away, sure that his instinctual animal stirrings were as obvious to her as to himself.

"It was just so stuffy in there."

Waxy nodded, staring down hard at the paved surface of the alleyway, trying desperately to think of anything besides the beautiful woman beside him.

"How is Albert doing?"

"Okay, I guess. Don't hear from him much." He was tempted to ask if she had heard from Albert, but didn't dare enter territory fraught with the danger of being on the wrong end of Beantown Bob's Louisville Slugger, like Eddie.

"I hope he's doing okay. He's a good guy."

"Yeah, deep down he is. A lot of folks don't see it, but he is a good guy."

CiCi nodded and smiled—as much to herself at her effect on men as to communicate non-verbally with the man sitting next to her.

"I guess I should get back in the kitchen. Another bus tray of dishes is probably ready to come in."

"Could you stay? Please?" CiCi touched his arm to keep him from rising. "Just for a minute or two so I don't have to sit out here, you know, alone."

"Uh. Yeah. Sure."

"Those dishes will still be there for you."

Waxy nodded.

"Do you like it here?"

"Here?"

"Here, in Alaska."

Waxy thought for a moment, more of Emma than of the fiftieth state to be admitted to the union. He nodded. "Yeah, I think so. It's different. Good different."

CiCi sighed heavily.

"I like the mountains and stuff. It is actually pretty incredible when I go along with Jimmi on his flights."

CiCi saw her opening. "I've never been up with him. Is it safe?"

"Oh, sure. He's a good pilot—of course, he's the only pilot I know—but I feel safe."

"Where do you boys fly to?"

"I, ah, you know, mostly help out with his deliveries up to the construction sites. Loading and unloading."

CiCi leaned in towards Waxy and half-whispered, "Are you in on the plan?"

Waxy exhaled heavily.

"I mean, I know *all* about it, of course," CiCi lied. "What, with, you know, Bob and me."

Waxy nodded.

"I just don't understand how they are ever going to find it. I mean, it's been so many years and all."

Somethin' for Nothin'

Waxy blew a long exhale. "Moe knows."

"What?"

"Moe the Eskimo. The cook. He knows."

"He knows where it is?"

Waxy nodded.

"You're sure?"

Waxy nodded.

CiCi nodded. She smiled, having confirmed that the 'How' of her leaving Alaska was now unquestionably real.

"Do you have an address for Albert? I'd like to send him a little note."

Waxy nodded.

"It might cheer him up to hear from a friend."

Waxy nodded, but in his mind snickered at the word 'friend.'

CiCi smiled and gave Waxy a huge hug in thanks, making sure that she pressed her breasts against Waxy's bicep. She got up and went back into the bar.

Ten minutes later, once his respiration rate returned to normal, Waxy followed her inside and went back to work.

~~~

The Search

The de Havilland droned on. The newness of the experience was gone. The initial awe and wonder that the unfamiliar perceptions avalanched over Waxy on his first few times in the cockpit melted into a grind of flight after flight after flight—as often as the weather would allow. The breath-taking vistas of lakes, glaciers, evergreen-carpeted forests and the bald caps of mountains reaching up above the timberline—even the majestic Olympian presence of Denali in the distance on clear days, failed to stir his soul, as before. Waxy sat in the back seat behind Moe the Eskimo, his eyes gazing upon the terrain below, but not discerning or absorbing any coherent mental map of the area. In those empty hours, he thought about Emma. He thought about *The Big Picture—his Big Picture.* He thought about sitting so close to CiCi and wishing he could break the wall of the *Lucky Wishbone Diner* counter between them and be that near to Emma, their bodies touching in ways and places he hadn't even yet dared to dream of. He pushed the headset microphone up over his head, so his sighs were absorbed by the rumble of the Pratt & Whitney radial engine and the rapids-like roar of the slipstream around the fuselage, rather than shared over the intercom.

Jimmi the Pilot, with a sectional chart on his lap marked up with the sectors of a search grid over the areas previously flown and those yet to be covered, nursed the *Beaver* at the edge of a stall, to loiter slow enough for Moe the Eskimo beside him to survey the land below in order to identify a landmark locating the crash site from his youth in the village. Of all of them, Jimmi the Pilot was the most patient, having so often observed the vastness of the earth first hand from high above and understanding the smallness of flying machines—even a four-engine, hundred-ton *Globemaster* cargo plane. He was grateful for Waxy's help with Moe the Eskimo, who on the first week of flights sat immutably mute, staring straight ahead, obviously not putting forth any effort at all. With Waxy as a minder, Moe the Eskimo at least began to swivel his head on his shoulders and, covertly reading his eye movements from behind his glacier glasses, could see that their native scout was finally actively searching.

If only he could keep a panicky Beantown Bob off the ledge about the fuel costs, Jimmi the Pilot was certain they would find the site of the wreckage as they slowly, but surely, eliminated squares on the sectional chart, narrowing the possible areas down until their payroll jackpot was found.

Jimmi the Pilot entered a shallow bank to shift their flight path over a quarter mile to the west, as always, positioning the right side of the airplane on the inside of the turn to keep Moe the Eskimo's eyes at work. When he rolled out straight and level again, he checked the Loran-C receiver and made a note of the latitude and longitude on his side window with a grease pencil. He would later transfer the location information to his sectional map to detail the areas searched and those yet to be searched.

He looked back over his shoulder at Waxy, who had the blank, zombie-like expression the weight of boredom and lovesickness typically pressed upon the visages of young men. Jimmi the Pilot knew that Emma knew of Waxy's attraction for her and also knew that the feelings were vaguely mutual, so on his regular morning stops for coffee at the *Lucky Wishbone Diner* he casually started talking Waxy up with ever so subtle dropped comments attesting to his good nature, and hard-working, but fun-loving character. The morsels he left on the counter appeared to give Emma pause to consider the boy in a softer, kinder light. To Jimmi the Pilot, it was like chumming bread crumbs to the giant goldfish in the decorative pond in the lobby of the whorehouse in Bangkok while he waited his turn for Kanchana, his favorite.

Jimmi the Pilot scanned the gauges and saw that they had burned off more than half their fuel load. He mentally planned to cover twenty more minutes of terrain before turning back towards Anchorage.

~~~

Brother and Sister

Dylan sat on the ragged sofa in the band house living room watching Saturday morning cartoons. He had yet to be to sleep and still had a buzz going from partying after the gig at *Fenway Park West*. Beside him snored a twenty-something brunette he had met between sets who was drunk enough to leave her friends and come home with him. Unfortunately, that meant when they got back to the band house, she quickly became so drunk and stoned that she fell asleep before Dylan could maneuver her to his bed. So now, he sipped a beer and watched Wile E. Coyote try scheme after scheme after scheme in vain attempts to catch the Roadrunner, sympathizing with the hungry predator's angst.

Nordo, the bass player, padded out from the front bedroom towards the bathroom dressed only in boxer shorts, rubbing his eyes with one hand and scratching his groin with the other. A shrill, descending glissando followed by a loud explosion caught his ear and grabbed his eye, yanking his head towards the television set. He stopped to watch Wile E. Coyote pull his charred carcass from a black, smoking hole in the desert floor and grunted primordially. He looked at Dylan, then at the slumbering beauty next to him, who suddenly thrashed in spasm of a dream breaking through to reality, like a writhing salmon might break the water's surface before falling back into the dreamy silence of its underwater world.

Dylan caught Nordo's careful inspection of the sleeping woman.

"No luck, huh?"

Dylan shrugged his shoulders and rolled his eyes. He shook his Coors beer can to gauge its fill. "Grab me another, would you?"

Nordo nodded as he padded on through the living room to pee, then fetch Dylan a beer.

Dylan had grown used to the lifestyle of a working musician. It wasn't a rock star's life—yet—but it was a hell of a lot better than cleaning up bodily fluids at the old folks home in Seattle. Even at the *Fenway Park West* level there was a cool unreality to not having to go to work at a regular job. The fact that after he was done playing music for the night, he was free not to do a damn thing, set extremely well with him. Plus, since they were the house band at *Fenway Park West*, he didn't have to waste his days and off evenings trying to talk to stupid bar owners to hustle up bookings during the day.

Dylan rarely rose before noon, which drove his sister crazy. But that was okay, since she wasn't there half the time anyway. Lately, though she was spending more and more of her nights at the band house instead of at Beantown Bob's cabin, which gave Dylan cause for concern for the future perpetuation of his current lifestyle, should her relationship with the man who was technically their employer ever come to an end. For the most part, Dylan avoided Beantown Bob, like a feline avoids a canine. No need to expose himself to the Boss Man any more than he had to. He had found them in the club in Seattle and had fallen head over heels for his sister's voice and her comely maiden looks, so he gave them the gig at *Fenway Park West*. Dylan didn't think too hard about their relationship—or any others, really—beyond his own self-interest, even if it did involve his sister's honor.

The toilet flushed and moments later the refrigerator door opened and closed. Nordo came padding back through the living room like a zombie, handing Dylan an unopened can of Coors, as he headed back to bed.

"Sorry man. Better luck next time."

Dylan looked at the brunette beside him and sighed. "Win some. Lose some."

Dylan reached for the bong and a lighter on the cable reel. Checking the bowl, he found it still half packed with unburnt marijuana. He lit up and took a few tokes, washing it down with Coors, then watched seven minutes of Foghorn Leghorn mentoring a young chicken hawk.

"Still at it, I see," CiCi said as she came in. She eyed the unconscious competition on the sofa carefully. "Nice. Is she still alive?"

"Barely," Dylan sighed heavily. "What time is it anyway?"

"Going on nine."

"Great. By the time she wakes up, *I'll* be ready to crash."

CiCi sat down across from Dylan in an overstuffed chair. She folded her hands on her lap in a way that reminded Dylan of their mother and gave him an earnest glare, also in a way that reminded him of their mother whenever she wanted to talk to him about his school grades, his non-existent college plans or his future employment prospects.

Dylan tried to narrow his field of view to the television.

CiCi eyed her brother and sighed.

Dylan tried to surreptitiously steal a quick look with only movement of his eyeballs, but knew he had been caught.

"He's up to something."

M.T. Bass

"He? Who?"

"Bob."

"Ah, what do you mean?" CiCi had his attention, as the conversation likely concerned the continuation of his current comfortably decadent lifestyle.

"Him and Jimmi. And, I guess, that creepy Eskimo guy in the kitchen is in on it, too."

Dylan waited for her to go on, but CiCi knew how to bait her brother—after all he was a man. She sighed again.

"What? What are they up to?"

"And the kid from Ohio. Maybe Albert, too, but I don't know how."

"Come on, sis, you're killing me."

"I think there's definitely something going on."

Dylan groaned. "What? Please, what? Do they have a big score coming in from Mexico?"

"No. Listen to me," CiCi looked at the sleeping brunette and listened for a snore, then leaned into Dylan. She waited for him to sit up and lean towards her, then whispered, "I think they found some long lost government Army payroll."

"Found? What do you mean found? Where? How?"

"I don't know for sure. The kid from Ohio told me that it's up in the mountains somewhere. There was a plane crash decades ago and the creepy Eskimo knows where it is."

"Yeah, so?"

"Don't you see? Bob's gonna find that stash and bolt, leaving us high and dry here in the Great White North."

"Come on, he loves you."

"He loves his money more." CiCi sat back and stuck out her bottom lip in a pout. "In case you haven't noticed, Bob's not really the sharing and caring type."

Somethin' for Nothin'

"I don't know. This all sounds crazy."

"I'm telling you they are up to something. Every day, Jimmi takes the creep and Waxy out flying. They're looking for it and if they find it and we're on the outside, we'll be on the outside with nothing—absolutely nothing, not even this shitty bar gig. That's for sure."

"You're crazy." Dylan laughed and tried to go back to watching cartoons.

"You want to go back to cleaning up piss, shit and vomit again?"

Suddenly, Dylan's voice was deadly serious. "No. No way."

"Then we have to get in on this thing."

"But you're already on the inside with Bob."

"Don't you think I've been pumping him to find out what's going on? He's being really tight lipped about this—and he's not even drinking as much as he usually does. That alone is a worrisome enough sign. Something's going on and he's not giving it up."

"What can we do?"

"Jimmi's no good. And no way that creep Moe would ever give us the time of day. We've got to get to those Ohio guys, somehow."

"Well, you were messing around with that Albert guy, right?"

CiCi glared down her brother's accusatory tone.

"What?" Dylan asked sheepishly. "I'm just saying…"

"He's up on the pipeline, so he can't help us."

"That leaves what's-his-name, the dishwasher."

"Right. And you need to get to him."

"Seriously? How?"

"He's a guy, right? What do guys want?" CiCi motioned her head toward the slumbering brunette. "Get him laid. I think that's what Albert did and, *eureka!* He followed him all the way to Alaska from Ohio."

"I don't know, sis."

"People are always pissing, shitting and vomiting—especially when they get old. And somebody's always got to be there to clean it up."

Dylan shuddered at the thought of returning to the very bottom rung of the healthcare services hierarchy.

"What's his name?"

"I don't know. Albert called him Waxy."

"Waxy? What the hell kind of name is that?"

"Who cares. Just do it."

Dylan nodded, suddenly stone sober.

The Letter

Albert fidgeted in the bus seat. He was tempted to read CiCi's letter again and reached toward the pocket on his flannel shirt, but it was back in his room at camp.

They had been sitting there for nearly two hours. Sully and Jack played gin rummy. Wil was reading *Breakfast of Champions*. A poker game raged on in the back of the bus and Mac was up front, pathetically trying to make time with Liz, the Teamster who had driven them out to the work site. Other workers slept, argued—mostly about sports, camp cafeteria menu items, pipeline management stupidity and the best Outside destination for their next R&R break—or pawed through the well worn pages of the collection of *Playboys*, *Penthouses* and *Hustlers*, yet again. Albert had been through them so many times on the daily drive from camp to work and back again that he had actually read all of the articles. Besides, most of the good pics had been torn out and taped up around the roof of the school bus.

After that first brutal week, Albert got used to the physical exertion required of laborers on the line: digging, filling, wrestling pipes and beams into position to form the Vertical Support Members which held the pipeline up off the ground so it wouldn't melt the permafrost. What he had not gotten used to was waiting idle at the job site—sometimes for hours—waiting for a broken down sideboom to get repaired or the truck delivering the next load of supplies to erect that day's section of Vertical Support Members to arrive or for some union boss to stop ranting on about safety to Alyeska management, as if that was really the point of his rant. All the union contracts had no-strike clauses in them, so impromptu safety meetings were the only legitimate way to stop work and resolve grievances. Since they got paid to read, converse, play cards and sleep, most of the workers didn't really care about sitting around doing nothing. For Albert, though, the labors cleared his mind of nagging thoughts and worries about CiCi, about Waxy, and about what he might be missing out on being stuck in the Alaskan wilderness somewhere between Fairbanks and Valdez. Sure, he was making good money—better than he had even imagined on the long drive with Waxy from Ohio to Alaska. But, now that he had time to think about it again, how much more could there be buried in that cargo plane? Would it really be enough to rescue CiCi from the clutches of Beantown Bob? Would she really leave him to go back Outside with Albert? Those were the thoughts that taunted him most, which laboring on the pipeline usually held at bay.

The letter hadn't helped sooth Albert's discontent, which was exactly CiCi's intent. He didn't have to physically hold the letter for its torment to work, because he had read it so many times nearly every word was memorized. Random phrases involuntarily percolated up into his consciousness again. CiCi had written that she loved Albert and wanted to be with him more than anything. He saw her smile. He heard her singing. He felt their naked bodies pressed together. Plenty of other girls had told Albert they loved him, but this was the first time he ever cared. Albert bolted out of his seat and stormed toward the front of the bus.

"Hey, Liz, could you open the door, please?"

The bus driver looked up into Albert's face, yearning for rescue from Mac's relentless advances. She wasn't as unattractive as she tried to make herself appear in a vain attempt to hold the tsunami of testosterone surrounding her at bay. Reflexively, Albert smiled weakly, though he had no real hunger for the hunt. Liz sighed and swung open the school bus doors.

"Thanks." Albert bounded down the steps and headed towards the pipeline right-of-way.

"You should come back in and sit down, man," Sully called out through the bus window. "Save your strength, dude."

"Yeah, you'll need it, man," Jack warned, hanging out the window next to Sully.

Albert stopped and looked back over his shoulder at Sully and Jack. Since he had not quit the pipeline work in the first few weeks like many of the other newbies, the veterans had accepted him as one of the crew and routinely razzed and harassed him like a freshman fraternity pledge.

Albert shrugged. "Guess it's hell being an old fart, huh?"

"Ahh, youth is wasted on the young," Wil said, appearing at the window on the other side of Sully.

"Doesn't your ass get sore just sitting there, wearing a pair of button holes into the seat?" Albert asked.

"Sore? You want sore?" snickered Sully. "I'll kick that smart ass of yours all the way back to camp, sonny."

"Sweet meat." Albert taunted his crew mates by slapping his ass and shaking it in the direction of the bus. "Gotta catch it first, old fart."

M.T. Bass

Albert walked out to the pipeline right-of-way. To the north he could see the parallel line of four-foot diameter pipe, waiting to be lifted and placed on the 'H' shaped VSMs he helped erect, then welded together by those insufferable 798ers from Oklahoma. He had learned to avoid the Tulsa Pipeliner local members of the Plumbers and Steamfitters Union as much as possible. Everybody's tempers were already short from the isolation and the long hours of work, and when a fight broke out on the line or in camp, the arrogant attitude of the 798ers was usually the spark that started it. Albert was glad his crew worked well ahead of the welding. He looked south down the empty right-of-way. Sidebooms, trucks and power shovels idled. Their operators milled about waiting for the signal to begin filling the pairs of twenty-four inch holes augered into the earth with eighteen inch pipe to start erecting VSMs.

The image of Liz's pained expression came back to Albert, especially the silent pleading in her eyes for relief from Mac's relentless abuse. With the help of the letter, Albert now recalled the same pleading in CiCi's eyes he had somehow missed seeing when they were together. Imagining Beantown Bob's abuses, sprouting like weeds between the words of CiCi's letter, hot embers of anger began to burn his gut, stoked by the helplessness of being hundreds of miles away from CiCi. He could not ignore her, like he had Liz. Besides, it was—for the first time—love.

So absorbed in his thoughts, Albert did not hear the crunch of gravel behind him.

"Taking in all of nature's beauty, are ya?" Wil asked, startling Albert as he stepped up beside him.

Somethin' for Nothin'

"Something like that, I guess," Albert answered with a heavy sigh. "At least it ain't as ugly as watching Mac trying to make time with Liz."

"Yeah, that is a sorely painful sight. But what are you gonna do? He's the boss man." Wil lit a cigarette and scratched at his beard. He looked thoughtfully up and down the line.

Albert followed his scan of the work site. "Finish your book?"

"Nah. It was getting a little aromatic on the bus—what with the beans and coleslaw for dinner last night." Wil looked south down the right-of-way. "Besides, fresh air is good for you. Least ways, that's what the VA docs told me."

"You sure came a long way just to get some fresh air."

"Well, you know, it's good coin and the hippy-dippy old lady didn't want this old war horse hanging around no more, so this seemed as good a place as any and far enough away to boot." Wil squinted as he took a long drag on his cigarette. "So, what the hell is a college boy doing digging ditches here in the middle of nowhere?"

"I don't know. Seemed like a good idea at the time. Of course, everything seems like a good idea when you're drunk."

"Well, at least this bad idea pays decent."

"I suppose," Albert agreed. "And I guess, like Mac says, we're making history. Like building the Panama Canal or the transcontinental railway—the one hundred thirteenth and two hundred forty-seventh wonders of the world respectively."

Wil shook his head. "Fuck Mac. I done made all the history I ever want to make, humping rice paddies."

"Nam?"

Wil nodded and crushed his cigarette out in the gravel.

"Well, at least there's nobody trying to kill us here."

"Just the work, son. Just the work."

Albert nodded.

Wil looked north toward the open end of the pipeline. "Damn. That's got to be one hell of a buried treasure."

"Wha—what?" Albert blurted out desperately, caught day dreaming about the payroll treasure.

Wil looked at Albert curiously, then answered, "The oil. Under Prudhoe Bay. Can you even imagine the enormous wealth that's paying for all this shit? The pipe, the equipment, the camps? Tens of thousands of guys getting paid crazy money to sit on their ass in the middle of the wilderness half the time?"

Albert shook his head. "I never thought about it."

"Billions and billions and billions, man. I can't even imagine it."

Neither could Albert. He was still stumped trying to imagine how much cash the fuselage of a cargo plane could hold.

A pair of flatbed semis rumbled past with the load of beams and shoes to support the pipe on the VSMs, the load Albert's crew had been waiting for.

"What are you two homos doing out here? Holding hands, watching the sunrise?" Sully asked as he and Jack walked by.

"Come on, girls. Time to go to work," hollered Mac. "Grab a shovel and get your ass on the line."

Albert turned and saw Liz close the door on the now empty bus with a look of temporary relief on her face. He should have done something to help. Then, he thought of CiCi one last time, before the day's work began.

~~~

Moe's Village

After weeks of droning over the endless forests, mountains and river beds, Waxy was amazed that the novelty of being up in the air never waned for Jimmi the Pilot, who constantly smiled as he scanned the horizon and dutifully annotated the sectional chart with the thus far unsuccessful search results. And nothing seemed to phase Moe the Eskimo, who stared straight ahead out the front windscreen from the moment they taxied out for takeoff until Jimmi the Pilot slowed the de Havilland to minimum controllable airspeed to loiter over that day's selected part of the search grid. Only then did Moe the Eskimo turn to squint out the window to his right impassively for hour after hour.

Waxy would look out the window, too, though he wished he knew what they were searching for so he could help speed up the process. Inevitably, as the forest became just a blur, his thoughts drifted to Emma and day dreams of how things could be if they actually found the plane wreck and it actually had money inside. Some days he thought through the idea of opening their own place. Sometimes it was a bar, like *Fenway Park West,* only better. Sometimes it was a diner, like the *Lucky Wishbone,* which Waxy could not imagine being better, only all their own—his and Emma's. At first, he envisioned Emma coming to live with him in the apartment now that Albert was gone, fitting her neatly into his daily routine, to be there in the morning when he woke and there at night to go to bed together. But that daydream often went awry when thoughts of Albert returning from the pipeline rudely intruded on his imagined domestic bliss, so he built a cabin in the woods for them to occupy. Every once in a while, he savored the reverie of bringing Emma back home to the farm in Ohio to show off to his parents and his small circle of outcast friends who were generally considered to be a boil on the student body of Rutherford B. Hayes High School in Delaware, frequently lanced by the verbal barbs of the more popular kids. Sometimes he built a life for them on a farm just like his mom and dad's, though he was not even sure if Emma was the agrarian type.

Most of Waxy's day dreams were platonic, filling an otherwise existentially empty chain of moments consumed with the rote motions of his daily routine with a meaningful, fulfilling relationship. Sometimes, though, more basic urges welled up in Waxy, like sitting at the the *Lucky Wishbone* counter watching Emma's body strain against her waitress uniform as she reached above her head for some napkins, to-go cups or condiments, the hemline rising to reveal the inside of her firm thighs; or catching a tantalizing glimpse of cleavage as she bent to deliver his pie or to top off Jimmi the Pilot's coffee. Wonder about what lie further beneath the checkered commercial food service uniform welled up to press against reality at odd and unpredictable times—when mindlessly sorting silverware; sitting on a bench in Elderberry Park, staring out over the waters of Knik Arm; or trapped in the rear seat of the de Havilland *Beaver*, staring at the back of Moe the Eskimo's head

Somethin' for Nothin'

clamped between the green ear muffs of a Dave Clark headset, wondering what in the world kind of thoughts might be swirling around in his native gray matter. Most times, Waxy suppressed those lurid thoughts and desires, except when they came to him after his shift at *Fenway Park West,* as he lay alone in bed in the apartment, staring at the ceiling, unable to drift off to sleep until those desires found satisfaction in completely different kinds of fantasies about Emma.

Waxy's attention was drawn to the movement of a grizzly bear along the bed of a river, the name of which Jimmi the Pilot had no doubt told him repeatedly, but he could not remember. He watched the bear look up at the plane as they passed overhead, then gallop quickly down the shore before taking a sharp left turn into a copse of woods. He sighed and looked at the jet-black hair on the head in the seat directly in front of him.

Waxy was the first to notice. Just as the peripheral edges of reality began to blur again for him, an ever so slight jerk of the green headset caught his attention. Something on the ground had hooked Moe the Eskimo's eye and pulled his head back and around.

Jimmi the Pilot noticed the same thing moments after Waxy and instinctively steepened the bank of the de Havilland to keep them over the area that had caught Moe the Eskimo's attention. He punched a button on the loran, then made a notation on his window with the grease pencil.

"Jimmi?" Waxy asked into the intercom.

"Do you see it?" Jimmi the Pilot asked, trying to look through the window behind Moe the Eskimo's shoulders for the landmark that had caught his eye.

Moe the Eskimo's head panned on his shoulders as he fixated on a point on the ground beneath the circling airplane.

"The village? Tuuluu—the village?" Waxy asked excitedly.

Moe the Eskimo slowly bobbed his head.

Jimmi the Pilot circled the last latitude and longitude he had written on his side window. He banked a little tighter around the focal point of Moe the Eskimo's stare.

"Are you sure?" Jimmi the Pilot asked. Then to Waxy, "Is he sure?"

"Tuuluuwag?"

"It is there," Moe the Eskimo finally confirmed.

Jimmi the Pilot circled the spot again and again, but neither he nor Waxy saw the remnants of Moe the Eskimo's long gone childhood village, which had been swallowed up by nature reasserting itself for the past quarter century.

Jimmi the Pilot rolled the de Havilland straight and level on a heading of due north. Snow capped mountains filled the windscreen. He looked to his left. North-northwest of their position was a gap in the mountains filled and paved with the smooth blueish-white shimmer of a glacier.

"There. It has to be there," said Jimmy the Pilot, pointing out the front windscreen. He turned the plane north-northwest and lined up their track to fly directly up the frozen river of ice.

"How do you know?" Waxy asked.

"He said that twenty dollar bills rained down on them that night, right?"

"Right."

"They had to be coming from there."

"How do you know?"

Somethin' for Nothin'

"They had to. The winds. The valley. The village. They had to."

"Did we find it?"

"No, but we know where it is." Jimmi the Pilot looked back over his shoulder at Waxy, a huge, shit-eating grin spreading across his face.

Jimmi the Pilot turned back towards the glacier and reduced power to take the plane down low above the icy, snowy surface. The valley it filled was narrow, so he tracked along the right side of the slender ribbon of ice, hugging so close to the wall of granite that Waxy reflexively leaned back from the window on his side of the plane. Jimmi the Pilot flew halfway up, scanning the pristine frosting of snow on the ice, then chandelled to reverse direction and dove back down close to glacier's surface to fly out of the valley. "It's buried down there. It has to be."

Waxy slid across the back seat to look out the same side of the plane as Jimmi the Pilot to see what he was seeing.

As they flew up and down the length of the glacier, Moe the Eskimo stared straight ahead and sighed heavily, while Jimmi the Pilot and Waxy tried to melt the ice with their glares to reveal the wreckage locked beneath the surface, buried by decades of ice and snow.

Jimmi the Pilot finally turned to head back towards Anchorage. He wondered where he could find a smaller plane to use, a Cessna or *Cub* fitted with skis to come back and test the surface of the glacier for landings.

Waxy smiled as broadly as Jimmi the Pilot, believing that the prospects for his fantasies about Emma to come true had suddenly gotten much better.

M.T. Bass

Moe the Eskimo simply stared straight ahead and lit up a Camel, unscolded this time by a distracted Jimmi the Pilot for smoking in the cockpit.

'X' Marks the Spot

Jimmi the Pilot sat in a chair in front of Beantown Bob's desk in his office above *Fenway Park West*, waiting and thinking. His eyes aimlessly examined the memorabilia that littered the room, cluttering his field of vision without really penetrating his consciousness. His mind churned with more practical thoughts of putting an airplane onto the surface of the glacier.

Beantown Bob came in the door and carefully regarded Jimmi the Pilot, who seemingly took no notice of his entrance. After a moment, he leaned his Louisville Slugger in the corner between his desktop and the typewriter wing, then sat down and pulled his chair up close to the desk. He waited, watching Jimmi the Pilot scan the cramped horizon of his life haphazardly scattered about.

Jimmi the Pilot's meandering eyes found Beantown Bob.

Beantown Bob spread his hands and opened his palms to the ceiling, silently asking, "Well?"

Jimmi the Pilot time-lapsed a smile across his face.

"You found it?"

Jimmi the Pilot nodded. "You bet your ass we did."

"Hot damn." Beantown Bob flipped his hands over like flapjacks and slapped the desktop.

Jimmi the Pilot grinned broadly and slowly bobbed his head up and down.

"You ain't shitting me, are you? Moe's village was really there?"

"Found it—or where it used to be, anyway."

"And the plane?"

"I know where it is."

"You saw it?"

"I know where it is."

"You know —"

"Look!" Jimmi the Pilot interrupted, launching himself out of the chair like a Navy A-4 *Skyhawk* catapulted off an aircraft carrier and shaking open the marked up Anchorage Sectional Chart.

"Okay…" Beantown Bob said warily as he leaned back out of the way while Jimmi the Pilot spread the map out in front of him.

"There!" Jimmi the Pilot's finger fired in to the middle of the map like a *Sidewinder* heat seeking missile. He made a cross and exclaimed, "X marks the spot, me matey."

"Okay…" To Beantown Bob, the section of the map Jimmi the Pilot pointed at appeared to be areas of tan and green randomly colored by a young child who could not stay inside the lines.

"We're here," Jimmi the Pilot pointed at an irregular yellow splotch representing Anchorage, then traced northeast towards Denali, then turned east, then north, finally tracing a thin blue line. "Moe's village used to be along this river…right…here. On the northwest side, towards the mountains."

"Okay…"

"Up this valley, to the Northwest, tucked out of the way is this little glacier. See it?"

Somethin' for Nothin'

"If you say so."

"You can't see anything from it and there's no peaks close by to climb or slopes to ski down, so I don't think anybody has ever really given two shits about it."

"And that's where the cargo plane crashed."

Jimmi the Pilot nodded and grinned.

"And you *saw* it, right?

"Think, B.B., *think!*" Jimmi the Pilot stood up straight and glared down at Beantown Bob. "If it could be seen, it would have been found by now. It's buried under thirty years worth of snowpack and ice."

"How do you know?"

"I just know it. I can feel it. And it all fits—the village, the valley, the winds. It's there, man. It's there."

"Okay…so, now what?"

"We get it."

"Right." Beantown Bob exhaled impatiently. "How?"

"I checked around," Jimmi the Pilot said, reaching into his flight bag on the floor beside his chair, "discreetly, of course."

"Of course."

"And nobody has ever tried to land there—I mean why would they? So I got the topo." Jimmi the Pilot spread out another map in front of Beantown Bob. "See?"

"What the fuck do I look like? Lewis and fucking Clark?"

"It's here." Jimmi the Pilot pointed to the glacier on the topographical map. "It's about forty-eight hundred feet up. Maybe a little less than a mile long usable and a little more than half a mile wide. Maybe. A bit of an upslope—"

"Get to the point already."

"Should be able to land on it. I'll try with a *Cub* first, then—"

"In an airplane? Are you nuts?"

"It's the only way. *That's why nobody's found it yet.* But I can do it. A walk in the park after jumping jets on and off the *Forrestal*"

"Yeah? Then what?"

Jimmi the Pilot ignored the skepticism in Beantown Bob's voice. "It won't be easy. I figure once we pin-point where it is under the ice, it'll be buried thirty—maybe forty feet down, but it'll be there for the taking."

"How?"

"Well, there's going to be digging involved, so we're gonna need some muscle—some young muscle."

"Waxy?"

"Too bad his buddy isn't around. Maybe he's hardened up some from pipeline work."

"Another wallet to cut in."

"You know, B.B., there's going to be plenty to spread around. Besides nobody said anything about equal cuts." Jimmi the Pilot winked.

"And Moe?"

"We're going to need him, too. Definitely. He's got native knowledge." Jimmi the Pilot pointed at his temple with his index finger. "I'm sure I can get us there and back with equipment and all, but once we're on the glacier, we're gonna need someone who can read the ice."

"Can we trust him?"

"We have to. As long as he doesn't wig out and start seeing dead relatives, we should be okay—especially with Waxy along to mind him."

Beantown Bob nodded. "So, now what?"

Somethin' for Nothin'

"I talked to Hawk at the airport and he's good with renting me his *Cub*. It's still got the skis on it."

Beantown Bob nodded, coldly calculating the costs of an airplane rental.

"He's giving me a good deal." Jimmi the Pilot paused. "But we're going to need our own plane. Cessna one-eighty or one eighty-five. I've got a line on one."

"Shit."

"I've got enough stash left to cover half the down payment, but we're going to need to move more product."

"Fucking Mexicans. I hate doing business with them."

"A means to an end, B.B. A means to an end."

Beantown Bob shook his head in resignation. "Just keep them out of my bar."

"Charge them double. That'll move them along. Those guys are cheap bastards. Always pinching their pesos."

"This'll be the last time, right?"

"I hope so. I'd mortgage the *Beaver* for this one—if I could. Again. You know."

Beantown Bob shook his head.

"How much can you pony up?"

"Ten grand, maybe."

"Don't know if that'll be enough." Jimmi the Pilot scratched the back of his head. "Gonna need a set of hydraulic skis. They're pricey."

"I'll see what I can do."

"One last big score with the cartel and then we'll be free of them once and for all."

"Better be," Beantown Bob barked. He thought for a moment, then asked earnestly, "You really think we can get it?"

"The tricky part right now is getting on the ice, since nobody's ever landed there. It doesn't even have a name. Of course, that's a good thing."

"How's that?"

"It means we won't have company. It's a pretty tight fit, which is probably why no one has tried it before. I guess there's never been a good enough reason…until now."

On Ice

On the first low pass, Waxy suddenly found himself scared shitless. Looking over Jimmi the Pilot's shoulder from the back seat of the Piper *Super Cub,* the windscreen overflowed with nothing but granite and glacier ice, blossoming into greater and greater visual detail as they flew directly into the jaws of death at seventy miles per hour. At one point his hyperventilating became so out of control that Jimmi the Pilot could hear it over the intercom.

"Hang on, sport," he reflexively told Waxy, trying not to break his concentration.

Trolling through the *Lucky Wishbone Diner,* Jimmy the Pilot snagged Waxy exactly where he expected him to be: in Emma's station at the counter, stuffing pie into his face. Getting him out of there was like yanking a salmon out of the water and on the trip north, his cockpit conversation had been little better than what could be had with a dead fish. So Jimmi the Pilot flew on, carefully consulting the marked-up map on his lap. He turned left at the river and flew up the valley until he got to the small, anonymous glacier above Moe the Eskimo's village.

As Jimmi the Pilot slowed the *Cub* and circled, Waxy dreamily gazed down on the sliver of the Alaska landscape lazily looping in the side window, but his thoughts were still back in Anchorage. Like a pivotal scene from a Hollywood movie he watched, rewound and watched again, in his mind Waxy saw an actor—who looked remarkably like himself—buck up his courage to ask Emma out on a date and she said...*Yes.* He replayed the scene over and over as Jimmi the Pilot empirically tested the breadth and depth of airspace that nature allotted above the buried treasure, surveying the terrain, the length of ancient ice that would be their runway and the turning radius distances between unforgiving granite peaks to either side.

Jimmi the Pilot's discrete inquires found that none of the other bush pilots at Merrill Field had been on the unnamed glacier—not that it couldn't be done. It was just that there had been no hires interested in paying for the hop to get there. So Jimmi the Pilot would be the very first one to land there. He flew out at least a mile away from the glacier and turned the *Cub* to the north-northwest on a long, one-way final approach toward the alleyway between the granite ridges. He needed to practice his approach to landing, gathering visual cues, sensing the swirls of wind in the seat of his pants, and gauging the upslope of the glacier. He needed to assess the surface of the snow pack and search for dangerous crevasses. He needed to clearly mark in his mind touchdown, turnaround and go/no-go points.

As Waxy scripted his upcoming date with Emma, he slowly realized they were no longer perched thousands of feet above the ground. Cragged peaks reached above the *Cub's* wings on either side and the sense of safely floating above the earth was replaced by a blurring rush of speed as they flew directly at the mountains. His fear amped up by the nearness of ecstasy with Emma, he lost control of his breathing.

Somethin' for Nothin'

"Hang on, sport. Hang on," Jimmi the Pilot said soothingly.

Jimmi the Pilot crossed the approach end of the glacier a hundred feet above the surface. The *Cub* sank softly a bit, until he smoothly added power and gently applied back pressure on the stick to follow the rising snow pack in a gentle climb, staying well above the surface. He allowed the plane to drift to the right side of the glacier.

"Jimmi! Fix it, Jimmi—Fix it!" Waxy panted, as rocks and boulders blossomed in the windscreen.

Jimmi the Pilot laughed as he firewalled the throttle, cranked the plane into a thirty degree bank to the left and yanked back on the stick to chandelle back down the glacier.

Waxy's stomach sank towards his belt to protest the maneuver, but when the plane leveled off he felt better seeing trees along the snaking river far below in the valley by Moe's abandoned village and an actual horizon with blue sky ahead of them again. "Are you trying to kill us?"

"A walk in the park, Waxy. A walk in the park."

"Son-of-a-bitch."

Jimmi the Pilot laughed, but the approach and landing wasn't really the "walk in the park" he made it out to be. The side walls funneled down to a sheer cliff face, so if he aborted an approach too late, they would likely stall-spin-crash-burn-and-die trying to avoid a head-on collision with a mountain range. And from a hundred feet the surface of the snow still looked deceptively smooth. He would definitely need to take a much closer, more careful look.

Just as Waxy could feel his bodily fluids calm themselves, taking comfort in at least a thousand feet of ground clearance,

Jimmi the Pilot cut the throttle and turned the *Cub* back towards the glacier for another practice approach. In pass after pass after pass, he came closer and closer to the surface until the skis cut through the tops of soft moguls, spraying snow crystals in their wake. Again and again, Jimmi the Pilot tested the blinding white surface, his eyes lost behind mountain climber glacier glasses stripped of their side shields. He did it so many times, Waxy became acclimated to the danger and was surprised when Jimmi the Pilot actually landed the *Cub* and cut a graceful arc at the end of his taxi to turn immediately around and take off again down the glacier towards Moe's village.

After several more landings, they headed back for Anchorage in silence, finding it hard to believe they had landed on top of their jackpot.

~~~

Emma

"That was fun," Emma said when they got outside the 4th Avenue Theater. "Did you like it?"

"Yeah, but I thought it was going to be a horror flick."

"Silly. It was Mel Brooks' *Young Frankenstein*...with Gene Wilder? And Madeline Kahn?"

"Yeah. I guess I didn't really pay attention to that stuff in the ad." Waxy was glad to hear Emma laugh out loud during the movie. By his on-going mental audit, he had, so far, narrowly avoided a total train wreck on their first date. "I thought you'd be disappointed it wasn't in color either."

"You're funny."

"I didn't mean to be," Waxy said as they loitered beneath a street lamp. Outside the darkness of the theater, he was able to savor her beauty again: the coy smile that seemed to push her cheek bones even higher, the sparkle that danced in her dark eyes and the jet-black hair that fell about her shoulders. He didn't realize how long it was, because he had only ever seen Emma with her hair pinned up in a bun at work. He liked it.

"Besides, I like black-and-white."

"What do you mean?"

"For my photos."

"What photos?"

"The ones I take. I like stealing souls."

"Stealing souls?" Waxy asked with a touch of alarm in his voice.

"It's what Indians thought happened when they got their picture taken. They believed the camera stole their soul." Emma searched Waxy's face for a glimmer of understanding. "Anyway, I like taking pictures. It's the only reason I keep taking a stupid class at the college—so I can use their dark rooms with my student ID."

"Photographs?"

"Yeah. I could show you them sometime."

"I'd like that," Waxy said, looking into Emma's dark eyes. He met her smile and grinned back, then looked up and down the street. "Do you want to get a drink?"

"Sure."

They started walking up Fourth Avenue, hesitantly and awkwardly trying to synchronize the gate of their steps. A couple of times, Waxy started to say something, but didn't. He looked up from the sidewalk cracks at his feet to assume an unfocused, faraway stare down the block, then checked the concrete again.

Emma was charmed by the effort Waxy put into their first date. She half expected that dinner would be at the *Lucky Wishbone Diner*, but he took her to the restaurant at the top of the Captain Cook Hotel for steak and crab legs, which must have cost a fortune. She chuckled to herself at the sound of his new corduroy pant legs rubbing together as they walked. His shirt, sport jacket and crudely knotted necktie were, obviously, newly bought as well. And, of course, he didn't wear his ever present Ohio State baseball cap, setting free a mop head of sandy-brown hair that he had, evidently, worked hard at combing somewhat into place. With a sideways glance, she caught Waxy absently smiling the same infectious grin he held throughout dinner, as he let her go on and on about her day at work and the colorful characters who frequented the *Lucky Wishbone Diner*, staring more at her than at the amazing view of the mountains and the inlet.

Emma sidled closer and hooked his arm in hers as they walked. "This is nice."

"Really?"

"Yes. Really." She nudged him with her hips.

Waxy smiled even more broadly, relieved…and aroused.

Emma got more than her fair share of attention from male patrons at the *Lucky Wishbone Diner*—and didn't hesitate to flirt with any one of them to pad her tips—but they were all too old or too rough or too crude or too lecherous for her to ever seriously consider dating. Jimmi the Pilot came about as close as any of them had, but a vague, nagging doubt held her at bay and their friendship never left the diner. Waxy did not get a second thought after he first came into the diner with Albert. She dismissed him as just another Outsider who wouldn't last long once he figured out that the odds of getting a pipeline job were slim-to-none; but his persistent, happy presence and humble, down-home innocence wore her down. Besides, Emma didn't meet a lot of men her own age outside of work, dividing her spare time between church functions and solo photo safaris, filling roll after roll of thirty-five millimeter film with images and souls.

Waxy slowed as they approached *Fenway Park West*.

"Where east meets west," Emma read the neon sign.

"Did you want to see where I work?"

"Sure. Why not."

Emma smiled as Waxy chivalrously held the door to *Fenway Park West* open for her. She liked that he treated her like a lady, opening doors, holding her chair and helping with her coat. They went in and he led her to a booth. She smiled, watching him eagerly retrieve a glass of wine for her and a beer for himself.

"Kind of a bus man's holiday, huh?" she asked as Waxy set down the drinks and slid into the booth across from her.

"What?"

"We both work in restaurants and here we are in one of them on our day off."

"Oh. I'm sorry."

She smiled. "It's okay. Kind of a joke."

Waxy looked at his beer.

"It's okay. Really." She touched his arm.

Waxy smiled at Emma, until he noticed that behind her Beantown Bob and Jimmi the Pilot walked into *Fenway Park West*, heading for the stairs up to the office. Beantown Bob took no notice of Waxy, but Jimmi the Pilot looked over, grinned his shit-eating grin and gave him a thumbs up.

"There goes Bob. He owns the place."

Emma looked over her shoulder. She saw Jimmi the Pilot quickly turn his attention back to following Beantown Bob in formation. "Hmmm…Let's finish our drinks and go someplace…else or something."

"Sure."

Moe the Eskimo came out of the kitchen, took his usual place at the end of the bar and lit up a cigarette. Exhaling a cloud of smoke, he looked over at Waxy. He nodded once.

Somethin' for Nothin'

"I just wanted you to see where I work."

"It's only fair. You've been to the *Bone.*"

Waxy shrugged his shoulders. "Yeah."

They finished their drinks and left, walking west down Fourth Avenue, going no place in particular.

Waxy smiled. "I'm having a real good time."

"Me, too." Emma grabbed Waxy's hand and laced her fingers with his.

Waxy savored the touch of her flesh.

"So…"

"So?"

"So, what are you going to do now?"

A moment of panic gripped Waxy. He had no plan for the moment, because he never imagined their date would last this long. "Now?"

"Now that you've found it—you know, the payroll." Waxy kept Emma regularly updated on their hunt while devouring all the pie *ala mode* she served him.

Relieved, he sighed. "Well, we still have to actually find the plane there under the ice. It's been, what? Twenty or thirty years or so. Moe said it could be fifteen or twenty feet down into the snow pack on the glacier."

"How are you going find it, then?"

"Jimmi says that he knows this mechanic genius—some guy named Sparks—who can make a supercharged metal detector somehow that we can use."

Emma laughed. "You mean like looking for quarters at the beach."

"Yeah. I guess. I never thought of it like that," Waxy mumbled, betraying embarrassment at how silly their treasure hunt suddenly sounded.

"What are you going to do with your share?"

"I don't know. I hadn't really thought about it."

"Well, think about it, silly boy. What would you do? What do you want?"

Waxy was genuinely stumped at the question. His brow furrowed in thought.

Emma was charmed by his truly guileless nature. "I can't imagine the freedom you'll have."

"Freedom?"

"Sure. I mean, you wouldn't keep washing dishes would you? You'd be free of that. Never have to work another day for the rest of your life—think about it. "

"I guess." Waxy hadn't thought about it.

"If it were me, oh, I would definitely quit the *Bone*. I'd be gone in a New York minute."

"Yeah? I—I…" Waxy was crestfallen at the sudden thought of not being able to see Emma every day.

"So, what about you? Would you go back to school?"

Waxy slowly started to shake his head, thinking about the failed Philosophy midterm left behind so many months ago. "Boy, I don't know. It all seemed kind of weird and so much useless information. I don't see how, like, any of it could help out running the farm."

"You'd buy a farm, then?"

Waxy slowly started to shake his head, again, thinking about how the rank smell of swine would fill his bedroom back home when the wind blew out of the east. "Yeah, I don't think so."

"I think I'd like to travel. Mmmm. Some place warm."

"Yeah. Maybe. As long as it wasn't far."

Somethin' for Nothin'

"What's the point of traveling, if it isn't far?"

"I mean, I just don't want to have to drive thousands and thousands of miles to get there."

"Silly. You can't drive to Hawaii or Tahiti."

Waxy's mind drifted into wondering what Emma would look like in a swimsuit on a beach in Hawaii or Tahiti. He caught himself and shuddered his thoughts back to Alaska. "No, I guess not."

"I've never been anywhere, but here and Oklahoma."

"Oklahoma?"

"Yeah, my dad is a welder and dragged mom and me up here when he came to work on the pipeline. Mom hated it, but there was no way I was ever going back to Stillwater, so I stayed when they went home."

"You mean, you're not from around here? Originally?"

Emma gave Waxy a stern, impatient look. "You didn't think I was an Eskimo, did you?"

Waxy concentrated hard on the sidewalk before him, trying not to step on any cracks. He didn't need any more bad luck, as it seemed as though his luck was quickly running out with Emma.

"I'm Cherokee, you silly." Emma punched his arm and laughed. "So, now you're going to dump me because I'm not a real Eskimo?"

"Dump you?" Waxy was confused. The prospect of him dumping Emma was as foreign to him as Sartre and Existentialism. "I don't understand—I mean, no. Of course not. No."

Emma leaned into Waxy and gave him a kiss on the cheek, then pulled his arm around her waist behind her. She felt his breathing quicken. "So, come on. What are you going to do with your millions and millions and millions? Buy a yacht? Build a mansion? See the world? Maybe with someone?" Emma poked his ribs. "Do you really think it will be millions of dollars? That you could be a millionaire?"

Waxy smiled at the prospect of being rich and maybe, just maybe traveling the world with Emma. "Where would you want to go, if you could, just, you know, quit the *Bone,* like you said, and just go wherever you wanted to?"

"I don't know."

"I mean first."

"First? Maybe Hollywood. Maybe New York City. Maybe Paris or London or Rome. Where would you go?"

Anywhere…with you. Waxy thought to himself. "Tahiti. That sounds kind of neat."

"Will you take me?"

Waxy slowly nodded, thinking of Emma on the beach.

"It's a date, then."

~~~

The Bridgewater Hotel

CiCi got to the airport early Sunday morning, leaving the band house long before anyone began recovering from Saturday night's gig. She would not have to be back until Wednesday. Everyone—even Dylan—thought she was going home to Seattle for a visit. She blankly watched the ground crews scramble to service the Alaska Airlines Boeing 727 parked at the gate, fueling the tanks, loading baggage and rolling catering carts into the cabin. Once they departed and were climbing north through the dark Arctic morning, she finally relaxed and allowed thoughts of Albert and his letters to fill her mind. She found it hard to believe she was on her way to meet him in Fairbanks. CiCi ordered a Bloody Mary and gave up tamping down physical, as well as emotional, feelings of anticipation: Beantown Bob's growing obsession with the treasure hunt had driven him into a maddening monk-like celibacy. Off the right wing, the horizon began to glow with the coming sunrise, which spread like the unconscious smile on her face.

CiCi's heart fell when she got to the Bridgewater Hotel and did not see Albert in the lobby.

Since receiving CiCi's last letter, Albert had spent many of the long hours in camp and on the job site thinking about the moment he would see her again. Unable to sleep, he came down from the room and parked himself in a lobby chair even before her plane left Anchorage to wait, imagining their reunion over and over, scripting every word, choreographing every movement of their bodies together in a hundred different scenes from tender to torrid—though mostly torrid. He was surprised when she first came into the lobby that he did not leap to his feet and race to her side, like the hungry wolf that he was. Instead, he remained sitting in the wing-backed chair, watching her search the lobby for him. He paused to absorb her innocent beauty anew. She looked gorgeous to Albert in a personal, meaningful way; definitely more real and intimate than in the eight-by-ten glossy band promo shot she had given him when he left for the pipeline…and even more arousing than in his fantasies.

CiCi desperately scanned the faces in the lobby.

Albert rose and slowly walked towards her, amused that she did not seem to recognize him.

Nine weeks of hard labors on the Pipeline had chiseled Albert's features to give him a lean, rugged look. At first glance, CiCi dismissed the stranger walking towards her, but her eyes were instinctively drawn back to him. Haunting familiarity gave way to recognition, as he closed the gap between them. He was much more handsome than she remembered. When they wordlessly embraced, she could feel through his heavy work clothes the muscles that months of wrestling steel cables, girders, dirt, gravel, and pipe had honed in him. The strength of his hug surprised her as he pressed the air from her lungs, but the dissonant counterpoint of memory and reality evaporated when he kissed her. She melted in the moment, forgetting her intentions of finally luring Albert into a conspiracy against Beantown Bob.

Somethin' for Nothin'

Albert cracked a half smile at the initial confusion on CiCi's face. The weeks and weeks on the pipeline had not only transformed Albert physically, but also mentally and emotionally, working away fatty adolescent thoughts and feelings to replace them with a more mature longing that he had not felt before, a yearning for more than just a warm, moist body beside him to satisfy his needs of the moment. He did not understand that yearning, but he understood the moment he saw CiCi again that she could fulfill it. When they embraced in the lobby, all of the dialog, blocking and action, mentally practiced and polished over so many hours evaporated from his brain, so he simply smiled, took her hand and silently led her upstairs to the room overlooking the Chena River.

Once in the room, the view was ignored as Albert pulled her gently to the bed and CiCi surrendered blissfully to his silent advances. Conscious, rational thought was left outside the door and they both reacted in an instinctual, animal way to the closeness of their bodies and the heat of their emotions, rekindled after the long gap since they last saw one another in Anchorage. They wrestled in a tender, athletic scrum again and again and again, until they expired in a throbbing, breathless tangle beneath the covers of the bed. Exhausted and emotionally spent, they fell into a long, lingering brunch-time nap that was broken only by arousal, another round of passion, then rest again, until the day had been spent as completely as their bodies.

When, finally, life-sustaining hunger caught up with them and room service delivered their daily bread, words were at last spoken.

"Mmmm, well, that was…*intense,*" Albert said as they sat against the headboard, hungrily devouring Delmonico steaks with *au gratin* potatoes and one of the half-dozen bottles of Cabernet Sauvignon he stocked the room with ahead of time.

CiCi looked over at Albert and smiled. She laid her head on his shoulder as she chewed and moaned, "Mmmmm."

Albert wanted to ask a hundred questions, but wanted more to savor their intimacy. And so, uncharacteristically, he held back as they shared their meal.

"I'm glad I came."

Albert smiled. "Glad doesn't really cover it for me."

"And we have three more days until we have to leave."

Albert closed his eyes and contemplated the next seventy-two hours of bliss. "And I won't have to share that time with anybody else. It just might be the end of me."

"Oh, you'll survive."

"Don't count on it."

"Don't be silly." CiCi slid her hand beneath the covers, between his legs, and squeezed gently. "Now, be a good boy and finish your dinner. There are children starving in India."

Albert swallowed hard. "But Hindus don't eat beef."

CiCi took another bite of steak and smiled slyly.

"You are bad, you know."

"When I'm good, I'm good. But when I'm bad, I'm better."

Albert laughed.

"You know, Waxy's got a girl, now—well, almost maybe."

"Really? He didn't say anything in his letter."

"Well, that's what Jimmi told Bob. He spends all his free time eating pie and mooning over some waitress at the *Wishbone.*"

Somethin' for Nothin'

"Oh yeah, I know which one. She waited on us when we first got to town. Cute, too," said Albert. "Sounds like I might have a bit of a project when I get back."

"So, did he tell you they found it."

"Found what?"

"He didn't tell you about the plane wreck?"

"No..."

"Oh, well, they found it. It's buried up on some mountain. Jimmi's landed there with Waxy and now they're trying to figure out a way to find it under the snow and ice."

"Really...When?"

"A couple of weeks ago, I think. Bob didn't come out and say so. I think he's afraid of jinxing it—or letting too many people find out about it—but they definitely found the place in the mountains where it crashed."

"But not the plane."

"Not yet."

Albert pondered the news, wondering why Waxy's last letter hadn't mentioned the plane...*or Emma*.

They finished their steaks in silence, then CiCi, still naked, moved their dishes back to the room service cart and crawled beneath the covers to coax a clearly distracted Albert into making love to her yet again.

But seventy-two hours was a long time. Inevitably their thoughts, like metal filings to a magnet, were drawn back to a treasure hunt they were not yet a part of and their conversations increasingly turned to how to satisfy their other desires.

To avoid raising suspicions, CiCi took the Wednesday morning flight back to Anchorage, while Albert waited for the one that left at twelve-thirty in the afternoon. As he waited in the airport, his determination had time to set and harden, as it did when he finally decided to take the fingerless man's union card in the dark downtown alley.

Anchorage

After landing in Anchorage, Albert called the apartment above *Fenway Park West*, but got no answer, so he grabbed a cab to take him there. He bounded up the steps, thinking how he was genuinely looking forward to seeing Waxy, again, but was taken up short by the appearance of the Holiday Inn 'DO NOT DISTURB' sign hanging from the door knob of the apartment at three o'clock in the afternoon.

Albert smiled, then went back downstairs to the bar, ordered a beer and waited among the afternoon regulars for Waxy to come down to work. It was funny that, like CiCi, none of bar flies recognized him from when he worked there pouring their drinks. Of course, none of them were ever within shouting distance of sobriety, so Albert nursed his way through a trio of Budweisers in undisturbed solitude.

"Well, well, well—look what the fucking cat dragged in," Beantown Bob growled as he came out of the kitchen, carrying a plate filled with a pulled pork sandwich and French fries. He sat down next to Albert and motioned to the bartender. "Bring us a couple of beers."

"Thanks, Bob."

"So, putz. You still got all your fingers and toes?"

Albert held up his hands and wiggled all ten fingers.

"Don't take off your shoes. The stink will drive out the clientele. I'll just take your word for it."

Albert smiled and took a pull off his freshly delivered long neck. "So, old man, what's shaking?"

Beantown Bob shrugged his shoulders and took a huge bite of his sandwich. Around the mouthful of bun and pork, he said, "Just fighting the good fight. You know."

Albert nodded. "How's my boy, Waxy?"

Beantown Bob chuckled. "Doing surprisingly well. Frankly, he was the last person I thought would ever get laid in this town."

"Emma?"

"Yeah." Beantown Bob squinted at Albert and said sarcastically, "They make a cute couple."

"Couple of what?"

"Exactly."

Jimmi the Pilot came in and sat on the other side of Albert from Beantown Bob. "Shit, B.B., I thought we had ditched this Rubber City loser once and for all."

"What do you say, Tex? Still porking the beef on a regular basis?"

"Sure beats self-abuse—or did you find yourself a husband up at camp?"

"Boy, Bob, I wish I could say I missed the old joint, but…"

Just then Waxy came out of the kitchen whistling a happy melody to retrieve the afternoon bus tubs full of dishes. He was looking down at his waist as he tied his apron. He pulled the knot tight, then looked up and saw Beantown Bob, Jimmi the Pilot and Albert staring at him with shit-eating grins on their faces.

"Hey! *SneezyDocDopey!*" Beantown Bob barked. "What the fuck are you so fucking happy about?"

"Hey, guys—*Hey, Albert.* When did you get back?"

"Evidently, just a bit before check-out time."

Somethin' for Nothin'

Waxy blushed.

"The way they go at it, she'll be lucky to be able to end her shift on her feet," said Beantown Bob, poking Albert in the ribs. "He forgets that my office is right next door to the apartment upstairs."

Jimmi the Pilot just smiled pridefully at Waxy. In the hours and hours they had spent together in the cockpit, a genuine fondness for the lad had grown on him, like ivy on a tree, until he caved in to his affections and took him under his wing like the little brother he never had.

The three men sat smirking and staring at Waxy frozen in place behind the bar.

The kitchen door squeaked loudly as Moe the Eskimo pushed it open. He took in the scene and acknowledged Albert's presence with a flick of an ash off his cigarette and a nod of his head. He silently motioned Waxy back into the kitchen.

"Yeah. I better get going…now."

"Sure, kid," smirked Beantown Bob. "Get back to work—*And stop that fucking whistling!*"

Waxy gathered the bus tub from behind the bar and went back into the kitchen under the watchful eyes of his friends and his boss.

"Our little Waxy is growing up so fast," Jimmi the Pilot said in a falsetto voice.

"Yeah. Right, whatever," growled Beantown Bob. He caught Jimmi's eye and motioned towards the front booths with his head.

Jimmi the Pilot nodded.

"Hey, putz," Beantown Bob elbowed Albert in the arm. "Walk with me. Talk with me."

Warily curious, Albert grabbed his beer and followed Beantown Bob to the booth furthest away from the bar along the front window. When Jimmi the Pilot slid in beside him, he barked, "What is this? A date? Gimme some room."

"Don't flatter yourself, slick."

"Stop your fucking bickering, you little school girls," Beantown Bob scolded, then took a bite of his sandwich. He nodded at Jimmi the Pilot.

"Got any friends up in Skinny City?" Jimmi the Pilot asked.

"Oh yeah. It's like one big sleep over, *mom.*"

"Hey, putz. Cut the crap. We know you know…*about the plane.*"

Albert got a sinking feeling in his gut that somehow Beantown Bob found out about him and CiCi. He suddenly felt trapped in the booth between Jimmi the Pilot and the window.

"I'm sure your happily little whistling dwarf friend has told you all about it."

The knot in Albert's gut loosened. "Yeah…so…"

"We're going to need some stuff to get it out of the ice," said Jimmi the Pilot. "You know, supplies, tools and equipment that just might happen to be laying around a construction site and, let's just say, might not be missed too terribly in such a large operation."

Albert nodded. "And what's in it for me?"

"A share."

"How big a share?"

"Hey, putz. Don't get greedy. Five percent—maybe ten—depending on if you can deliver what we need."

"We'll give you a shopping list. You cozy up to the Teamsters in the yard, and I'll schedule a run to the camp to pick it up," said

Somethin' for Nothin'

Jimmi the Pilot. "If you need some weed or coke to grease the skids, we'll work it out."

"Why don't you just skim what you need off your deliveries?"

"I gotta deliver what's on the manifest. But once it's in camp…"

"Yeah. Shit goes missing all the time."

"Exactly," Beantown Bob said finishing the last bite of pulled pork and licking the bar-b-q sauce off his fingers. "And nobody around town here gets curious about our sudden need for dynamite and blasting caps and such."

Albert slowly nodded, trying not to smile. Getting in on the treasure was easier than he and CiCi thought it would be. "How much cash do you think is there?"

"Enough," grunted Beantown Bob.

"How do you know?"

"Look, are you in or out?" Jimmi the Pilot asked impatiently. "I can find somebody else, but—since you already know—we'd rather hold our cards close to the vest."

"Sure. What the hell," Albert held out his hand towards Beantown Bob, who reluctantly shook on the deal. "I'm in."

Just then CiCi slid into the booth beside Beantown Bob and gave him a peck on the cheek, catching Albert completely by surprise. "What are you 'Little Rascals' up to this time?"

"Nothing," Beantown Bob answered sheepishly. "How was Seattle?"

"Good. Good to see mom—Oh, hey," she said nonchalantly to Albert. "When did you get back?"

"Today." Albert was amazed at how easily CiCi's act of indifference came to her.

"Yeah? Me, too. That's nice."

"Come on. I'll have Moe cook you up a steak," Beantown Bob nudged CiCi out of the booth with his hips. "These two have some things to work out."

Jimmi the Pilot slid around to the opposite side of the booth and watched Albert's gaze as he followed CiCi walking away. Beantown Bob did not see it, but Jimmi the Pilot noticed the change in Albert's expression when she first sat down. He said nothing, but filed it away for future reference.

When Jimmi the Pilot left after they finished working out the details of their equipment embezzlement from Alyeska, Albert stayed parked in the booth, nursing Budweisers and wishing CiCi and *Torchlight* were playing that night at *Fenway Park West*. If he couldn't lay beside her, he longed to hear her sing.

Albert left well before last call and went up to the apartment to wait for Waxy to close, but fell asleep. When he woke at ten the next morning, Waxy was not in the apartment. He had not come home after work, but Albert knew where to find him, come lunchtime, so he shaved, showered, dressed and headed out, on foot, towards the *Lucky Wishbone Diner*.

"Say hey, Casanova," Albert snickered as he parked himself on the stool next to Waxy at the counter.

"Hey," Waxy answered around a mouthful of banana cream pie.

"You didn't come home after the prom last night. What gives, young man?"

"You know…"

They watched Emma scurry by with a tray full of food to serve. Her smile at Waxy turned into a smirk when she noticed Albert beside him.

"Yeah. I know." Albert sighed. "Hope I didn't cramp your style any."

Somethin' for Nothin'

"Nah, we stayed at her place." Waxy leaned back and surveyed his friend closely. "You look...different. How is it working on the pipeline?"

"Good. Hard, you know. 'Making a man' out of me, I guess." Albert flexed a bicep. "Lots of food and porn when you're not busy throwing gravel around."

"Black, right?" Emma said curtly as she slid a cup of coffee towards Albert. "You gonna order something, slick?"

Albert nodded. "Yeah, just a cheeseburger and fries."

"Got it." Emma wrote out the order and put it through the window to the kitchen. She grabbed a couple of plates to deliver.

"She's still kind of peeved you just up and left me," Waxy said with a sly grin, watching Emma head out on the floor again. "But I'm not."

"I love it when a plan comes together." Albert sipped his coffee. "And speaking of plans..."

Waxy quickly shoved a forkful of pie into his mouth and stared down at the plate.

"Hey, I know all about it—"

"From CiCi?"

"Yeah, well—but from Bob and Jimmi, too. They talked to me last night about getting them stuff you guys need out of camp."

"Oh yeah?"

"Yeah. So, I'm in on it."

"Good," Waxy said with a big sigh of relief, clearly uncomfortable at the prospect of deceiving his friend.

"Yup. Maybe, just maybe, we'll strike it rich even beyond our wildest dreams."

"I think I'd like that."

"Yeah, take that Kragies, you old hag, you." Albert watched Waxy watch Emma and laughed. "I'm glad for you, man."

"Huh?"

Emma wordlessly slid a cheeseburger and fries in front of Albert, then grabbed a bottle of ketchup and mustard for him from below the counter. She whispered to Waxy, "It's almost noon."

"Oh, shit. I gotta meet up with Jimmi," Waxy said to Albert. "How long are you going to be in town?"

"You know, I think I'm going to change my ticket and head back north today," Albert said.

"But you just got here."

"Yeah, but I've got some things to take care of for...*you know.*"

For the first time since Albert got to the *Lucky Wishbone Diner,* Emma smiled.

~~~

Sparks

"Who the hell is this idiot?" hollered Sparks, the Airframe and Powerplant mechanic, when he opened the man door to the hangar.

"This is Waxy," answered Jimmi the Pilot.

"Who the hell is a Waxy?"

"He rides shotgun for me and helps load and unload."

"Hell's bells. Come on, already."

Jimmi the Pilot entered the dark hangar and Waxy followed. Dimly lit, it took their eyes a few moments to adjust and in those passing seconds, Sparks had already hobbled deep into the piles and piles of junk—both aviation and non-aviation related—that filled the huge open space like an indoor junk yard. Landing gears, propellers, wings and empennages were the largest of the carcasses, but there was also a Ford F-100 pickup truck and an ancient Chrysler sedan in varying states of disassembly and decay. God only knew what else occupied the boxes, crates and pallets that were piled high enough to create alleyways and tunnels like a huge metallic ant farm.

"Hey, Sparks," Jimmi the Pilot called out into the depths of the hangar.

"Idiots. Come on, come on. I ain't got all day."

Jimmi the Pilot led Waxy deeper into the junk pile, navigating off of the mechanic's voice. Waxy could not understand how Sparks could move so quickly, not only because of his limp, but also because at every turn, some sharp object grabbed at Waxy and got caught in his clothes. He followed Jimmi the Pilot as closely as he could, sure that if he lost contact with him, he'd never find his way out. Jimmi the Pilot moved slowly and deliberately to keep from getting his leather Naval aviator jacket caught and torn on unforgiving metal.

"So, you got a mining detector in here somewhere?" Jimmi the Pilot sounded out.

"God damn it. I told you I did. Now keep up," came the reply from Sparks.

"How'd you come to get it?" Jimmi the Pilot adjusted his path through the wreckage and Waxy followed, watching every step he took.

"God damn idiot miners ran off and shafted Hawk on the charter fee—"

"So to speak." Jimmi the Pilot winked at Waxy.

"—so we cleaned out their camp and kept their shit. It's a pisser."

Jimmi the Pilot looked back over his shoulder at Waxy, smiled and shook his head. They burrowed on after Sparks.

"So, what makes this one so good?"

"P-I."

"What's that?"

"Pulse Induction. Heavy duty. Lots of juice. Course you might still have to drill some to drop it down a hole, depending on what you're looking for."

"Lost my keys." Jimmi the Pilot chuckled to himself.

"Yeah. Right. *Idiot!*"

Somethin' for Nothin'

Jimmi the Pilot and Waxy caught up with Sparks in the back corner of the hangar where he was already pawing through the contents of a pallet and shelving unit, examining every piece of junk before he moved it out of his way, as if memorizing and cataloging it for future reference. Jimmi the Pilot leaned against an aluminum wing propped up against the wall and watched, knowing that Sparks would not allow him to handle any of the stuff.

Waxy watched Sparks mumble to himself as he dug through the clutter, until he eventually unearthed a large orange case that looked like miniature foot locker.

"Here you go. A MinePro Excalibur II." Sparks pulled the case out into the alleyway between the piles of junk. "Not the best you can buy, but it gets the job done."

"How deep?"

"How deep you need to go? What, did you drop your keys down a god damn well?"

"I don't know. Fifty? Maybe a hundred feet."

"That might be touch and go. I could look at souping it up some. More battery juice, you know. Or you could just auger down and drop the head into the hole." Sparks limped off into a different section of the junk pile. "I got an auger over here somewhere."

"Great." Jimmi the Pilot winked at Waxy. "You're the best, Sparks. The best."

"How'd you lose those keys anyway?"

"You know, just fell out of my pocket."

"*Idiot.*"

"Yeah. I know."

Sparks came back dragging a gas-powered auger. "I got some extensions, too. I figure a buck and a half."

Jimmi the Pilot nodded and pulled a wad of bills out of his pocket. He counted out ten twenty dollar bills. "Here's two. See what you can do to soup up the old Excalibur Two, eh?"

"You got it. I'll have it done by Friday."

"Deal. See you then."

"Just help me bring the shit up to my workbench."

Jimmi the Pilot and Sparks lifted the metal detector together and carried it through the piles of junk. Waxy grabbed the auger and followed.

"So, how's business for you and Hawk?"

"Well, you know him. Don't do business that don't make him smile. So, could be better. I seen it worse. It's a pisser, but, you know, it's not like he needs the dough either."

"Taking any pipeline work?"

"Not much. Bores the shit out of him. Doing mostly hunting and fishing charters."

"I get it. Droning back and forth on the same path gets old quick."

They came to a cleared out area that was markedly neater and more organized than the rest of the hangar, centered around a long work bench and a couple of sets of large drawered tool boxes. The area was well lit and clean. It was Sparks' work area.

"What do you really need this shit for, Jimmi?" Sparks asked. "You ain't going into the mining business are you? Good way to make a small fortune…out of a big one, that is."

"Nah. I got some salvaging to do. Say, you wouldn't happen to have a set of hydraulic skis in here somewhere—for a Cessna one-eighty?"

Sparks gave Jimmi the Pilot the once over up and down. There was no telling which one of the hundreds of legends

Somethin' for Nothin'

and village folklore tales of buried riches that Jimmi the Pilot intended to chase and it wasn't any of his business. Two hundred dollars was a fair price and it was a lot easier to make money supplying the fools going out after the gold, than panning there out in the wilderness himself, like a damned fool.

"You bet. Fluidyne thirty-two hundreds." Spark pointed toward a far corner of the hangar. "Set you back six grand. Manual pump."

"Installed?"

"Yeah, what the hell. Won't take me that long."

"I'll take 'em."

Sparks took a long hard look at Jimmi the Pilot, then over his shoulder at Waxy, who hung back and away from the conversation. "Just be careful out there, Jimmi."

"You know me, Sparks, old buddy. Don't you worry your pretty little head."

"It's a cold, hard world."

Jimmi the Pilot gave Sparks a two-fingered salute and led Waxy back out the man door of the hangar.

"*Idiot,*" Sparks mumbled to himself and got to work on metal detector.

~~

Pigs on Ice

Jimmi the Pilot loitered above the glacier in the Cessna 180 he and Beantown Bob had acquired with a down payment using the cartel's drug money. Slowly and gracefully circling, he scanned the surface carefully as he pumped the skis Sparks had mounted down into position before landing. Moe the Eskimo sat beside him, expressionless—staring straight ahead. Waxy sat behind Moe the Eskimo, peering down at the severely white surface of the stream of ice frozen in mid flow down the valley between two unnamed mountains. Beside him was the metal detector that Sparks had "souped up." Behind him was the auger and the rest of the tools they would need. It would be their first venture outside the cockpit to stand on the surface of the glacier.

"Well, boys, I've got a good feeling about this," Jimmi the Pilot said cheerfully over the intercom.

Moe the Eskimo grunted.

"Are you sure it's safe?" asked Waxy.

"Safe is for sissies." With that, Jimmi the Pilot rolled the Cessna out on a long, high downwind leg, reduced power and slowly drifted down towards the surface as they flew away from the peaks of the mountains. He could feel Waxy squirming in the back seat. "So, what do you think we ought to call this place? It's got to have a name."

Silence back on the headsets.

Moe the Eskimo stared straight ahead.

Waxy squirmed in the back seat, watching the ice flow get closer and closer.

Jimmi the Pilot made a gentle arcing turn one hundred and eighty degrees until the Cessna was lined up on final approach to the glacier. "I say Bahammy Mammy—those peaks look like a pert young set of breasts I once knew intimately and we'll be landing right in the cleavage."

Silence back on the headsets.

"Cessna Six-Six-Golf, short final, runway six-nine, Bahammy Mammy," Jimmi the Pilot reported to an imaginary control tower.

Jimmi the Pilot worked the throttle to gently lower the Cessna towards the snowy surface, then just above touchdown added power to climb with the gradual incline, letting the Cessna inch its way down.

Waxy watched the plane's skis cut the crust of snow, sending up rooster tails of powder until they found firm footing.

Jimmi the Pilot kept the engine RPMs up, the tail high and the plane light on the skis as they taxied quickly up to the top of the upsloping glacier. As speed and distance ran out, he turned the Cessna sideways and pulled the power to idle.

"Holy shit," Waxy blurted out. "I guess this is it."

"Fenway West Airlines welcomes you to Mount Bahammy Mammy. We hope you enjoy your stay and fly with us again real soon," replied Jimmi the Pilot as he turned off the radios and pulled the mixture, shutting down the engine. He switched off all the electrical systems, flipped off the master switch and turned the ignition off. They sat for a moment, savoring the silence. "Well, Moe, time to do our thing—Waxy, get our snow shoes."

Waxy handed two pairs of snow shoes over the seat, one at a time, first to Moe the Eskimo, then to Jimmi the Pilot. He braced for a blast of cold air once they opened the doors to the airplane, but the wind was surprisingly calm.

"You wait," Moe the Eskimo instructed Jimmi the Pilot as he swung his legs out and slipped on his snow shoes. He gently lowered himself to the snow's surface, testing its strength with his weight, holding on to the wing strut. Jumping up and down a bit, he found the surface solid and walked slowly towards the tail of the plane, keeping his hand on the fuselage for support if needed. On other side of the plane, he motioned for Jimmi the Pilot to get out.

"Wait here kid," Jimmi the Pilot instructed Waxy as he unlatched his door and let gravity pull open it open. He pushed his seat all the way back and swiveled his legs out to put on his snow shoes. He joined Moe the Eskimo and they walked out to the end of the left wing, surveying the broad expanse of ice that sloped down to a sheer cliff face, beyond which lay a valley filled with pine and spruce trees thousands of feet below.

Waxy wanted to get out, but he was trapped by the front seats being pushed back on their tracks, so he watched Moe the Eskimo lecture Jimmi the Pilot, pointing at different places down the slope, while Jimmi the Pilot nodded and asked an occasional question. He could see their breath in the cold, even though it was officially summer, and could hear their muffled voices, but could not make out any words to follow their conversation. Finally, Jimmi the Pilot walked back up to the door and slid the seat all the way forward.

"Come on out kid and enjoy the view."

Waxy grabbed his snow shoes. He strapped them to his dangling feet and gingerly lowered himself to the snow, hearing it crunch as it took his weight. He awkwardly shuffled down to the end of the wing. The tip of the snow shoe dug into the surface, sending him tumbling face first into the glacier.

"Pick your feet up. Step high," Moe the Eskimo instructed a moment too late.

Jimmi the Pilot laughed out loud.

"Wow," was all Waxy could say after he stood up and brushed himself off, taking in the full panorama of the mountain scene without having to view it from behind the tightly framed Plexiglas of the airplane cockpit. The air was crisp, quiet and bracing, but not uncomfortably cold. He could feel warmth from the bright sun on his face. He shielded his eyes from the glare.

"Glasses," said Jimmi the Pilot. "Get them on."

Waxy pulled the glacier glasses from inside his parka and put them on. He could see now without squinting and shielding his eyes.

"Well, boys, shall we get at it?" Jimmi the Pilot asked, opening the cargo door and pulling out a canvas tarp.

They spread the tarp out and staked it down in the snow, then unloaded the metal detector, the auger, gas cans and bundles of brightly colored climbing rope on top of it. Jimmi the Pilot covered the airplane cowling with a blanket, then took two bundles of rope and started wrapping them around the hub ends of the propeller blades, then tied them off.

Somethin' for Nothin'

"Is that safe?" asked Waxy.

"If the prop blades are strong enough to pull you, me, Moe and the whole damn airplane through the air, it should be strong enough to keep us from falling off the damn mountain."

Waxy nodded and continued to unload the plane. The work was not hard, but the altitude stole his breath.

While Waxy and Jimmi the Pilot busied themselves about the plane, Moe the Eskimo assembled the two halves of a long, slender rod and carefully walked an arc from the tail of the plane to its nose, then back again, slowly increasing the radius by a stride, probing the snow with the rod every other step. On the third arc back to the nose of the plane, Jimmi the Pilot tossed him one of the ropes, which he tied to the 'D' ring on the chest harness he wore and continued pacing and probing in an ever expanding arc around the parked Cessna.

Meanwhile, Jimmi the Pilot and Waxy took shovels and began to clear a path in the snow in front of the plane to prepare for their eventual departure back down the slope of the glacier. When they finished they sat on the tarp to catch their breath and watched Moe the Eskimo map the area around the plane.

"I've got a good feeling about this, kid. A real good feeling."

"You think it will be hard to find?"

"Well, Sparks said our trusty Excalibur will find a brass tack at a hundred yards, so with the auger we should have no problem going back in time through the ice to find it."

"How deep do you think it could be?"

"I don't know. Thirty years of snow pack could put it down a ways. We'll see."

Waxy and Jimmi the Pilot assembled the metal detector. Jimmi the Pilot put on the headphones and signaled Waxy to turn it on. He tested it on the wheel strut and gave Waxy a thumbs up. Waxy took the other rope that Jimmi had tied to the airplane propeller. He tied it to the chest harness he wore and Jimmi the Pilot tethered himself to Waxy with a shorter length. Moe the Eskimo had warned them about the dangers of crevasses, which could be hidden with layers of snow hardened and strong enough to hold one man, but would quickly give way and swallow up two or three.

"It's good," Moe the Eskimo told them as he walked back by them towards the plane. He would probe the next quadrant around the plane, while they searched for the aircraft wreckage.

Jimmi the Pilot began tracing over the arcs of Moe the Eskimo's tracks in the snow, sweeping the metal detector's head back and forth over the surface, listening intently to the headphones, while Waxy lumbered behind him carrying the modified electronics and battery pack. Halfway through Moe the Eskimo's tracks they rested.

"Anything?" Waxy asked with anticipation.

Jimmi the Pilot gave him a chagrined look and a shake of the head. He silently swept his arm across the horizon at the broad expanse of the glacier, then back towards the minuscule area they had searched just downhill from the plane. After catching their breath, they finished the first quadrant and moved back to the plane to start searching again to the west. When they finished searching all four sides of the Cessna, they wearily returned to the tarp, exhausted from trudging through the snow and carrying the metal detector for several hours.

Somethin' for Nothin'

"It's a good start," said Jimmi the Pilot, as they rested.

Moe the Eskimo stood, looking down the slope of the glacier towards the site where his boyhood village once stood, smoking a Camel cigarette.

After a while, Jimmi the Pilot retrieved a topological map and a solar compass from the cockpit. Waxy held the chart and watched Jimmi the Pilot take readings and make markings on the map to pinpoint the area they had just searched. They then packed the equipment into the plane. With Waxy at the right wing tip and Jimmi the Pilot on the left, they see-sawed the wings up and down to make sure the skis were unstuck from the ice. They wearily joined Moe the Eskimo in the Cessna.

"I am bushed," said Jimmi the Pilot as he went through the starting engine checklist. "It takes it out of you."

"We have much ground to cover," said Moe the Eskimo.

"Yeah, and then what about when we find it?" asked Waxy. "How hard is that going to be to get at it?"

"We're definitely going to need some help." Jimmi the Pilot shook his head slowly. He pushed the mixture full rich, pumped the throttle twice, flipped the master switch on and turned the ignition. The Continental engine coughed and belched, finally coming to life. As the engine idled to warm the oil, Jimmi pulled the cabin heat full on and rubbed his eyes. After a few deep breaths, he looked over Moe the Eskimo and Waxy to make sure their seat belts were buckled, then advanced the throttle, revving the engine until the skis began sliding. He turned downslope to begin his take off run.

Waxy was already dozing in the back, dreaming of Emma, as they lifted off and banked towards Anchorage.

~~~

In a Fog

Waxy, Moe the Eskimo and Jimmi the Pilot went back to Bahammy Mammy Glacier nearly every day going on three weeks, methodically mapping the metal content—or lack thereof—of the ancient ice. They had canvassed less than a quarter of the surface.

Waxy never figured just walking around on snow shoes could be so tiring. Though Moe the Eskimo was indefatigable, returning to stand for eight or nine hours, loading and unloading the dishwasher at *Fenway Park West* so sapped the last bit of strength out of Waxy's body that he was barely able to climb the stairs to the apartment, where he immediately collapsed into bed to sleep like a hunk of immovable granite—too tired to even dream—before getting up early the next morning to meet Jimmi the Pilot again at Merrill Field.

He snored softly. Emma lay naked beside him and gently rubbed his shoulders. Lately, she had seen him literally doze off halfway through his milk and pie, when Jimmi the Pilot dropped him off at the *Lucky Wishbone Diner* after returning from a day of searching for the hidden treasure for a quick meal before he had to go to work in the kitchen at *Fenway Park West*. And yet, every time Waxy came through the diner door, his eyes lit up and his face beamed when he saw her, until the fatigue slowly enveloped him like a fog rolling in off Cook's Inlet.

Emma, like Beantown Bob, battled back the gnawing doubts that the cargo plane could be found buried in the ice or that they were searching on the right mountain or that the wreckage even existed. Like Beantown Bob, she harbored those doubts from the searchers. She simply wished for a Sunday of rain and low clouds to shroud Anchorage and the wilderness south of Denali with unflyable weather to give Waxy a much needed break. If the TV weathermen were right, they would get that break tomorrow and she planned a home cooked meal with a home baked apple pie for Waxy.

For now, she let him sleep.

Queen's Gambit

CiCi sat across from Beantown Bob at the kitchen table in his cabin sipping at her morning cup of coffee, plotting her move. The silences between them grew longer and longer as the search for hidden treasure dragged on and on. The conversational crevasses were not completely unwelcome, as CiCi often filled them with memories of her days at the Bridgewater Hotel in Fairbanks with Albert and felt the warm yearnings rise within her breast to be with him again. While Albert satisfied her more immediate physical needs, he was also slowly growing on her emotionally like mold on cheese—unwanted, but inevitable. In his absence, she pulled compulsively at the thread of an obsession to leave Alaska, which Beantown Bob might not even notice any more—but would surely disappoint Dylan, whose stunted ambitions were beginning to aggravate her seriously. It was great to be free of the enslavement of a day job, but CiCi couldn't help but feel her dreams were being slowly smothered, trapped as she was so far away from a real music scene back in a real civilization.

She sipped her coffee and studied Beantown Bob studying the marked up U.S. Geological Survey topological map as intently as he used to study the box scores and stats on the sports pages, while eating his cereal in the morning. He ran his eyes over the slowly metastasizing search grid and the dates scrawled inside each square.

Within CiCi, emotion wrestled ambition. She would not allow herself to doubt that the wreckage of the plane crash existed and the unbounded wealth within would be found. Her doubts swirled about the fear that she and her ambitions would not share in the windfall and she would be chained to the stage at *Fenway Park West* forever—or at least until Beantown Bob no longer needed her youthful beauty to fill the bar with customers who consumed mass quantities of his liquor. She harbored no illusions that he would eventually lose even more interest in her than he had lately indulging his obsession with the activities of Jimmi the Pilot on top of some stupid mountain somewhere.

CiCi wondered how she could convince Beantown Bob to cut in another full partner on the search and salvage operation. She had to be careful. Of course, she knew Albert was stealing construction equipment and supplies for the venture, but Beantown Bob never told her anything about it. She often fretted whether she could keep from tipping him off to their relationship, thereby fatally sabotaging her pay-off. Her wonderings evaporated into moist memories of physical satisfaction in Fairbanks, until she shook herself mentally back to the moment.

"You are turning into a grumpy old man," CiCi whined emphatically to Beantown Bob.

"Huh? What?" Beantown Bob froze in mid cereal scoop, a spoonful of Frosted Flakes existentially suspended between bowl and bowel.

CiCi put on a coy smile. "You're not turning into my grandfather are you? That would be weird."

"What do you mean?"

Somethin' for Nothin'

"You sit there every morning staring at that stupid map, mumbling to yourself like he used to do as he read the newspaper."

"Grandfather?"

"Well, you know." CiCi exhaled loudly. "He was like in his own little world. Who knew what he was thinking or saying. It didn't seem intended for anyone else but himself and if you interrupted him, he'd snap at you."

"Hmmm." Beantown Bob shoveled the Frosted Flakes into his mouth and considered it. "Maybe I've been a bit distracted lately."

"A bit?"

He shrugged his shoulders and gave CiCi a sheepish look.

"Are you worried?"

"Worried about what?"

"About finding…it."

Beantown Bob scooped another spoonful of Frosted Flakes into his mouth.

"How long has it been?"

"Too long," he grunted.

"Any luck? At all? I mean, you never say anything—well, at least nothing for me to be able to understand, *Grandpa.*"

Beantown Bob looked at the map and slowly realized that he had been foolishly hiding his secret in plain sight. He sighed and nodded his head. "I guess I've been a bit preoccupied."

"A bit?"

"Yeah, well…"

"Come on, Bob. These things take time. It's only been a month. Right?"

"Almost two. Who would have thought it would take this long to find a huge fucking airplane. Not to mention what this is costing me in gasoline alone for the stupid plane. And, once we do find it, we're going to need time to work the site before winter closes down on us."

CiCi nodded. She hadn't thought about racing the seasons.

"Meanwhile, Jimmi still has to take regular charters and his special freight flights to keep some cash flow going with the...you know, the weed and blow."

CiCi pondered for a minute. "Maybe you need more help."

"Huh?"

"Wouldn't more people looking find it faster?"

"What? You mean Dylan? If he ever woke up in time to see the ass end of the morning it'd be a miracle—and even if he did get up by the crack of noon, I don't know how much help he would really be."

CiCi sighed and nodded. Beantown Bob was right about her brother.

"You haven't said anything to him, have you?"

"No. Of course not," CiCi shook her head. "But isn't there *anyone* else?"

"Darlin', I don't really want to put a want ad in the *Daily Snooze* classifieds for help on our treasure hunt. Then, like, the whole world would know what we're up to and we don't want that kind of company."

"There's nobody else?"

"Like who?"

"Nobody else knows about what you're doing?"

"Better not be—not besides you. I warned those guys."

"Are you sure?"

He paused to consider the possibilities. There was only one other person. While Albert had come through with the needed

Somethin' for Nothin'

supplies skimmed from the Camp Delta inventory, the thought of putting up with his obnoxious attitude and smart mouth brought a scowl to Beantown Bob's face.

"Winter, huh?" CiCi sipped her coffee, waiting for the seed of doubt she had planted to sprout.

"Son-of-a-bitch," Beantown Bob whispered to himself, bowing to the inevitable.

"Hmmm?" CiCi asked innocently.

"Son of a bitch."

"What?"

"Albert. He knows."

"You think Waxy—yeah, of course, you're probably right. He had to have told him. But what does it matter? He's hundreds of miles away somewhere on the pipeline working construction."

"Construction, yeah. Construction," Beantown Bob growled lowly, almost to himself.

"Do you really think you have to worry about him?"

Beantown Bob just grunted. He had some vague, unsettling vibe about Albert. He didn't know exactly why, but he knew he didn't want that asshole hanging around. "Knowing him, he'll probably figure out a way to weasel his way in anyway. But I sure wish there was someone else."

CiCi hid her smile of self-satisfaction behind a sip of coffee as she saw her gambit unfold successfully.

~~~

Crime and Punishment

Albert pushed his tray down the serving line rails in the cafeteria of Camp Delta, loading up on vital calories in the form of sweet rolls, French toast, scrambled eggs, bacon, hash browns and whole milk before his shift on the line. It was more than just a saying in Skinny City that breakfast was the most important meal of the day. Albert groggily tried to sort out blurry images from the porno movie he watched the night before with Jack and Sulley, snippets of erotic dreams from his slumbers and warm, moist memories of CiCi from the Bridgewater Hotel.

Suddenly, his reveries came crashing back to reality when his tray was jolted from the right by the tray of the worker behind him.

"Yeah. Sorry, pal." The tone of the voice betrayed a total lack of remorse.

Albert looked back, then up.

A much taller, burly worker in his late thirties dressed in a flannel shirt and heavy tan construction overalls with four days growth of red beard, looked down with malice at Albert.

Albert smirked and moved down the line, grabbing a cup of coffee, then heading quickly to the table where Wil, Sulley and Jack from his crew were already sitting, shoveling down their breakfasts in silence. With the growing daylight, the work day started earlier and earlier. No matter whether it was in Ohio or Alaska, five o'clock in the morning always came way, way too early for a notorious late sleeper like Albert.

Albert dug into the food on his plate, like a backhoe scooping up tundra. He tried to resurrect warm memories of CiCi as he absently bit and chewed a slice of bacon.

The burly, red-headed worker noisily slammed his tray down across from Albert and sat next to Sulley, who took minimal notice between sleepy bites of flapjacks.

Albert frowned as he tried to figure out a possible reason for this harassment. He was well beyond what Wil called his Official Unofficial FNG—"Fucking New Guy"—Probation Period and had long ago been accepted by Mac and his crew. He was popular with other workers in his dorm—thanks mainly to the marijuana and cocaine he skimmed and shared from the stash Jimmi the Pilot provided to bribe the Teamsters who ran the warehouse and supply yard. Besides, there was plenty of new blood in camp that came back after the long shift drawn, drained and bone weary; walking dead who never showed their faces in the rec room, instead, hitting the rack immediately after dinner to quench their exhaustion in a deep coma of fatigue-induced slumber, just as Albert had done upon his arrival. Those zombies were easy pickings for hazing by the seasoned vets.

Albert studied the hard-set face of the bully in vain for any hint of recognition, trying to figure out if he had gotten sideways with this guy some time before—maybe in a poker game or at one of the pool tables in the rec area. Though he looked vaguely familiar, Albert couldn't place him. Usually it was the Pipeliners who caused trouble, based on their inflated egos and stratospheric regard for themselves as God's gift to welding, Alyeska and civilization in general. Albert had, long ago, learned to avoid them. But the stalker wasn't wearing one of their trademark colorfully patterned hats and didn't have their typical red-neck Okie drawl.

The man stared back at Albert, his bared teeth tearing into the grilled ham steak he was eating with his fingers.

Though he'd regret it later in the day, Albert was put off enough that he grabbed his tray and left without finishing breakfast. He decided to check in at the tool crib to see if Jess and the boys needed anything from his stash, then joined Wil, Sulley and Jack on the bus heading out to the work site. On the ride, Albert tried to coax daydreams of CiCi back into his head, but the red-headed bully kept intruding on his thoughts.

Their progress through the wilderness towards Pump Station 10 seemed imperceptible, but the work kept going on and on, day after day, with Mac's crew mindlessly pushing gravel, erecting beams and wrestling pipe in their section of the zig-zag scar being cut from Prudhoe Bay to Valdez. The brisk air dissipated the last wisps of dream debris and erotic memories from Albert's mind, serving to help him focus on the hard and sometimes dangerous tasks at hand. Albert had long ago absorbed the orchestrated chaos of construction that surrounded him into an awareness of noise, men, and huge diesel machines that ever lurked on the periphery of his consciousness. The crew helped erect the vertical beams for the next VSM, then stepped back to allow the backhoe and tank truck to fill the hole with gravel and water. Albert mindlessly stared down into the augered hole as it filled up, waiting to shovel the last of the gravel up around the base.

Suddenly, Wil pushed Albert down to the ground, as a Caterpillar sideboom working the other side of the pipeline right-of-way swung its hook directly towards Albert's head.

Albert reached out to grab his hard hat, which had tumbled off his head. He put it back on and rolled to look behind him. There in the cab of the sideboom pipelayer was the bully from breakfast, who stared at Albert sprawled out on the ground for a moment, then jerked the hook up and back.

"You okay?" Wil asked Albert, once the modified CAT dozer lurched down the line.

"What the fuck was that all about?"

"Aw, nothing. Probably."

Albert watched the sideboom roll away. The operator stared back. The squeaking clatter of the sideboom's tracks raised the hair on the back of Albert's neck.

"You know, he probably just got distracted or something. Come on. Help me fill this bitch up."

Albert got up slowly and grabbed his shovel. With every other scoop of gravel, he glanced back over his shoulder at the other side of the right-of-way.

At breakfast the next morning, the driver sat down with the crew again across from Albert. The two regarded one another warily.

"Hey, you know, sorry about yesterday," the driver said flatly. "I thought I was further over."

"Yeah," Albert responded after a weighted pause. "No problem...I guess."

"Funny thing," the operator said, then filled his mouth with a huge bite of flapjacks.

Albert waited.

Somethin' for Nothin'

The driver stared at Albert and chewed slowly, deliberately.

"What's a funny thing?" Albert finally asked.

"My mom's brother was working up here." The driver loaded and worked another mouthful of flapjacks. He squinted at Albert.

"Yeah? So?"

The driver swallowed to clear his mouth. "His name is Elroy. They call him Roy."

Albert shrugged his shoulders and skated a piece of French toast through a puddle of maple syrup on his plate.

"He lost his job, 'cause of an accident."

"Yeah? So?" Albert put the forkful of French toast into his mouth.

"Your name is Roy, isn't it?"

It took a moment to register, then Albert stopped in mid-chew. He remembered the name on the union card in his wallet: Roy Walsh.

"Kind of... *coincidental*, wouldn't you say?"

Albert shrugged and took a drink of milk.

"Anyway, my uncle lost all the fingers on his right hand except for his thumb."

Albert and the red-headed driver regarded one another from across the table in light of the new information they now both shared. Albert knew for sure the incident the day before was no accident. "Tough break."

"Yeah... I tried to find him when I got up here, but nobody seems to know where he went to."

"Alaska's a big place."

"He was in Anchorage, last my mom heard."

Albert shrugged. "Maybe he moved on... went home."

"Yeah, but no. He was still waiting for his disability settlement and when it finally came through Alyeska couldn't find him either."

"Sounds like a real mystery." Albert got up and picked up his tray to turn it back into the kitchen. "Hope he turns up."

"Yeah." The driver nodded, then called after Albert as he walked away. "Hey, real sorry again about yesterday. I'll, you know, try to be more careful next time."

Albert just kept walking away from the table. He knew his time on the pipeline was at an end.

Desierto del Altar

Waxy slept in the co-pilot's seat as Jimmi the Pilot steered a southerly heading through the night across the vast emptiness of western Utah. They had been in constant motion since leaving Anchorage, flying down the coast, eventually turning east at Seattle to cross the Cascade Mountains before turning back on course towards the southern border of the United States again. Jimmi the Pilot had put ferry tanks into the space where the rear seats should be to extend their range. The fixed base operator at the Pocatello, Idaho, airport was extremely happy at the fuel bill paid in cash after the wing and ferry tanks gulped up hundreds of gallons of avgas.

On the many trips they had taken together to the pipeline construction camps to deliver supplies, Jimmi the Pilot instructed Waxy on the bare basics of piloting an airplane; on interpreting the airspeed, altimeter and directional gyro instruments on the panel; and how to adjust the autopilot to keep the *Beaver* on its intended track. He was glad he had, as Jimmi the Pilot could feel his eyelids growing heavier and heavier. Now that they were flying across empty canyon lands and desert, when the dawn came he could nap and let Waxy babysit the plane as they droned on towards the Mexico border. It was a nice luxury having a co-pilot. Jimmi the Pilot did not have to eat so many white crosses to stay awake, especially on the way back, when, loaded up with contraband, he was usually uncomfortable spending any more time than necessary on the ground.

Once the sun finally broke the horizon to the east, Jimmi the Pilot roused Waxy from his slumbers.

"Hey, Lindberg. You up?" Jimmi the Pilot asked Waxy.

"Where are we?"

"Utah."

"How can you tell?"

"That's what they make maps for, you know."

"Oh."

"You can spell me a while."

Waxy rubbed his eyes and worked to bring the instrument panel into focus.

"This heading should work out for the time being. First Officer Aztec has the helm. Steady as she goes, Mr. Chekov."

"Aye-Aye, Captain."

"Wake me if you see any big mountains or cities—'cause you shouldn't. Not for a long while"

Waxy nodded and sat himself upright a little straighter in the seat to scan the vacuous horizon.

Jimmi the Pilot pushed his seat back and pulled his baseball cap down over his eyes. In just a few moments he was deep asleep and Waxy was on his own.

"This is crazy," Waxy said out loud to himself as he took note of Jimmi the Pilot's audible slumbers. He smiled to himself, absorbing the fact that being the only one awake in the de Havilland made him the pilot—*a real pilot*. Flying airplanes was something he had never even dreamed of doing before, though now he found it quite exhilarating. He couldn't wait to get back and tell Emma all about it.

Somethin' for Nothin'

At first, Waxy had the instinctual hesitancy of a normally law abiding citizen not to get involved in Jimmi the Pilot's trek to the southern border to smuggle drugs back up to Alaska. But the search and salvage operation was sucking up Beantown Bob's capital and they needed an infusion of cash to put avgas in the tanks to keep on commuting back and forth to Bahammy Mammy Glacier. Besides, Jimmi the Pilot promised, there would be an immediate and healthy cash infusion into Waxy's back pocket that he could use to further his relationship with Emma.

As mile after mile of the rock hard face of Utah passed below in the dawning light, he mentally stepped back and surveyed his current circumstances and how far he had come since bailing out of Ohio State University with Albert. He had an apartment. He had a job. He had a girlfriend. He was there, piloting an airplane towards Mexico to make a drug deal to generate cash to fuel the treasure hunt that would make him rich beyond his wildest dreams. *Crazy. Just plain crazy.*

But in the end, Waxy concluded, Albert had made good on his drunken, High Street promise of adventure.

Waxy scanned the empty horizon and indulged himself with fantasies of a future together with Emma, with all the money they would ever want or need. Maybe he could take real flying lessons. Maybe he could get his own plane and they could fly off to anywhere they wanted, whenever they wanted to do whatever they wanted to do.

Those thoughts occupied his mind in a very satisfying way until Jimmi the Pilot woke ninety minutes later and took over as Pilot-in-Command again. He landed at Cedar City, Utah, to fuel up, then took off, heading for the empty spaces west of

Tonapah, Arizona, hugging so close to the rugged terrain that Waxy, even after all the hours spent in the cockpit with Jimmi the Pilot, began to squirm uncomfortably in his seat.

On the last leg, Jimmi the Pilot pulled out a duffel bag filled with money from behind their seats.

"You ever shot a gun?"

Waxy nodded. "I've hunted with my dad and my uncle was a policeman. He took me to the range a few times."

"Good." Jimmi the Pilot reached in and pulled out a Beretta M9 semi-automatic pistol and checked the magazine to make sure it was fully loaded. He handed it to Waxy.

"What's this for?"

"This ain't Duck, Duck, Goose, kid," Jimmi the Pilot said grimly as he checked the load on another pistol and put it into a holster he had wrapped around his shoulders. He covered it with his Naval aviator's jacket. He took out a third and fourth gun, checked them, then set them down on the cabin floor between the seats.

Jimmi the Pilot punched coordinates into the Loran-C receiver and engaged the autopilot to find the empty spot on the Sonoran desert floor where they would land to meet their cartel connection. They droned on in silence. The sun shined as bright as the sunniest of days on the Bahammy Mammy Glacier, harsh, dry and hard, yet without the sharp, piercing intensity that reflected off the snow and ice.

Jimmi the Pilot turned west towards Los Angeles, then turned off the transponder to reduce their signature on air traffic control radar screens. Ten minutes later he turned southwest. He throttled back the power and let the Beaver slowly drift down even closer to the desert floor. At a hundred feet above the sandy, rocky surface, he turned back toward the destination loaded in the Loran and hand-flew the rest of the way to the rendezvous site.

Waxy did not know if he were dizzy from the increased sense of speed from the terrain rushing by in a blur or from the hard reality of having a pistol stuffed into his waist band and the suddenly very real danger inherent in the crime he was about to commit. Waxy was so disoriented, he didn't even know if he was still in the United States anymore.

They flew in silence for nearly an hour until Jimmi the Pilot slowed the plane to approach to landing speed and, after only a few more minutes a black dot ahead grew into a black Chevy *Suburban*. Jimmi circled the SUV twice, before rolling level to fly out a half mile. He did a low one hundred and eighty degree turn to land back towards the vehicle.

As he taxied up, he instructed Waxy on how he wanted the transaction to go down. "You hang back under the wing on your side of the plane with the duffel bag, until they bring the stash out of the truck. Then I'll signal you to bring over the cash. We do the deal and get the hell out of here. You watch those guys close—real close, the whole time. See anything that looks wrong, then call out the 'bogey' and say ten o'clock if it's on my left, two if it's on my right. Got it?"

"Got it."

Jimmi the Pilot gave Waxy a determined look. "If I say 'Geronimo,' then just start shooting. Don't think. Just shoot. Got it?"

Waxy looked at Jimmi the Pilot.

"Got it?"

Waxy nodded slowly. "Got it."

"Just be cool. Just be cool, but keep your damn eyes open. They're drug smugglers. And not to be trusted any farther than you could throw 'em. Do exactly like I say, and you'll get back to Emma."

Suddenly, there was a deep hole in the pit of Waxy's stomach.

"Yup. We're playing for keeps." Jimmi the Pilot pivoted the plane to the left, so Waxy would have a clear view of the *Suburban* from under the right wing. He shut down the engine and looked over at Waxy one last time. "Ready?"

Waxy felt the grip of his pistol in the waistband of his jeans through his t-shirt and nodded.

"Grab the cash and let's do this thing, then get the hell out of Dodge."

Jimmi the Pilot shut down the engine and they got out of the plane.

"*Hola,*" Jimmi called out with a big grin as he stepped around the landing gear and prop to walk towards two Mexicans leaning on the front fender of the SUV.

Waxy circled back around the tail and stood in the shade of the right wing. He dropped the duffel bag of money at his feet. He watched Jimmi the Pilot approach the men. They talked and pointed towards Waxy. Jimmi the Pilot waved at Waxy. Waxy waved back, then slid his hand down slowly, closer to his belt line near the grip of the pistol. Then, Jimmi the Pilot and the Mexicans seemed to get down to business.

Waxy watched closely. Something in his peripheral vision caught his attention. He looked right and saw a third man peer around the rear of the *Suburban* with shotgun.

"Two o'clock," Waxy called out, feeling his heart rate ramping up. Then, he remembered, "Bogie."

Somethin' for Nothin'

Jimmi the Pilot waved back casually over his shoulder without looking, but Waxy noticed the slight cock of his head towards the back of the vehicle and his right arm move to his chest and rub his sternum.

The man lifted the shotgun towards Jimmi the Pilot.

"Geronimo!"

The shooting was over before Waxy even realized it.

He unloaded his pistol, shooting out the back window of the SUV and spinning the man with the shot gun around, bringing him to his knees. The man desperately clawed at the desert floor to crawl for cover behind the *Suburban*.

At the same time, Jimmi the Pilot drew his pistol and double-tapped the two men he was talking to point blank. He then looked over at Waxy, who pointed at the rear of the SUV.

His back against the vehicle, Jimmi the Pilot slid slowly towards the rear bumper and peered around.

The man awkwardly crawled away on his knees and one hand, clutching his abdomen with the other. He was visibly losing strength as he bled out.

Waxy saw Jimmi the Pilot step around the rear bumper and aim downward. He only heard the report of the pistol when Jimmi the Pilot put a bullet into the back of the wounded man's head, then disappeared completely.

"Assholes," Jimmi the Pilot spat out as he came around the front of the *Suburban*, having cleared the vehicle of any more smugglers. "Fucking assholes."

"What the—"

"Come on. We've got to haul ass." Jimmi the Pilot went to the back of the SUV and yanked opened the rear doors. He began to pull out duffel bags full of marijuana and cocaine, tossing them at Waxy's feet. "Come on, man, come on—get this shit in the plane. We've got to get the fuck out of here. *Pronto.*"

Waxy grabbed the bags, carried them to the plane and threw them in back. After a few trips, they had gotten all the drugs, so they scrambled back into the plane.

Jimmi the Pilot's hands flew across the switches, mixture, prop and throttle controls to start the plane, skipping the checklist he usually followed religiously. Before Waxy knew it, they were airborne, heading due west, fifty feet off the deck.

It had all happened so quickly, Waxy hardly comprehended the events of mere minutes before.

He and Jimmi the Pilot flew in silence as they serpentined across the desert floor, eventually heading north-northwest, towards the Mojave Desert.

"Now you know what the gunfight at the O.K. Corral was really like," Jimmi the Pilot finally said wearily.

Waxy just stared at the desert as it passed beneath them in a blur.

~~~

The Darkroom

From the kitchen, Emma saw Jimmi the Pilot come into the *Lucky Wishbone Diner* and sit down at the counter. She watched as he ordered a cup of coffee and stared wearily down into the blackness in dark concentration. A tempest of emotions began to swirl within her.

Waxy was probably already at *Fenway Park West* washing dishes after spending all day on the mountain. The long summer daylight allowed more and more hours of searching whenever the weather allowed. They left earlier and returned later, which meant less time for Emma and Waxy to be together, but that did not stoke the heat of anger she felt rising in her cheeks. As tired as he surely must have been, Waxy slept fitfully ever since returning from Mexico, often waking in a sweat from his dreams—dreams he refused to talk about.

Emma studied Jimmi the Pilot's drawn and haggard expression, trying to read the reason for Waxy's nightmares.

Before going south with Jimmi the Pilot, Waxy and Emma had drifted into a comfortable and intimate routine. She asked for evening shifts, so they could meet up when the weather was not flyable to spend the day together. Depending on the severity of the forecast, they might plan a trek into the mountains for a hike or photo safari, go to a movie matinee or just hunker down in the apartment to ride out the inclement weather in each others arms. Sometimes when a storm or fog rolled in unexpectedly, Waxy surprised her by showing up at the campus with a picnic lunch Moe the Eskimo fixed for them that they shared under a pavilion by Goose Lake. Afterwards, Waxy would sit on a stool in the darkroom and watch her work, keeping her company with earnest questions, anecdotes from the family farm and tales of his adventures with Jimmi the Pilot on the glacier or hauling freight to the pipeline construction camps. Emma missed him terribly on the days she worked alone developing her pictures. Since Mexico, she sometimes felt that same emptiness during lulls in their conversations, when the haunted expression on Waxy's face made clear his thoughts were drawn away from the present.

Jimmi the Pilot had long been a regular fixture at the *Lucky Wishbone Diner,* breezily swinging by on his way to the airport to grab a cup of coffee to go or on the way back at the end of the day to hungrily shovel down the daily special to quell his appetite after a long day of freight and charter flights. He chatted and flirted with all the waitresses, most of whom indifferently dismissed his advances. Emma, though, parried back in a friendly, but sassy way, engaging him in flirty dogfights which led to a friendship that teetered on the brink of something more—something Jimmi the Pilot clearly yearned for—but their relationship remained strictly platonic. A nagging voice in the back of her head held Emma back from ever seeing Jimmi the Pilot outside the diner. She never figured out why, but it was certainly something more than the difference in their ages. He reluctantly seemed to understand and never violated the boundaries of their customer-server relationship. In fact, Jimmi the Pilot took notice of Waxy's not

Somethin' for Nothin'

unrequited attraction to Emma and dragged him into the *Lucky Wishbone Diner* over and over again to dine after their day's flights, until he had pumped and primed their relationship to the point where it freely flowed.

Since they started flying to Bahammy Mammy glacier, Jimmi the Pilot did not seem to have the energy to spar with Emma like before, though he was not unfriendly. At first she thought it might have been out of respect, even envy for her relationship with Waxy, but as the weeks wore on, he became less and less animated. His feasting on the daily special took on a lethargic necessity, instead of his usual hearty gusto. Their conversations were lean and punctuated with uncharacteristically longer and longer pauses. And since coming back from Mexico, starting a conversation with him had become as hard as firing up the vapor locked engine on her Chevy *Vega*.

From the kitchen, she watched Jimmi the Pilot wait alone for his meal to be served, wondering what thoughts and worries were bearing down upon him. Emma felt storm-tossed by genuine concern for her friend, anger at what he had gotten Waxy involved with in Mexico and worry that the grand scheme which was going to free them all—Waxy, Jimmi the Pilot, Beantown Bob, Moe the Eskimo, and her—free all of them from the beartraps that held them fast there in Alaska, might fail.

Emma waited for Jimmi the Pilot's dinner to arrive, then went out to lean on the counter and speak lowly with her friend. "Jimmi."

Jimmi the Pilot apathetically breached the crust with his spoon and stared into the steam rising from the filling.

"Jimmi," Emma whispered. She gently stroked the top of his left hand which was balled in a hard fist.

He looked up from his chicken pot pie and smiled weakly.

Emma smiled back. She felt his fist relax as he exhaled wearily.

"I thought it was going to, you know, be all right," he finally whispered, hesitantly. "Just another run...to the border...like all the others. No problem."

Emma nodded and listened.

"I didn't mean to get him sideways, like this. It was supposed to be another milk run."

Emma squeezed his hand gently.

"Is he doing okay?"

She shook her head. "What happened?"

Jimmi the Pilot told her about the ambush in the desert.

She listened, working hard to mask the rising fear and anger gripping her inside from showing on her face or from causing her hand to clench, digging her nails into the fleshy sides of Jimmi the Pilot's hand.

"What happens now?" Emma asked softly.

"I don't know, exactly."

"What will they do?"

"The cartel?" He stirred the steaming pot pie filling aimlessly. He shook his head. "Not good...nothing good."

"Jimmi? What are we going to do?"

"Find the wreck and get the hell out of Dodge. That's what I'm going to do."

Emma nodded. She patted Jimmi's hand softly and went back into the kitchen. At the counter, Jimmi the Pilot stirred his pot pie.

Somethin' for Nothin'

Emma looked at the clock, agonized at the hours still left before her shift was over and she could be with Waxy.

The next day, alone in the darkroom, she caught herself weeping.

~~

Eureka

The long meticulous hours scanning the surface of Bahammy Mammy glacier gnawed at Jimmi the Pilot like a cold wind. Since coming back from Outside, the treks to the mountain were undertaken with more intensely focused determination. Still, he could not keep his mind from wandering as he swung the metal detector back and forth over the areas cleared of crevasses by Moe the Eskimo, followed by Waxy, carrying the case of souped up electronics. The casual banter and laughs shared between Jimmi the Pilot and Waxy that once helped pass the time were replaced by crisp, mountain silence.

Waxy filled the empty hours by repeatedly watching, rewinding and watching again the shootout in his mind like a football game film, trying to make sense of the action by simplifying it to Xs and Os. He took little comfort in the fact that, though he shot a man, Jimmi the Pilot had delivered the *coup de grâce*. He fretted over how he could ever explain it all to Emma, then witnessed again men dying in the sand as he trailed along, lugging the control box of the Minepro Excalibur II.

Jimmi the Pilot's conscience was clear of any remorse for his actions in the desert, just as it was for every one of the five-hundred pound bombs he dropped on the jungles of

Southeast Asia from his A-4 *Skyhawk* before getting shot down. The past did not haunt him, but the future did. He knew eventually, inevitably the cartel would come for them and he was determined to punch out of Alaska with a golden parachute before they did. Up on the mountain, he allowed the hard white surface of the glacier to blank out his mind of such thoughts as he meticulously swung the probe back and forth across the ice in a near meditative state.

And so, Jimmi the Pilot mentally missed the first interruption of his temporary nirvana by the theremin-like squeal in the headsets of the metal detector, though by animal instinct his arm muscles froze and his feet stopped dead in their tracks. Waxy, trailing closely behind and lost in his own thoughts, nearly collided with him like a bad sitcom bit.

"What?" Waxy asked.

"Shhh." Jimmi the Pilot slowly swung the probe of the metal detector. In his headsets, a scratchy squeal assaulted his ear drums. A smile crept over his face. After so many long weeks, days and hours on the ice, the metal detector had finally come alive. "Holy shit…We got something."

"What?"

Jimmi the Pilot knelt down and affectionately rubbed the surface of the ice.

"Are you serious?"

Jimmi the Pilot nodded. He looked back over his shoulder at Waxy and smiled. Then he pulled a piton out of his backpack and plunged its blade into the surface of Bahammy Mammy glacier, like a stake to the heart.

Waxy waved his hands over his head to signal Moe the Eskimo, then took the headset from Jimmi the Pilot and heard

Somethin' for Nothin'

for himself the electric squeal of discovery. He wearily sat down on the ice and laughed out loud for the first time in a long time.

Moe the Eskimo came up to the pair and surveyed the happy looks on their face, but did not crack a smile himself.

"We found it," Waxy gushed. "I think we found it."

Moe the Eskimo squinted to scan up and down the glacier. They were nearly a half mile down from where the Cessna was parked and five hundred yards west of the centerline of the glacier that had become hard packed from all of their arrivals and departures. As if sensing the presence of the wreckage through an internal, spiritual metal detector, Moe the Eskimo began nodding his head, too, and for the first time in Waxy's recollection since meeting him at *Fenway Park West*, cracked a smile so big it bared teeth across his broad flat face.

Moe and Waxy hiked back to the Cessna to retrieve the power auger and the bit extensions, while Jimmi the Pilot triangulated the exact position of the find with the sun compass. With the auger, they drilled a hole six feet down into the ice at the spot that the metal detector had come alive. Waxy switched the box of electronics back on and Jimmi the Pilot put the probe down into the hole as far as he could, listening to the electronic squeal become louder and louder in the headsets, confirming the presence of the metal beneath the ice.

Waxy and Moe the Eskimo watched the grin on Jimmi the Pilot's face grow. He pulled the headsets off and handed them to Waxy who listened, then passed them to Moe the Eskimo, who heard the technological confirmation of the tribal legends he had listened to in his youth.

"EUREKA!" Jimmi the Pilot yelled at the top of his lungs. His voice echoed faintly off the far mountain cliffs. "YOU-FUCKING-REEK-AHHHHHHH!"

Moe the Eskimo lit a cigarette and simply stood by, watching Jimmi the Pilot and Waxy fall to the face of the glacier to roll about laughing and making snow angels above the spot where an Air Force cargo plane's final flight came to a deadly end, killing its crew and, eventually, destroying Moe the Eskimo's village.

After Waxy and Jimmi the Pilot regained their composure, they spent the rest of the afternoon working with renewed vigor to map the debris field, documenting on the topographical map that already had so many grid squares X'ed out as empty.

Exhausted, but exhilarated at the end of a long day, they piled back into the Cessna. Jimmi the Pilot goosed the throttle and turned the plane back down the glacier. As they barreled downhill, gaining flying speed, their heads all instinctively swiveled to the crash site as they passed by.

Once airborne, Jimmi the Pilot circled over Bahammy Mammy glacier several times before pointing the aircraft back towards Merrill Field.

The three flew back to Anchorage in silence with new and very different thoughts running through the minds of Waxy and Jimmi the Pilot.

~~~

Gone

"Are you shittin' me? *Finally!*"

CiCi heard Beantown Bob's exclamation from his office all the way down to the first floor on the stage. Jimmi the Pilot bounding up the stairs two at a time had first caught her attention and made her wonder what was going on.

The door to Beantown Bob's office slammed shut, confirming her suspicions.

"God damn it," CiCi snarled.

"What's your problem?" Dylan asked as he spun the wing nuts down on the cymbals of his drum kit.

CiCi just glared at her brother.

Dylan shrugged and tested the tension on his snare.

Upstairs, Beantown Bob sat at his desk and watched carefully as Jimmi the Pilot spread the topographical map out before him and pointed to the grid sector that was not X'ed out. Jimmi the Pilot pulled another, smaller piece of paper that had his hand drawn notations he had not yet transferred to the chart, showing the boundaries of where the metal detector squeals had waxed and waned.

"We drilled down about six or eight feet and didn't see anything, but the signal strength got loud enough that I think it might only be fifteen or twenty feet down."

"Jesus. So, we're going to have to mine it out? How fucking long will that take?"

"Not sure, B.B. We're gonna have to do the tunnel rat thing for sure. I guess it depends upon how broken up the fuselage got in the crash and where the cargo hold ended up. The auger will help get us started, but it's going to be a lot of hard digging."

Beantown Bob absorbed the markings on the map, staring hard as if he could bore down beneath the surface to find the wreckage and see the cash inside. "When can we get started?"

"As soon as this front pushes through. The weekend, maybe."

Beantown Bob grunted his grudging assent. "We can't afford to waste any time or, before we know it, old man winter will fuck us over."

Jimmi the Pilot nodded.

Below, CiCi obsessed on Beantown Bob's closed office door, stoking her frustration into anger that flushed her cheeks. It would be another three weeks before she could meet Albert again at the Bridgewater Hotel. *Too long*.

Seeking relief from the heat of her rage, CiCi stormed off the stage towards the back exit to the alley, kicking a microphone stand out of her way.

Dylan started to make a snide comment about her menstrual cycle, but thought the better of it.

The next day CiCi sent Albert a postcard of a Klondike prospector panning for gold. She wrote on it only, "They found it."

By the time the postcard was delivered to Camp Delta, Albert was gone.

~~~

The Tunnel Rat's Tale

Emma had never seen Waxy so talkative and animated, excitedly interrupting Jimmi the Pilot, who sat backwards on a chair at the end of the back booth in *Fenway Park West*, telling Beantown Bob, CiCi and her about their day up on Bahammy Mammy Glacier. Emma pressed against Waxy, rubbing and squeezing his thigh, sometimes dangerously close to inducing ecstasy, all the while carefully surveying CiCi, who sat beside but not close to Beantown Bob on the other side of the booth. The two women took careful measure of one another as Beantown Bob grudgingly listened to Jimmi the Pilot. He occasionally glanced across the table at Waxy, who pounded down his second Yukon Jack and gulped Moosehead Lagers when he wasn't interrupting Jimmi the Pilot to help tell his tale.

Emma hadn't seen Waxy drink so much either. She searched his face for clues to understand his odd behavior, then looked around the table to see if she was the only one who had noticed the change.

Beantown Bob's eyes lingered over Emma's pretty face, then her breasts, which CiCi caught out of the side of her eye, inducing a ripple of annoyance across her face, giving Emma cause for a sly smile.

The bartender delivered a third round of drinks and Waxy

pounded down another shot of Yukon Jack. "Tell them about the cre—"

"I'll get to it," Jimmi the Pilot said, motioning with his hands for Waxy to slow down. "I'll get to it."

Emma knew Waxy hated being a tunnel rat, but since he was the smallest one, it made sense. He still didn't like it. Even though the ice was white, it weirdly got kind of milky dark the further he went in—not to mention how cold it was deep inside the glacier. Waxy could only take being inside so long before he had to come up and when he did he felt more physically tired than seemed right for the work he did and the progress he made.

A hole was started with the auger, drilling at a slight angle into the ice six feet. Waxy, Moe the Eskimo and Jimmi the Pilot then worked with picks and shovels to widen the mouth to a manhole sized diameter three feet down, until Waxy could go in to open up the end of the tunnel, with Jimmi the Pilot and Moe the Eskimo pulling up the buckets he filled with chiseled chunks of ice. Every twenty minutes or so, they would pull Waxy up by the rope tied to his body harness for a break to sit by a kerosene space heater and drink coffee or hot chocolate from a thermos at their mini version of a construction camp set up close to the spot where the metal detector had first squealed.

After hours of chiseling, digging and scrapping, Waxy got to the face of the hole. Jimmi the Pilot and Moe the Eskimo pulled him up and lowered the auger down into the shaft, then lowered Waxy down behind it. He drilled down another six feet, coughing on the engine exhaust that made him even more tired and gave him a headache. When the second drilling was

Somethin' for Nothin'

done, they pulled him and the auger out and sent him back down with the metal detector to slide the probe further into the glacier for aural evidence of the aircraft fuselage.

After two weeks, a half-dozen exploratory shafts had been drilled into Bahammy Mammy Glacier. The metal detector waxed and waned, but never grew significantly louder in the headsets, confirming that they were getting no closer to the treasure. Sometimes, the squeal faded and in his exhaustion, Waxy got discouraged.

"You didn't think becoming a millionaire was going to be easy, did you, slick?" Jimmi the Pilot repeatedly teased.

Jimmi the Pilot never seemed to lose his broad grin and Moe the Eskimo never seemed to tire from the labors on the glacier. Waxy didn't understand. He was always brutally exhausted at the end of the day. And it wasn't as if Jimmi the Pilot and Moe the Eskimo just sat around. They lowered and lifted him and equipment into the tunnel. They lifted out buckets of ice. Sometimes they slid down feet first to chip away at the face of the tunnel with a long metal pole to loosen the ice while he was resting and getting warm again.

The latest tunnel dug that day had, again, not raised the decibel level of the metal detector, even though they had gone down nearly twenty feet. Losing the light, Jimmi the Pilot and Moe the Eskimo pulled Waxy out from inside the glacier one last time and they began to pack up their equipment.

"I wish we could just blow open this damn thing with dynamite," Waxy said wearily.

"Say, maybe that's not such a bad idea," Jimmi the Pilot said.

"Avalanche," Moe the Eskimo grunted and Waxy's brief

shimmer of hope at the prospect of explosively eased labors was snuffed out.

"Shit," said Jimmi the Pilot. "Sounds like a Wile E. Coyote deal."

"Shit," sighed Waxy.

They loaded up their equipment and donned their snow shoes, then headed single file back towards the plane at the top of the glacier. Waxy dreaded the long walk at the end of the day. Bone weary from digging, he not only still had over a half a mile to trudge uphill to get off the mountain, he had to drag a sled weighted down with tools, gas cans, and the auger.

Waxy fell into line behind Jimmi the Pilot who followed Moe the Eskimo to trek to the Cessna. He marched like a zombie on a death march, barely able to lift the snow shoes strapped to his feet. He thought it was just the fatigue making each step harder and harder, but he had actually veered off from the trail that Moe the Eskimo scouted for them and into fresh, untested powder. Weary themselves from the day's labor's, Jimmi the Pilot and Moe the Eskimo drove on, heads down, towards the Cessna lost in their own thoughts until Waxy screamed as his left foot broke through the surface of Bahammy Mammy glacier. A crevasse swallowed his leg up to his hip.

"Help me!" Waxy's wail echoed weirdly off the mountains. "Help me!"

Jimmi the Pilot and Moe the Eskimo, aroused from their thoughts, stopped in their tracks and looked back in confusion at the sight of Waxy clawing desperately at the ice.

"Hang on," Jimmi the Pilot called out, finally grasping the danger of the situation. He staked his sled to the ice and headed back towards Waxy being careful to stay on the path that Moe the Eskimo had cleared for them. "Hang on, kid. Hang on."

Moe the Eskimo staked his sled, grabbed a coil of rope and shuffled after Jimmi the Pilot. He barked out at Waxy, "Stay still! Don't move."

"Hurry up! Come on! Hurry!" Waxy hollered ever more frantically, as he heard cracking sounds come from the ice around him.

Moe the Eskimo caught up to Jimmi the Pilot and tossed the end of the rope to Waxy.

"Easy kid. Easy," instructed Jimmi the Pilot as Waxy grabbed at the rope. "Get it tied to your harness."

Waxy was fifteen feet or so off the safe trail. He couldn't reach the rope, so Moe the Eskimo pulled it back and tossed it again. This time it went behind Waxy. On the third toss, the end of the rope fell within Waxy's reach. He quickly pulled it towards him and tied it off to the D-ring at his chest.

Before Jimmi the Pilot could tie the other end around his waist to act as an anchor, Moe the Eskimo grabbed his hand and subtly shook his head. If Waxy fell in and the crevasse was deep enough, he might pull Jimmi the Pilot in behind him, killing them both and stranding Moe the Eskimo on the glacier.

Jimmi the Pilot understood and nodded. He wrapped the rope around his arm and behind his back like the anchorman on a tug-of-war team, so he would be able to quickly let go of Waxy and not be pulled into the crevasse himself. Moe the Eskimo motioned him back. Jimmi the Pilot dug his snow shoes into the snow and slowly pulled the rope taut.

"Pull me out. I can't get out. Pull me out of here."

"Easy," Moe the Eskimo said to Waxy. "Easy."

Moe the Eskimo slowly probed the surface between the trail and the spot where Waxy had fallen through. He found the edge of the crevasse. He pulled out his pick ax and dug two foot holds, then took off his snow shoes and laid out towards Waxy, sticking the toes of his boots into the holes he had dug to give him leverage. He looked back over his shoulder at Jimmi the Pilot and nodded. Jimmi the Pilot dug in to brace himself to hold Waxy's full weight if the surface suddenly collapsed.

"Easy." Moe the Eskimo reached out towards Waxy with the metal pole he used to probe the ice. With a back and forth motion, across the surface, he cleared away loose snow, then slid his pick ax across the ice to Waxy.

The ice creaked and cracked loudly.

"Hurry, please," Waxy pleaded softly.

Moe the Eskimo nodded. "Try to pull yourself out with the pole."

The ice crackled.

"Use the pick to free your leg."

Waxy hammered at the ice around his leg.

"Easy...Easy."

Waxy chipped carefully around his thigh. Bahammy Mammy glacier protested with a loud crack. They felt him—Moe the Eskimo on the pole and Jimmi the Pilot on the rope—lurch down into the crevasse.

"Moe...*Please...*" Waxy bleated fearfully.

"Pull yourself towards me." Moe the Eskimo looked back at Jimmi the Pilot and called out. "Back. Easy. Back."

Somethin' for Nothin'

Waxy pulled on the pole and felt himself slowly come out of the crevasse. He kicked his leg to free his foot from the snow shoe and felt himself come out faster. Finally, he was prone on the surface and pulling himself towards Moe the Eskimo. Once beside Moe the Eskimo, he scrambled on his hands and knees towards Jimmi the Pilot, hearing a loud cannon-like crack from behind him.

Moe the Eskimo slid himself backwards towards the safety of the trail, pulling Waxy's sled with the auger and gas cans behind him.

"Jesus Christ, kid. You scared the living shit right out of me," Jimmi the Pilot told Waxy as he pulled him into a bear hug by the rope attached to his harness. "Don't you ever fucking do that again."

Waxy panted heavily against Jimmi the Pilot's chest.

Moe the Eskimo came up behind Waxy and merely put his hand on his shoulder.

"And then from behind us—it was like the worst thunderstorm thunder you ever heard," Jimmi the Pilot slapped the table, startling a now captivated audience in the booth, "and the surface where Waxy had just been trapped collapsed into a huge sink hole. And there it was…"

"What?" asked Beantown Bob, annoyed at the drama.

Jimmi the Pilot took a long pull off his Budweiser, peering down the length of the longneck at Beantown Bob.

"What, God damn it. What?"

"I found it!" Waxy blurted out loudly, tensely. "I found the fucking plane."

Startled, Beantown Bob and CiCi turned their heads towards Waxy.

Emma finally understood why Waxy was drinking so much and behaving so strangely. She glared accusingly at Jimmi the Pilot.

Jimmi the Pilot grinned broadly and nodded his head.

"I found it." Waxy pounded down yet another shot of Yukon Jack. "I found that mother fucker."

"The wing of the plane was there, down about twenty or thirty feet, bridging the gap of the crevasse," Jimmi the Pilot explained. "He's right. He found it."

"But he almost died," scolded Emma.

"But he didn't," replied Jimmi the Pilot.

"But I found it," Waxy slurred. He stared at the label of his Moosehead lager. "I found it."

A long, pregnant pause settled over the table.

"Is it there?" CiCi finally asked, unable to endure the unknown any longer. She wanted to know—she needed to know for sure. Her future depended upon it.

Emma scowled at Cici.

Just then the bartender served another round of drinks, but Emma pushed theirs away into the center of the table. She slid out of the booth pulling Waxy along with her.

Jimmi the Pilot patted Waxy on the shoulder as he slid by.

Beantown Bob and CiCi watched silently as Emma helped steady Waxy on his feet then lead him towards the rear exit. When the door slammed shut behind them, Beantown Bob stared off into space, absorbed in thought.

CiCi looked back at Jimmi the Pilot.

"Well, we'll find out now," Jimmi the Pilot answered her, then took a long thoughtful drink off his fresh Budweiser.

Emma struggled to help Waxy up the stairs to the

apartment. At the top, she leaned Waxy into the corner to use her key to unlock the door and let them in.

The television was on and Albert sat on the sofa with his feet up on coffee table. He froze in mid gulp of his beer at the sight of Emma.

Emma stared back in surprise.

"Is that Albert?" Waxy slurred heavily. In the duel between coherence and alcohol, the Yukon Jack prevailed. Waxy lurched clumsily towards the bedroom.

"I've seen that look before," Albert said.

Emma just scowled at Albert and helped Waxy to the bedroom, where he collapsed on the bed fully clothed and began to snore loudly. She closed the door and sat beside him, gently stroking his hair. She stared at the door, as if looking directly at Albert out on the couch for a long while, until she wearily lay down beside Waxy and held him in her arms, thinking for a long while about Albert, CiCi and the treasure buried beneath Bahammy Mammy glacier.

When Emma woke in the middle of the night to go to the bathroom, Albert was gone.

Emma hung the Holiday Inn 'DO NOT DISTURB' sign on the outside of the apartment door, then went back to bed with Waxy.

The Prodigal Son

"So, you trust that fucker?" Albert asked Waxy as they stood by the gaping yaw of the crevasse on Bahammy Mammy Glacier, watching Jimmi the Pilot barrel towards them on his take-off run down the face of the glacier to go get Moe the Eskimo and return with more equipment.

"He'll be back. We're standing on his future," Waxy answered grimly.

The Cessna's engine grew louder as it approached. Lighter now, the plane's skis broke away from the surface as it passed by and climbed out. Waxy and Albert tracked the plane as Jimmi the Pilot turned back towards the small village airstrip twenty miles down the valley that they used as a staging area. He would be back with Moe and the rest of the equipment in less than an hour. Once Jimmi the Pilot rounded the mountain peak and was out of sight, the surface of the glacier was smothered in silence. Waxy and Albert could hear only the sounds of their own breathing.

"I like it," said Waxy.

"What?"

"This. The quiet. The calm." Waxy turned and scanned the ridges and peaks that surrounded them there on Bahammy Mammy Glacier. "I like it."

Albert shrugged his shoulders and stepped towards the

crevasse to look over the edge at the exposed portion of the cargo plane's wing. "A bit chilly for my liking."

"Moe says not to get too close. The sides can give way sometimes…like a calving glacier."

Albert looked back over his shoulder at Waxy, then down at the buried plane again "Damn. That fucking Moe was right, huh? We're going to be rich, my friend. Rich."

Waxy scanned the silhouette of the ridgeline to the east. "I can't believe you're here."

"Yeah, well, I guess now that we found the plane, Bob is getting even more frantic about getting the loot out since summer's gone. At least that's what Jimmi claims."

"No. I mean, why did you come back from the pipeline?"

Albert peered down into the crevasse. "You know me and hard work…kind of like cats and dogs sleeping together. You know?"

Waxy looked at his friend, then back to the ridge line. "You staying with CiCi?"

"Yeah. At the band house."

"Thanks." Waxy sighed. "But you better not let Bob find out. I don't think he'd go easy on you like Eddie."

"She said he never comes around. Ever. Besides, he can't fire me, 'cause I don't really work for him anymore."

Waxy shook his head. "He'll tattoo your ass with his baseball bat."

Albert shrugged. "So, what are you and Emma gonna do with your share?"

"Emma?"

"She's nice. And though I've only seen her calves under the hemline of that waitress dress, I imagine she's got a great set of legs. Go all the way to the top, I'll bet."

Somethin' for Nothin'

Waxy shuffled his feet uncomfortably. He nodded. "I haven't gotten so far as to be spending money I ain't got in my hands yet."

"You're not going to stay up here, are you?"

Waxy shrugged his shoulders. "I don't know. I think Emma would like a change."

"I'm not. That's for sure."

"Why's that?"

Albert grabbed a handful of powdery snow and threw it towards Waxy. It sparkled in the morning sun.

"There's snow in Ohio, too."

"Not as much as here, though." Albert kicked at the surface of the glacier. "Who said anything about going back to Ohio? Besides, I don't know if enough time's passed for the Field Marshall to forgive the liberties I took with his Visa card."

"Where does CiCi want to go?"

"LA. To be a rock star." Albert sighed and smiled at Waxy. "Looks like we both have a female problem to deal with. Yeah, I don't see her settling into domestic tranquility in the Rubber City."

Waxy came over and stood next to Albert. They looked down into the crevasse at the section of aluminum wing jutting out from the ice. Each contemplated what the future might hold, once they found and breeched the fuselage and deposited its contents into their bank accounts.

It wasn't long before the drone of the Cessna's Continental engine echoed up the valley and Jimmi the Pilot lined up with the makeshift runway on Bahammy Mammy glacier. As they tracked the Cessna's approach, Waxy and Albert watched the plane descend gently until the skis bit the snow and slid up the slope.

Waxy and Albert began the trudge up the slope to unload.

They put the equipment—picks, shovels, saws, sledge hammers, rope, a chainsaw and more—onto sleds to pull back down to the crevasse. Like ants, they scurried back and forth on the path between the small plane parked above the ice and the much larger one trapped below. Moe the Eskimo and Waxy spread out a canvass tarp and began to unload the tools on to it. Albert and Jimmi the Pilot assembled the large tripod with a hand winch, securing it to the ice by driving long spikes deep into the surface of the glacier first to anchor each of the tripod legs. A second set of spikes was pounded in ten feet out in a semi circle away from the crevasse. They tied climbing ropes from the spikes to the top of the tripod.

"Okay, men. Who's first over the edge?" Jimmi the Pilot asked when they had finished setting up the tripod.

Albert and Waxy looked at Jimmi the Pilot like he was crazy. Moe the Eskimo pulled a saw, a pick, a shovel and a long crowbar from the pile of tools on the tarp and, ignoring the other three men, began walking away from the crevasse, towards virgin ice.

"He's got to build the snow shelter to store the stuff," Jimmi the Pilot explained, pointing his thumb over his shoulder at Moe the Eskimo. "And, hey, I'm the pilot. Remember? I'm the only one that can get any of us back off this iceberg. If something happens to me, you guys are fucked."

Albert looked at Waxy, who was looking over the edge of the crevasse with fear spreading on his face.

Somethin' for Nothin'

"I'll go," Albert said.

"And we have a winner," Jimmi the Pilot announced. *"Ding-Ding-Ding-Ding-Ding*—Come on down. You're the next contestant on *The Price is Right."*

Waxy watched Albert put on the body harness and strap the metal spikes and toe treads to his boots.

"You owe me," Albert said to Waxy and winked.

"Boys, boys, boys—there'll be plenty of fun to go around. Right now, time and daylight are a wastin'," said Jimmi the Pilot. He motioned towards the tarp. "Get him the climber's hammer and a bag of pitons."

Waxy grabbed the tools and followed Jimmi the Pilot and Albert towards the edge of the crevasse.

"Man, that's a long way down," Albert said looking over the edge.

"Ah, you big baby, it's only fifteen feet or so," Jimmi the Pilot answered.

"No. I mean down, down—past the wing. Gotta be a hundred feet or so."

"Yeah, well, don't think about that. Just concentrate on the task at hand. Besides you'll have the safety rope on. So, don't worry about it. And don't look down."

Albert gave Jimmi the Pilot a grim look. They attached Albert's body harness to the manual winch. Waxy handed Albert the climbing tools and pitons and went back to the tripod to crank his friend down into the crevasse.

"Aren't you glad I came back?" Albert asked Jimmi the Pilot.

"You are a ray of fucking sunshine."

"I knew you missed me."

Albert stepped to the crevasse and looked over the edge again.

"What did I tell you about looking down?" Jimmi the Pilot scolded.

"Fuck you, cowpoke."

Jimmi the Pilot smiled. "You'll be fine. Honest. Now, let's do this thing."

Albert turned away from the edge and got down on his hands and knees.

Waxy cranked the safety line taut, then gave Albert some slack.

Albert crawled backwards until he felt his feet over the edge of the ice. He spiked his climber's pick into the surface and lay flat on his stomach. He slid his legs over the edge until the safety rope pulled taut again. He gave Jimmi the Pilot a nod.

Jimmi the Pilot looked back at Waxy and nodded. "Easy. Nice and easy."

Waxy nodded back and ratcheted Albert out a half turn. The tripod groaned as Albert's weight shifted from the ice to the winch. Only his head and shoulders were still visible to Waxy.

"Hang on," Jimmi the Pilot called out. He did a quick walk around of the tripod to make sure the spikes anchoring the legs were holding and the ropes holding the top had not slipped.

"God damn it," Albert shouted out. "Let's go. Let's go."

Jimmi nodded to Waxy. Waxy nodded to Albert and cranked the winch back then forward to let Albert down a notch at a time. Until he disappeared completely over the edge.

Somethin' for Nothin'

Jimmi the Pilot went to the opposite side of the crevasse to be able to see Albert dangling just below the surface.

Albert dug the spikes on the toes of his boots into the side of the crevasse and began to dig out hand holds in the ice to help him climb back up. Once he was done, he signaled Jimmi the Pilot, who signaled Waxy to crank him down another few feet, where he stopped to dig more steps in the wall of ice. Taking Jimmi the Pilot's advice, Albert did not look down and concentrated at the immediate job at hand of chipping out a ladder in the face of the crevasse.

The minutes passed painfully slow for Waxy as he waited for the next signal from Jimmi the Pilot to winch his friend down deeper into the crevasse that had nearly swallowed him whole. Now, the quiet was more unsettling than soothing, punctuated as it was by the creaking of the tripod and the ratcheting of the winch, then Albert's faint muffled chiseling. Waxy's mind wandered between cranks to Emma. Now that they were so close, he allowed himself to ponder Albert's question about what they would do with the money and what their future together might be.

Waxy was startled when the tension on the safety rope was suddenly released. He looked at Jimmi the Pilot, who grinned broadly and gave him a 'thumbs up' signal.

The arctic silence was broken by a yell loud enough to bring Moe the Eskimo up short from his labors digging out a makeshift snow shelter fifty yards behind where Waxy stood at the tripod, as Albert celebrated reaching the cargo plane. The aluminum wing formed a ten foot by twenty foot ledge which spanned the crevasse. The wing tip and the fuselage were still embedded in the glacier, but the outboard engine nacelle stuck out from the ice on the far side.

M.T. Bass

Waxy shuffled carefully to the edge of the crevasse and saw Albert standing on the wing of the cargo plane.

"Fuckin' A" Albert yelled, looking back up at Waxy.

"Be careful."

"Get him the tools," Jimmi the Pilot called out to Waxy. Then down to Albert, "Start placing those pitons."

Albert saluted Jimmi the Pilot with his climbing hammer, then began pounding pitons into the face of the crevasse. "Gimme some slack, Waxy."

Waxy reeled Albert out, then brought a pick, a shovel and a chainsaw to the edge. He tied lengths of rope to the handles. When Albert was done pounding he began to lower them down one at a time. When Albert got them, he set them out on the wing and tied the other end of the ropes to the pitons he had driven into the ice, so if any of them slipped and fell off the wing, they could pull them back up from the depths of crevasse. Finally, Waxy began lowering the chainsaw.

"Don't you drop that thing," Jimmi the Pilot warned. "They don't grow on trees and it's the only one we got."

Albert flipped Jimmi the Pilot the bird as he tied off the chainsaw. "Hey, this aluminum is slick with ice. How about if I melt it off with the torch?"

"Hey, numb nuts, how about if you just blow us all to smithereens? They were heading to Japan—no doubt filled to the brim with avgas—which you might just be standing on."

"Oh." Albert looked down at his feet.

"That's right. The fuel tanks are in the wings. No telling what's left in them, but there's no sense in taking any chances."

"Never mind."

"Right."

Somethin' for Nothin'

Albert grabbed the pick and carefully shuffled across the wing towards the buried fuselage.

"The cabin is probably about twenty feet in or so," Jimmi the Pilot called out.

Albert looked over his shoulder, then carefully set his footing. He began to swing the pick at the face of the crevasse, digging out chunks of ice with each swing.

Jimmi the Pilot walked over to Waxy. They stood shoulder-to-shoulder watching Albert work. His days working on the pipeline had prepped him for these labors by strengthening his muscles and acclimating him to hard work outside in the cold.

"You're going to have to spell him at some point," Jimmi the Pilot said lowly to Waxy.

A pained expression flashed across Waxy's face.

"You'll be tethered up." Jimmi the Pilot patted Waxy on the shoulder.

Waxy took a deep breath. He nodded slowly.

In silence, they watched Albert work the face of the glacier, slowly opening a hole into the ice.

"You've used a chainsaw before right?"

"Yeah. On the farm, helping my dad."

"Right. Was your other uncle a lumberjack?"

"Huh?"

"Never mind."

They stood together, blankly watching Albert swing the pick, but both were thinking hard about not thinking about the treasure they were seeking.

After another hour, Jimmi the Pilot called down into the crevasse, "Hey, slick. Take a break."

Albert waved and shuffled back to the other face of the crevasse. He waited for Waxy to ratchet up the slack in his safety line, then climbed up the wall using the steps he had dug in the ice, assisted by the pull of the winch. At the top, Albert panted loudly and smiled broadly. His cheeks were rosy red.

"Go on over to the igloo with Moe," said Jimmi the Pilot. "He's got a heater set up. Warm yourself a bit while I get the kid hooked up."

Albert trudged off to the heater. He warmed his hands first, then turned himself in the heat, first side-to-side, then front-to-back, as if on a vertical rotisserie.

Moe the Eskimo stopped to watch Albert intently.

"Fuckin' A, Moe. You were right," Albert said excitedly.

Moe the Eskimo lit up a Camel cigarette. He nodded and cracked the slightest of smiles.

"Fuckin' A, man. Fuckin' A."

Moe the Eskimo blew a long stream of smoke and breath into the crisp air. "Don't stay too close, too long."

Albert smiled back at Moe the Eskimo. *"Fuck-in-A."*

Jimmi the Pilot silently helped Waxy into the body harness. "He got a good start. I think you can probably start carving with the chain saw."

Waxy nodded as he cinched his body harness a little tighter.

Jimmi the Pilot tied the rope connected to the winch to the D-ring on the harness. "Maybe you could carve me out an ice swan, while you're at it—it'll be good practice for when you and Emma get hitched."

Waxy looked at Jimmi the Pilot with a confused expression on his face. "You know for the reception—Come on, kid, lighten up already. You'll be fine. You'll be fine."

Waxy nodded weakly.

"Hey, slick, let's go," Jimmi the Pilot called out to Albert. "You're on the clock and it's ticking."

Somethin' for Nothin'

Albert jogged back over to the tripod. Waxy marched slowly to the edge, turned around and got on his hands and knees. Albert lowered him down. Jimmi the Pilot watched him go down to the wing, shuffle over to the beginnings of their mine shaft through the ice. Waxy inspected Albert's progress and began to work the face with the pick.

"The chainsaw. Use the chainsaw. Carve us a nice swan or something."

Waxy looked back up at Jimmi the Pilot grimly, but set down the pick. Soon the growl of the gas powered chainsaw echoed loudly through the ravine of ice and unnaturally up across Bahammy Mammy Glacier.

Halfway done with the snow shelter, Moe the Eskimo came over to the crevasse to assess the progress. Waxy dug into the face of the ice with the tip of the chainsaw with a grim determined look on his face. Before long, he had begun to move into the ice, first up to his elbows; then up to his shoulders until he finally was swallowed up completely in the five foot tall tunnel he was boring towards the fuselage of the cargo plane.

Inside the shaft, Waxy focused intently on working the blade of the chainsaw. His mind was sponged clear of all other thoughts, as he dug deeper and deeper into the ice of Bahammy Mammy Glacier. All extraneous thoughts of Albert, of Jimmi the Pilot, of riches, of Emma, of the danger of falling deep into the crevasse were gone, replaced by the work and the roar of the chainsaw. He did not think to measure his progress. He only juiced the throttle on the chainsaw as he dug into the ice again and again, kicking the hunks of ice wrenched from the face back behind him with his foot. The glacier gave way easily and before long Waxy was completely out of site of Albert, Jimmi the Pilot and Moe the Eskimo. Waxy hardly noticed himself, as the shaft he cut was comfortably larger than the exploratory tunnels bored out with the auger.

"He should take a break," Moe the Eskimo said.

"Hey, Waxy, take a break," Albert yelled down into the crevasse.

"You do realize, he can't hear you," Jimmi the Pilot said to Albert. "Give him a tug on the line."

Albert gave the safety line three quick tugs.

"Jesus! Easy, man. Don't pull him off his feet—he's got a chainsaw in his hands."

Waxy vaguely sensed the tug on the rope, but didn't recognize it as a signal from above. He kept working the face. Up ahead, the color of the ice appeared to be changing ever so slightly. Although he could not see clearly through the scarring from the chainsaw cutting, the face of the shaft was a bit darker, like the shadow cast by a cloud on a sunny day. It was something he perceived, but did not comprehend. Waxy just continued to cut, ignoring the second series of tugs at the safety line. He cut again and again, thrusting the chainsaw tip forward towards the shadow. His eyes watered. His breathing became labored as he worked harder and harder, chasing the shadow. His mind began to wander from the task at hand, drifting away from reality in an invisible current like an unmoored boat. It wasn't rational thoughts or even coherent memories that filled his mind, rather the brief flashes of frozen scenes like a bad movie montage—with his dad working a tree line on the farm; a luscious warm piece of the *Bone's* Dutch apple pie; the soft caressing lips of a strange

Somethin' for Nothin'

woman on his genitals in Las Vegas, Emma's smile—that filled his fading consciousness as he was being slowly poisoned by carbon monoxide.

Waxy stubbed his toe on the inboard engine nacelle, then suddenly realized that the dark shadow in the ice ahead was the fuselage of the cargo plane. He switched off the chainsaw and pushed up his safety glasses to rub his burning eyes.

"Waxy," he faintly heard Albert call out from above through the ringing in his ears.

"I think I see it," Waxy said softly, almost to himself, then louder and louder and louder, as he backed out slowly from the shaft. "I see it. I see it. I see it."

As he emerged from the ice tunnel and stood up straight, a wave of dizziness crashed over him and he crumpled to his knees.

"Waxy," Albert yelled.

"I see it," Waxy answered. "I think I see it."

In a bowling motion, Waxy slid the chainsaw into the tunnel to keep it from falling into the crevice, then bent over onto his hands and knees, resting his throbbing forehead on the cold aluminum of the airplane wing.

"Get another rope," Jimmi the Pilot instructed Albert. "Moe—Tie the kid off."

Up above on the surface of Bahammy Mammy Glacier, Albert, Moe the Eskimo and Jimmi the Pilot scurried to help Waxy.

Waxy rolled his forehead on the aluminum wing, trying to concentrate and think of Emma. He did not know what happening to him. He only knew that he longed for her smile and for her embrace.

Once he was connected to the tripod, Moe the Eskimo quickly winched Albert down into the crevasse to help Waxy. Albert crawled the fifteen feet over to Waxy and grabbed him tightly as his friend finally lost consciousness and collapsed off of his hands and knees.

"I want to go home," Waxy murmured as he slowly regained consciousness. He looked up and saw his friend. "Albert? Man, my head hurts bad."

"Hang on, Waxy. You'll be all right. We'll get you out."

"But, Albert—I saw it."

Albert looked into the tunnel and saw the dark mass of the cargo plane's fuselage and understood. He looked back up at Jimmi the Pilot and Moe the Eskimo peering down over the edge of the crevasse and nodded.

"Tell Emma I saw it."

Albert sat with his friend, until he came to his senses enough to move back to the ice ladder, where Jimmi the Pilot and Moe the Eskimo cranked him out of the crevasse. Moe took him over to the heater by the snow shelter to get warm. Jimmi the Pilot helped Albert get the tools out of the crevasse then winched him out as well.

When they joined Waxy by the heater, he was asking Moe the Eskimo, "You'll tell Emma I saw it, right?"

Moe the Eskimo rubbed Waxy shoulders. "Sure, kid. Sure."

Waxy sat by the heater while the others packed up the camp, storing the equipment in the snow shelter. Jimmi the Pilot went on ahead to preflight the Cessna. Albert and Moe the Eskimo, flanking Waxy for support, helped him up the slope and loaded him into the back.

Somethin' for Nothin'

Shortly after Jimmi the Pilot took off from Bahammy Mammy Glacier, Waxy was sound asleep and dreaming of Emma.

~~~

Double Cross

"ARRRRGGGGHHH, Excedrin headache number sixty-nine," Waxy moaned weakly as Albert and Jimmi the Pilot helped him up the stairs to the apartment above *Fenway Park West*.

They ushered him into bed. Albert got him some Tylenol, then turned out the light and closed the bedroom door.

"His head is going to be aching for a day or two," said Jimmi the Pilot. "Takes a while for the body to expel the carbon monoxide out of the bloodstream."

"He's going to be okay, though, right?"

"Yeah. No brain damage—no more than usual, anyhow—if that's what you mean. Just a Texas-size migraine."

Albert looked back at the closed bedroom door. "Should we take him to a hospital?"

"Nah. He'll be fine. He's a tough little cookie."

Albert looked at Jimmi the Pilot skeptically.

"You know, I don't mean to be callous, but as long as we have a window of weather, you, me and Moe should go back up and get done what we can," Jimmi the Pilot said. "We'll give the kid a break—he needs it. But, you know, summer's gone and we still got a shit load of work to get done before we get snowed out."

Albert glared at Jimmi the Pilot.

"For now, we just let him rest, okay?"

Albert nodded.

"Anyway, I worked me up an appetite. You hungry?"

Albert shook his head. "I think I'll hang out and make sure he's okay."

"Suit yourself, but I'm starved." Jimmi the Pilot went to leave, but paused at the door. "He'll be fine."

"Whatever you say, Jimmi."

Jimmi the Pilot started to say something, but just nodded, then left.

Albert restlessly paced the apartment. He sat and tried to watch TV, jumping up to impatiently flip through the channels, then sitting back down to squirm on the couch for a few more uncomfortable moments, before going to the kitchen for a beer or a bag of chips or any excuse to look on the door of the bedroom, behind which Waxy slept.

It had not even been an hour before Albert heard footsteps coming up to the apartment door. He was trying to figure out why Jimmi the Pilot was back so soon, when he was further confused by the jangle of keys unlocking the door.

Emma barged into the apartment and froze in her tracks at the sight of Albert standing in the kitchen by the refrigerator.

"Jimmi came by the *Bone* and told me what happened."

"He said that Waxy's going to be okay."

"How could you let this happen?" Emma dropped her purse and her keys to the floor.

"Huh? I didn't know. It was Jimmi's chainsaw. And I wasn't even down there with him."

Emma marched over to Albert and pushed him hard in the chest with both hands. He stumbled back against the kitchen counter. "Asshole. He could have been killed—*Again!*"

Somethin' for Nothin'

"Jimmi said—"

Emma took a wide roundhouse swing at Albert. He ducked, but her fist clipped the left side of his jaw. She began to flail wildly, beating him about his head and shoulders. "He's your friend, God damn it. He's your friend."

Albert grabbed Emma in a boxer's clinch, pinning her arms to her sides. He felt the adrenalin collapse as her muscles went limp and she leaned into his chest. A moment later, he felt the weak spasms of her weeping.

"But you're supposed to be his friend," Emma sobbed.

Albert loosened his grip on her and gently held her head to his chest.

"Where is he?" Emma suddenly demanded sternly, pushing away from Albert and wiping the tears from her cheek.

Albert pointed over her shoulder at the bedroom.

Emma turned and went in to check on Waxy, closing the bedroom door behind her.

Albert rubbed the side of his face where Emma's punch had connected with his jaw. He quietly slipped out of the apartment. At the bottom of the steps, he paused in the alleyway, wanting a drink badly, but not wanting to deal with any of the personalities he was sure to find inside *Fenway Park West*. So, Albert wandered the streets of downtown Anchorage, stopping at different bars around town for an anonymous boilermaker at each place, before moving on. He avoided the west end of town, where the Alaska State Employment trailers were, eventually drinking his way back east to *Fenway Park West*, which was closed when he got there. He knew the back door would still be unlocked as Moe the Eskimo closed up the kitchen. Too drunk to make his way to the band house, Albert sneaked quietly into the bar—in spite of his state of inebriation—and found his way to the over-sized booth in the back for parties of six or more. He wearily crawled onto the padded bench to sleep for the night—just as Waxy had so often done when he got off work to find the Holiday Inn 'DO NOT DISTURB' sign hanging on the outside door knob.

Albert listened to the faint clanking of pots and pans from the kitchen and just started to doze when he heard Beantown Bob's office door slam shut and footsteps overhead. He reeled himself back to consciousness enough to follow the conversation between Beantown Bob and Jimmi the Pilot as they came down the stairs.

"Seriously, the kid didn't think it might not be a good idea to use a chainsaw inside the tunnel?"

"Come on, B.B. Lighten up, man. It happened before any of us realized what was going on. He was making hellashious progress. Before he passed out, he said that he could see the fuselage through the ice."

"But he's out of commission, right?"

"Yeah, for a few days at least."

"Shit," Beantown Bob rapped his Louisville slugger down hard on the floor. "Shit—fuck—*son-of-a-bitch.*"

"I know. I know. I know. Me and Moe and the Mouth will get up there in the next day or two."

"But down a man, you'll only get half as much done."

Jimmi the Pilot nodded.

"It's fall and we're not even inside the plane yet. And any day, I expect the Burrito Boys to be showing up to settle the score."

Somethin' for Nothin'

"What choice did I have, B.B.?"

"Man, you really screwed the pooch on that one."

"Yeah, but what choice did I have?" Jimmi the Pilot retorted weakly.

"And screwed us royally in the process." Beantown Bob led Jimmi the Pilot over to the bar, where he went behind to grab a couple of beers out of the cooler for the road. "And if I have to go on the lam from the cartel before I can unload this joint, I'm totally fucked."

Jimmi the Pilot took the Budweiser longneck from Beantown Bob and followed him towards the rear exit. "We're almost there. We're almost there."

"Yeah, and then what?"

"Then what, what?"

"I keep thinking there's gotta be a way we can increase our shares," Beantown Bob grumbled.

"What are you saying?"

"A five-way split is definitely going to cut into our personal profit margin. Maybe there's a way to deal with the situation."

Hearing this, Albert yanked himself back into full consciousness and listened closely.

"You mean, like Carlos?"

"No, no, no. Nothing so dramatic. But, you know, I'm sure that once the recovery operation is wrapped up there will be, you know, *stuff* left behind."

Jimmi the Pilot did not answer.

"Think about it. You're going to need it to pay off your plane and find someplace far, far away from the Burrito Boys. And don't forget I've been financing this not so little adventure which is seriously draining my bank account."

Albert held his breath. He listened to Beantown Bob and Jimmi the Pilot leave through the back door. When the key turned in the lock, he lifted himself up on his elbows and peered across the booth's table, not quite believing what he had heard Beantown Bob propose, but knowing that he was certainly capable of it.

A sliver of light cut into the darkness of the bar as the swinging door to the kitchen slowly pushed open.

Moe the Eskimo slid halfway out the door and saw Albert's head in the back booth, silhouetted by the street light outside the front window. He put a cigarette in his mouth and struck a match. He held it at bay beyond the tip of the Camel filter, so that Albert could see him shake his head.

Albert imagined Moe the Eskimo as a weird jack-o-lantern.

He lit the cigarette, shook out the flame of the match, then went back into the kitchen.

"Holy fuck," Albert whispered to himself. He lay back down in the booth and stared into the reflected glow of the streetlight. "Holy fuck."

Blackmail

Dylan pouted on the couch in the band house living room. He squinted at the blank screen of the television set and drank slow, measured sips of his Coors. He was primordially aware of evolutionary changes taking place about him and felt an instinctual, animal fear rising at the threats to the existence he had come to enjoy since leaving Seattle with CiCi and the band.

He knew all along his sister was not always faithful to Beantown Bob, but, until now, none of the affairs had ever come close to being a genuinely competing "relationship"—until now. In fact, she rarely saw any of her extracurricular lovers a second time, except for Eddie the ex-bartender, which had also worried Dylan at the time. She never before brought any of them to the band house either, even though the chances of Beantown Bob showing up there were about as good as Janis Joplin rising from the dead. Dylan looked up at the ceiling, where on the second floor his sister was sleeping with Albert.

The gig at *Fenway Park West* had been a great run, epic "Sex, Drugs & Rock 'n' Roll." Dylan did not want it to end, but he knew that it soon would, though he did not comprehend exactly why or how or when it ever started imploding. The one thing he knew for sure was that he did not want to move back home to Seattle and get another dead end job at a nursing home. He could practically smell the stench of elder urine and feces. He locked his stare on the dead television and pouted anew over that prospect.

Thumping upstairs drew his eyes upwards again. He followed the footsteps across the ceiling and locked his gaze on the stairway.

CiCi stopped on the bottom stair.

Dylan stared at his sister down the length of the beer bottle.

"Well, I guess there's no coffee made," she said, knotting the belt of her bathrobe tight around her waist.

Dylan shrugged.

CiCi sighed, took the last step down and padded off towards the kitchen. She cleaned and loaded the Mister Coffee machine to start a fresh pot. When she switched it on and turned around, Dylan stood at the doorway to the kitchen. He had come up behind her so softly, his appearance took CiCi aback. "Creep!"

"I want in."

"In? What are you talking about?"

"In. I want in."

"I don't know what you're talking about."

Dylan scowled. "I am not a fucking house plant. I hear things. I see things."

"Yeah? What do you think you hear? What do you think you see?"

"I see you stepping out on Bob, big time." Dylan looked up towards her bedroom.

"That's none of your business."

"It's my business, because the band is my business and Bob is the band's only gig."

Somethin' for Nothin'

CiCi folded her arms across her chest. "Well, maybe it's time to move on."

"I want in."

"In on what?"

"I see those Buckeye Bozos coming and going with that pilot guy. I see them huddling up with Bob in the back booth. They got something going on." Dylan stared at CiCi, then contorted his face into a dopey expression. In an exaggeratedly moronic voice, he half-yodeled, "I ain't stupid, ya know."

CiCi met his stare and thought, recalling the conversation Albert overheard between Beantown Bob and Jimmi the Pilot, *maybe you are stupid.*

"If this gig is going to end, I need something, too. I ain't going back." He took a last drink out of his beer. "I ain't."

The Mister Coffee gurgled loudly as it finished the brewing cycle. In the silence between brother and sister, the dripping slowed, then ceased.

CiCi poured two cups of coffee and breezed past her brother on her way back up stairs, saying, "I don't know what you're talking about."

Dylan watched her over his shoulder, then went to the refrigerator for another beer. "Bitch."

He parked himself back on the couch to pout and wait.

Before long the shower started and footsteps—heavier footsteps—came down the stairs.

"Hey, man," Albert said as he passed through to the kitchen with two empty coffee mugs.

Just like with his sister, Dylan appeared stealthily behind Albert at the Mister Coffee. He watched him pour two more cups of coffee.

Albert was startled when he turned around. "Shit, man. What are you, some kind of fucking ninja?"

"I want in."

"Huh?"

"I want in."

"In on what?"

"You know."

Albert shook his head and started to move past, but Dylan stepped into his path.

"You're doing my sister," he said in a low, threatening growl.

"Your point being?"

"Last time I checked, she was still Bob's girlfriend. You know Bob—your, um, *partner,* right? So, you screw her, you're screwing him, too—aren't you?"

Albert stared down Dylan, wondering how much CiCi's brother really knew about the treasure on Bahammy Mammy Glacier.

The plumbing shuddered with water hammering as the shower shut off, drawing their looks toward the ceiling.

Dylan scowled at Albert. "I want in."

Albert looked back down from the ceiling. "I gotta go."

"I will fuck you up."

Albert exhaled wearily and stepped past Dylan, pushing him out of the way with his shoulder.

"We'll talk more later," he called out after Albert.

Dylan got another beer out of the refrigerator and leaned against the counter. He flipped off the cap with the church key hung around his neck and took a long, long pull.

~~

Kudzu

CiCi spent as little time as possible in Beantown Bob's office above *Fenway Park West*. In fact, she could not remember if and when she had ever actually sat down in there, but now she clearly remembered why: it was dark, cluttered and borderline claustrophobic. The room reeked of grandparent houses and made her skin crawl like hugging a creepy old uncle whose hands were prone to indecent wandering. She struggled to put aside such thoughts as she sat across from Beantown Bob behind his desk, coyly trying to get her brother hooked up into the treasure hunt gang to buy more time by keeping his mouth shut about her affair with Albert. CiCi had no doubt that the self-destructive little shit would do it. Dylan always had been a pain-in-the-ass little brother and still was.

It's getting crowded in here, Beantown Bob thought absently, ignoring CiCi's pleadings. He gazed around his office, but this particular thought was about more than cluttered shelves and piled up floor space. Since his cabin was, well, a cabin, the office was his attic. He looked at it like an objective curator of the Beantown Bob museum, reading biography in each item of junk, like a tea leaf reader. How in the hell did his high school football jersey ever even get there from his mom's house in Massachusetts? No telling. As his ears mindlessly absorbed CiCi's words, he flipped back through the eras of

Beantown Bob, using layers of dusty paraphernalia like counting tree rings, until he came crashing into the dead end that was the long overdue and still incomplete manuscript on his desk.

Beantown Bob sighed. It's getting crowded in here, he thought, pondering now about his present day life, filled as it was with crazy characters and wild plot lines that seemed lately to press in hard upon him. Jimmi the Pilot was always a wild card; but CiCi, Dylan, those guys from Ohio, Mexican drug dealers and now this whole crazy Air Force cargo plane treasure hunt that he had bet his entire life on like a lucky number at a Vegas roulette table, were suffocating him like kudzu vines on an oak tree. He shook his head at his own foolishness.

"No? Why not?" CiCi screeched. Her entire future, starting with her escape from Alaska geographically and Beantown Bob relationally, just then depended on meeting the extortion demands of her sibling.

"Sorry. Just shaking off a random thought."

"Are you even listening to me?"

Beantown Bob nodded, then promptly drifted off again from their conversation about CiCi's pain-in-the-ass brother, whose bar bill always exceeded his earnings as a drummer. Originally, that had been part of the plan to snare her into staying well beyond her youthful attention span for him and for playing gigs at *Fenway Park West*. So far, the plan had worked great.

He definitely did not need her making waves right now with all he had to deal with.

Beantown Bob nodded again, agreeing to let Dylan in on the treasure hunt. Besides, with the kid down, the extra hands would be sorely needed at the site to keep things moving forward as quickly as possible. And when all was said and done, Dylan could be left up on the mountain, just like the others.

"Thanks." CiCi stood up and hesitated awkwardly, then walked out of the office.

"Close the door, will ya?"

She did.

Manifest Destiny, Beantown Bob thought. He would not regret it—whatever it takes to get the job done—but, in the end, Dylan just might be sorry. Beantown Bob smiled in self satisfaction, but his scheming was interrupted by a random thought: how long had it been since he had bumped ugly with CiCi? He looked at the closed office door, through which she had just left and tried to remember.

"Son-of-a-bitch," he whispered softly to himself.

The memory of how CiCi always made love like a hungry animal crashed over him like a storm surge wave. It was a genuine hunger, often wearying, not one which could be ignored for long.

"That mother fucking Albert son-of-a-bitch," he whispered again. "It'll serve him right to freeze to death on that God damn mountain."

Agitated, Beantown Bob got up to go downstairs to pull the cash from the register drawer. He paused on the catwalk outside his office and peered down into the bar area. In the booth close to the front door were three Hispanic men, dressed in stiff new flannel shirts, khakis and hiking boots—so new, he thought that their clothes no doubt still smelled of the cardboard boxes they had been shipped in. He squinted to see if the L.L. Bean tags still hung from their shirts and pants as a way to distract himself from more unpleasant thoughts about why these Outsiders—not even lower forty-eighters, but actual foreigner outsiders—had shown up in his bar. "Fucking Jimmi. You really screwed the pooch this time, didn't you?"

Beantown Bob leaned his Louisville Slugger quietly against the railing next to him in the pool of shadows where he knew he was not visible from below. Leaning with his elbows on the top rail, he watched the Mexicans with a predatory, big cat-like intensity. Cocking his head, he could just catch snippets of Spanish rise from below, their meanings completely lost on him, but the import of which gripped his gut.

Beantown Bob instinctively reached beneath his New England Patriots jersey to his belt line to adjust the Smith and Wesson revolver he had started to carry ever since rumors of a gang of Latinos prowling up and down Fourth Avenue started circulating among neighboring shop proprietors and bar owners.

~~~

Striking Aluminum

Dylan sat in the back of the Cessna next to Albert and whined the whole way up to Bahammy Mammy Glacier. It was worse than even when the Field Marshall would load the entire Stiles family into the station wagon for a vacation road trip and Albert had to endure the suffocating presence of all of his sisters at once within the confines of his mom's Volvo. It got so bad that, thankfully, Jimmi the Pilot unplugged Dylan's headset microphone from the intercom, though Albert could still faintly hear murmurings of his pathetic monologue above the roar of the engine as he watched the Alaska wilderness pass by out the side window. It made him angry to have Dylan replace Waxy, but, in the face of her brother's extortion demands, what choice did he and CiCi have?

It grated on Jimmi the Pilot to see Waxy replaced, too. The kid had saved his life in the desert. He was a hard worker and not bad company during all the long hours they had spent together in the cockpit. And although his feelings for her had never completely gone away, Jimmi the Pilot felt downright big brotherly in his successful match-making efforts to bring Emma and Waxy together. But Beantown Bob was also right that they could not afford to lose a single day of work on Bahammy Mammy Glacier. Somehow time had slipped quickly by without him really noticing and now, not only was the hard breath of winter starting to blow down from the Arctic Circle, the God damn Mexicans were closing in on Jimmi the Pilot. He was growing tired of looking over his shoulder all day long, everywhere he went. He even considered moving the de Havilland *Beaver* and the Cessna off Merrill Field to a private airstrip off to the east after they found the padlock on front gate cut. Frankly, Jimmi the Pilot would be surprised if the Burrito Boys didn't just torch the hangar if they found it. They were too stupid and too impatient to convert an asset like an airplane into cash, even though its value was two or three times that of the drugs he and Waxy had pulled out of the *Suburban*. Of course, maintaining a clean balance sheet was never the cartel's strong suit—at least on paper.

Jimmi the Pilot looked over towards the co-pilot seat. He could see Moe the Eskimo's jaw line work as he ground his teeth and knew that they were of a like mind on the situation with Waxy. The two were close. But they needed a maximum effort to beat the winter and beat the Burrito Boys. With Bahammy Mammy Glacier up ahead, Jimmi the Pilot began working the hydraulic pump to lower the plane's skis into place.

"Jesus H. Christ on a cracker," Jimmi the Pilot said out loud as Dylan's squeals of terror filled the cockpit as he landed up the slope. Damn, he was glad he had unplugged the mike or all their ear drums would have been ruptured.

Once out of the plane and into their routine of moving equipment to the edge of the crevasse and setting up the tripod, winch and ropes, Albert, Jimmi the Pilot, and Moe the Eskimo traded impatient knowing looks at Dylan's laggardly contribution to their efforts. For every two or three trips they

Somethin' for Nothin'

made between the snow shelter and the crevasse, he made one, complaining the whole time about the weight of his load, about the cold or about the difficulty of trudging through the snow. When they were ready to get to work, they had no choice but to station him at the winch. After Jimmi the Pilot briefed him thoroughly on his duties in cranking the winch to raise and lower Albert in and out of the crevasse and, especially being careful to keep the slack on the safety ropes to a minimum, he vowed to monitor Dylan much more closely than he had ever had to watch either Waxy or Albert.

Albert went down to the surface of the wing. They lowered the chainsaw down to him, then a Scot Air Pack that Jimmi the Pilot had "borrowed" from the Merrill Field fire station, which would allow Albert to work the face of the shaft without getting carbon monoxide poisoning from the chainsaw's engine exhaust. He soon got to work parrying and thrusting at the ice like the chainsaw was a sabre, pausing only to kick the frozen debris behind him like a mole burrowing beneath a garden. Albert soon lost all sense of time as he became absorbed in his labors. It was hard to see most of the time, because he had given up as hopeless keeping the fireman's face mask clear of ice particles thrown off by the chainsaw blade. Instead he kept pressing ahead lost in churning thoughts of the imminent danger presented by Dylan's threat to reveal his and CiCi's relationship and Beantown Bob's intent to leave him and Waxy on the top of Bahammy Mammy Glacier to die so he could keep their share of the loot. Albert pressed on and on, trying to get his labors to fog away his worries. The only thing that would have stopped him was running out of breathing air or fuel in the chainsaw's tank. Before that happened, though, a horrific metal grinding and a shower of sparks filled the ice shaft. The chainsaw bucked back hard in his hands.

"What the fuck?" Albert asked himself out loud. He backed away and pondered in confusion, goosing the throttle of the chainsaw until he realized he had struck the fuselage of the cargo plane.

"Now what's wrong?" Jimmi the Pilot asked himself as he peered down into the crevasse when the chainsaw's furious growling suddenly calmed to idling purring.

"Holy shit. I found it," Albert yelled into his face mask. Of course, no one else could hear him.

"Hey, Slick!" Jimmi the Pilot called out. "What's wrong?"

Albert tore off the face mask and yelled at the top of his lungs, "I GOT IT! FUCKING A, WE'RE THERE!"

Jimmi the Pilot leaned on his knee to look over the edge of the crevasse.

Curious, Dylan shuffled over next to Jimmi the Pilot to see for himself what was going on.

Not thinking when he tore off his mask to call out and to be able to finally see and touch the aluminum skin of the plane with his hand, Albert began coughing and gagging at the exhaust fumes which filled the tunnel. He dropped the chainsaw and quickly backed out of the shaft for fresh air.

Jimmi the Pilot, distracted by what was going on down in the crevasse, failed to see that Dylan had left his post at the winch. When he noticed him standing at his side, Jimmi the Pilot barked angrily, "Hey, God damn it, get your ass back on the winch. Get that slack up. Pronto."

Dylan hurried back to the winch and began cranking wildly.

Somethin' for Nothin'

As Albert coughed and hacked, trying to clear his lungs, he did not pay attention to the safety line as it was quickly reeled in, until it caught his foot and tripped him off his feet. He hit hard on the surface of the wing and quickly slid off the slick aluminum, free falling into the crevasse until the slack in the safety line ran out with a hard jerk to his harness. He swung sideways and slammed into the hard ice wall of the crevasse, knocking breath out of his lungs and consciousness from his mind.

The load on the winch caused it to suddenly snap back against Dylan's furious cranking and broke his arm. He went down in a wail of whining anguish, writhing in snow while Albert dangled helpless, twenty-five feet below the surface of Bahammy Mammy Glacier.

Jimmi the Pilot and Moe the Eskimo rushed to the tripod to grab the creaking legs to make sure that they did not pull loose from the anchors in the ice. They kicked the moaning and crying Dylan out of the way and worked quickly to rescue Albert from the crevasse. Moe slowly cranked the winch. Jimmi the Pilot tossed a second safety line down to Albert, who had regained consciousness and desperately grabbed on to it. Together Jimmi the Pilot and Moe the Eskimo slowly lifted Albert back up to the level of the wing.

Albert climbed up on the wing, panting on all fours to catch his breath. When the load came off their rope lines, Jimmi the Pilot rushed back to the edge of the crevasse.

Albert looked up, a grimace on his face. Haltingly, between heavy gasps, he exhaled, "We're…there…it's really…there…"

Jimmi the Pilot grinned broadly.

Albert smiled back through his pain and laughed almost

maniacally to himself, "We're there. There. Fuckin' A, we're there."

Jimmi the Pilot ignored Dylan's whimpering behind him. "Come on, Slick, let's get you out of there."

~~~

Armed and Dangerous

In his enthusiasm, Albert took a leap to charge up the steps to the apartment above *Fenway Park West,* forgetting about his injuries. The pain in his side brought him up short, and he stopped on the second step up, setting down the small duffel bag he carried, to catch his breath. Recovered, Albert grabbed the bag and slowly climbed the stairs. He instinctively reached for the door knob, but hesitated, then knocked three times. Too impatient to wait for a response, Albert tried the door. It was unlocked, so he let himself into the apartment.

Waxy and Emma were sitting at the kitchen table eating macaroni and cheese. They paused mid-bite to absorb Albert's entrance and the somewhat wild look in his eyes.

"Albert? What's going on? I thought you were up working Bahammy Mammy."

"Waxy, I fucking A found it, man. I found it."

"But, didn't you already find the plane?" Emma asked.

"I mean I got to it. We're at the fuselage, Waxy. We're there. We're there." Albert sat down across the table from Waxy with Emma to the side between them. "I touched it. I actually touched the aluminum. I touched it. So fucking close, man. We are so close."

"Did you get in?"

"We're going to need cutting torches or something to get through the metal—but we are fucking A there." Albert looked at Waxy, then Emma with a huge grin on his face. "You gotta get back in the saddle."

Waxy and Emma traded glances.

Waxy looked down and nodded.

"But what about Dylan?" Emma asked.

"That fucking maroon almost got me killed—tripped me with the safety rope and I fell into the crevasse." Albert untucked his shirt and pulled it up to reveal a massive bruise on the side of his abdomen. "Thank God, I didn't break anything. That son-of-a bitch Dylan broke his arm, though, when the winch handle started back-driving before it caught. We just got done dumping him off at the emergency room. Couldn't've happened to a nicer guy, huh?"

Waxy started tapping his fingers on the table. "Wow. You're there. Wow. Great."

Emma held her tongue, but the look of obvious concern on her face revealed her worries for Waxy's safety.

"When are you going back up?"

"Tomorrow. You up for it, man?"

Waxy nodded, slowly, then faster and faster. He saw Emma's care fraught face. "It'll be okay. It'll be good. We're there—now all we have to do is pull out the cash. Then...You know, like we talked."

Emma just sighed. She rubbed Waxy's arm gently.

"One thing we gotta talk about, though," Albert, changing his tone and reflexively lowering his voice. He looked towards the wall that the apartment shared with Beantown Bob's office.

"What's that?"

"Hang on."

Somethin' for Nothin'

Albert leaned over and opened the duffel bag. He retrieved a pair of pistols and set them on the table. The three stared down at the weapons.

Waxy looked over at Emma, recalling his gun battle with Jimmi the Pilot against the Mexican drug dealers. "What are those for?"

"We have to start carrying them."

"Why?" asked Emma, alarmed at the prospect. "And why do you even have these?"

"Well, ah, I had a little trouble up at Delta that I thought might follow me back here," Albert said wincing, as he recalled the operator's threats and assault with the sideboom over the disappearance of his uncle, the fingerless man Albert had killed for his union card.

"What kind of trouble?" asked Emma.

"That's not important now."

"But what do we need guns for?" Waxy asked.

"'Cause Jimmi's got one."

Waxy nodded knowingly. "And?"

"And I'm sure Bob does, too."

"So?"

"So, the other night—the night that you got monoxide poisoning up on Bahammy Mammy—after Emma came by…" Albert paused and exchanged a glance with Emma, both recalling their altercation that night. "I, ah, left and got a little drunk and ended up sleeping down in *Fenway Park*. You know, on the bench of that big booth in the back. Well, anyway, I overheard Bob tell Jimmi that they should, you know, 'take care of us' and that way they could keep our shares."

Emma gasped softly, but audibly.

"Come on. Jimmi wouldn't…" Waxy's thought drifted off as he pictured Jimmi the Pilot coldly putting a bullet into the head of the Mexican drug dealer Waxy had only wounded behind the Chevy *Suburban* in the desert.

"Waxy?" Emma asked.

"Yeah, maybe. Maybe not. But I am absolutely positive Bob would do it—in a heartbeat," Albert said. "Just leave us up there to die in the cold on that fucking hunk of ice once the last bag of cash is loaded up. You know it, too."

Waxy nodded grimly.

Emma looked at Waxy, then to Albert and back to Waxy.

Waxy reached out and pulled one of the Walther PPK pistols towards him. He picked it up, released the magazine, checked that it was empty, then pulled the slide back and locked it open to inspect the weapon. His familiarity handling the firearm surprised both Emma and Albert.

"You got ammo?" Waxy inquired, suddenly in a very business-like manner.

Albert nodded. He reached down into the duffel bag and pulled out two boxes of cartridges and stacked them up on the table.

Waxy opened one of the boxes, then began to push cartridges into the magazine.

"Moe was there that night cleaning up. He heard it, too," Albert said. "If you don't believe me."

Waxy just nodded, focusing his attention on loading the magazine. "I believe you."

"Waxy?" Emma asked, her voice heavy with worry.

Waxy released the slide and slid the magazine back up into the grip. He pulled and released the slide to chamber a round.

Somethin' for Nothin'

Waxy flipped the safety down to uncock the hammer, flipped it up to set the trigger, then set it on safe again. He released the magazine and loaded another bullet to fill it, then slammed it home into the gun again. Waxy looked at Emma. He set the pistol down and reached out to stroke her cheek gently. She bent her head down to meet his hand, closing her eyes. "We'll be okay. We've come too far."

"But—"

"We will be okay. I promise. We're too close to turn back now."

Emma only nodded.

Albert reached for the other pistol.

~~~

The Globemaster

The next day, they were back on Bahammy Mammy Glacier. Moe the Eskimo and Jimmi the Pilot lowered Albert, then Waxy down onto the wing of the C-124 *Globemaster*. Waxy shuffled over and peered into the mine shaft through the ice. He saw the silver aluminum of the fuselage and smiled. He went back to help Albert receive the torch, hoses, sledge hammers and oxygen and acetylene gas tanks.

Donning the Scot Air Packs, Waxy went into the shaft followed by Albert. Albert opened the tank valves. Waxy struck the ignitor, adjusted the flame, and began cutting into the aluminum skin of the airplane. Steam from the sublimating ice cast a rainbow around the tip of the torch.

From the edge of the crevasse, Jimmi the Pilot and Moe the Eskimo watched intently in silence as the flame and sparks glowed eerily through the ice. The ice cracked loudly every so often in a painful protest from the heat transfer off the metal, drawing their eyes to meet and share their worry. Inside the glacier, Waxy and Albert ignored it.

Waxy lost himself in the mesmerizing work of cutting out the aluminum end of the tunnel. When he finally connected the oblong, rounded rectangle he was cutting around the frosted over window in the fuselage, he stepped back and cut off the gas to the flame. He smiled broadly behind his mask, then nodded at Albert.

M.T. Bass

Albert's muffled voice answered from behind his mask, "Fucking A, man."

Albert shut off the gas valves and they pulled back the torch and tanks. Outside the shaft, they doffed their Air Packs and awkwardly, but carefully traded places. Waxy handed Albert the short handled sledge hammer and followed him back to the fuselage of the plane. The aluminum crumpled and caved a bit with each blow, as Albert worked the edge inside the scorched line that Waxy cut with the torch to attack the airframe underneath. After pounding relentlessly at the fuselage until breathless, Albert passed the sledge hammer to Waxy, who slid past Albert to the plane. They traded places again and again, tag team style, until before they knew it the cutout section suddenly gave way to one of Albert's blows and fell into the inside of the aircraft cabin.

Albert stuck his head through the hole and peered into the darkness inside without seeing. "Hand me a flash light."

Waxy grabbed a flashlight out of the duffel bag and passed it forward.

The beam cut into darkness sealed beneath Bahammy Mammy Glacier for decades, revealing a surreal scene of United States currency blanketing the cargo hold like identical rectangular flakes. Albert scanned the beam back and forth across four pallets secured to the floor of the plane.

"Holy shit. Waxy…"

"What?"

Without answering, Albert plunged into the hole. He did not even flinch when he stepped on the corpse of a dead airman and snapped the frozen, brittle bones of his rib cage.

"Albert, what is it?" Waxy shuffled forward to the hole. All he could see was the beam of the flashlight skittering crazily about the cabin, first away, then back towards him.

Albert suddenly appeared at the hole in the fuselage with the flashlight tucked into his armpit. The beam swept across Waxy's eyes causing him to reflexively look away. When he looked back, Albert was holding up one of the many gold ingots from the pallets.

"Arrrrrhhh, matey," Albert growled. "We found the bleedin' booty."

He handed the gold bar to Waxy and they began to laugh hysterically.

At the edge of the crevasse, hearing the muffled laughter from beneath the ice, Moe the Eskimo and Jimmi the Pilot looked at each other quizzically.

"Hey, kid," Jimmi the Pilot called out.

Albert pointed at the duffel bag. Waxy grabbed it and dumped out the contents, then put the gold bar into the bag.

"Hang on," Albert disappeared into the *Globemaster* and returned with two thick bundles of hundred dollar bills. He tossed them into the duffel bag and nodded his head.

Waxy zipped up the bag and crawled out of the tunnel. He waved at Jimmi the Pilot and Moe the Eskimo to toss down a rope for the duffel bag. He tied it off and watched them haul it up to the surface of Bahammy Mammy Glacier.

Albert appeared at the entrance to the ice shaft and watched the grin explode on Jimmi the Pilot's face as he opened the bag.

"How about them road apples, you fucking cowpoke?" Albert called out.

Jimmi the Pilot just grinned back.

M.T. Bass

Moe the Eskimo lowered the empty duffel bag back down with two more to use for a bucket brigade to start extracting the cash and bullion from the cargo plane's hold.

The Burrito Boys

After the first flight of the Cessna off Bahammy Mammy Glacier packed up with a load of cash and gold, Jimmi the Pilot and Waxy dropped off Albert and Moe the Eskimo, then flew back to the area around the mountain to find a place in the wilderness to hide the loot. They eventually found a nearby stretch of shoreline along the Tamalaheena River, just long enough for the Cessna to land and take-off again, but short enough to discourage any regular visits by other bush pilots. It was at least twenty miles from any man-made structures visible from the air, whether inhabited or not. Jimmi lined the Cessna up on short final, dumped full flaps in and slowed the plane to the very edge of a stall. He aimed to use all the available length of the sand bar, flaring out over the water, skimming the waves with the back ends of the skis hanging from his landing gear. He taxied to the edge of the woods and shut down the engine. He and Waxy got out of the plane and began to explore into the tree line.

"Hot damn, kid. Hot damn," Jimmi the Pilot said, when they reconvened at the plane. "Do you believe it?"

"Yup. Moe was right."

"Hot damn, kid."

"So, what are you going to do with your share?"

Jimmi the Pilot looked at Waxy. "Don't know. I'm definitely

thinking some place warm—island warm, I mean, not desert warm. I don't need another winter pounding. What about you?"

"I kind of like it up here."

"What about Emma?"

Waxy hemmed and hawed. "She might be ready for a change of scenery."

"Yeah, well, sticking around might not be that good of a plan, anyways."

"Why's that?"

"Mexicans."

"In Alaska? Oh…" Waxy answered his own question with a sudden realization, remembering again the trip to the border with Jimmi the Pilot. "Yeah. Maybe not."

"Come on. This spot will work, *primo.*"

They got back into the Cessna and took off, barely getting airborne at the end of the sand bar. Jimmi the Pilot flew in ground effect down the river, then climbed and headed towards Anchorage.

When they got back to Merrill Field and finished tying down the Cessna, Jimmi the Pilot silently shook Waxy's hand, gripping it extra tight it seemed. They parted without words and Waxy looked back over his shoulder at Jimmi the Pilot as he walked dreamily around the plane gently caressing the wings, tail and control surfaces, with no apparent purpose at all.

Waxy stopped at the *Lucky Wishbone Diner* to see Emma. Instead of sitting at the counter, as usual, he took a booth in an empty corner of the dining room.

Emma spotted him in someone else's station and waved him over to the counter. He shook his head, so she told the other waitress she would take care of him, grabbed a piece of fresh blueberry pie and a glass of milk, then headed his way with an inquisitive smile on her face.

She set the pie and milk down in front of Waxy. "Hey, screwball, I'm over at the counter."

"Oh, and, miss, keep the change," Waxy said as he slid a ten thousand dollar bundle of hundred dollar bills across the table to Emma, who involuntarily squealed at the sight of the money.

"Waxy! Put that away!"

"And there's plenty more where that came from." He smiled broadly.

"Really. Put it away."

He shook his head. "No."

"But-but—"

"Put it in your pocket. Carry it around. It won't be long now. It won't be long."

Emma grinned. She quickly scooped up the cash and put it into her pocket with her tip money. She patted the bulge and giggled. "I, ah—I, geeze—I have to get back—you know."

Waxy smiled. He took a bite of pie and washed it down with a big gulp of milk, watching Emma practically tiptoe like a ballerina back to the kitchen.

She looked over her shoulder at Waxy and smiled a smile that slowly melted with doubt and worry.

Waxy winked at her and smiled back, then patted the Walther PPK beneath his jacket.

~~~

Jimmi the Pilot was in a great mood as he walked out of the office of the Fixed Base Operator. He was intercepted by Sparks, the mechanic.

"You had some visitors," Sparks said, sidling up alongside and squinting at him. "It's a pisser…wetbacks."

Jimmi the Pilot stopped dead in his tracks and the grin drained from his face. No explanation was necessary. The cartel had found him and was now coming after him. "Thanks, Sparks."

He slapped the mechanic on the shoulder. He climbed in and started his GMC pickup, parked on the side of the building. The engine idled loudly as Jimmi the Pilot pondered his situation. He put the truck in gear, but instead of turning left at East Fifth Avenue, Jimmi the Pilot went right, heading north towards the Chugach Mountains.

~~~

Beantown Bob sat in his office counting the night's receipts. *Fenway Park West* was empty, except for Moe the Eskimo and Waxy, clattering around, cleaning and closing down the kitchen. A shattering of glass caught his ear. It was different from the sound of ten inch rounds or beer mugs crashing into the tile floor behind the bar or at the dishwashing station in the kitchen. He stopped counting and listened. The front door creaked, a sound that was normally impossible to hear when the bar was open. Footsteps echoed up from the bar. Beantown Bob grabbed the pump action shot gun leaning against the wall behind him next to his Louisville Slugger and went to peer around the corner of his office door and down into the bar area.

Somethin' for Nothin'

The leader directed two men into the kitchen and two other men to clear the game room, the restrooms and the dance floor area. The leader then cleared behind the bar.

Just then, Beantown Bob heard the familiar unmuffled exhaust of Jimmi the Pilot's pickup truck pass by out front to circle around the block and park out back in the alley. Beantown Bob grabbed a flashlight and went to the back window on his office as quickly and as quietly as he could. He slid the window open and began flashing S-O-S in Morris Code up the alley, praying that Jimmi the Pilot would notice. When he heard the pickup's engine shut down still a block away, Beantown Bob went back to the doorway to his office and saw Waxy and Moe the Eskimo sitting at the bar facing the men holding them hostage with their pistols. The leader was in Waxy's face, obviously threatening and interrogating him. He heard the pebbles tossed by Jimmi the Pilot against the window pane behind him. Just as the leader raised his arm to pistol whip Waxy, Beantown Bob kicked his desk chair hard and toppled it. Everyone's eyes rose to the catwalk leading to his office.

Leaving a man to guard Moe the Eskimo and Waxy, the four men started quietly padding up the stairs towards Beantown Bob's office.

Moe the Eskimo tapped the pack of Camel cigarettes in his shirt pocket. His guard nodded, then quickly glanced over his shoulder at the four men slowly climbing up step-by-step in a line.

Moe the Eskimo put a cigarette between his lips. He slowly reached into his pants pocket for his lighter.

Beantown Bob waited behind the door jam, counting the number of steps the men had climbed.

Waxy did not see Jimmi the Pilot in the shadows of the hallway leading to the restrooms and the rear entrance, taking aim with his Beretta M9, until the instant before *Fenway Park West* erupted in the roar of gunfire.

Jimmi the Pilot shot first, hitting the man guarding Waxy and Moe the Eskimo in the leg. Before the guard could pirouette to return fire, Moe the Eskimo leaped off the bar stool, simultaneously grabbing the guard's right arm and slashing his throat with the switchblade which was in the same pocket as his lighter.

The second he heard Jimmi the Pilot fire, Beantown Bob came out of his office and raced across the catwalk to the top of the stairs where he fired four shots in quick succession down the stairway, tumbling the four intruders backwards like dominoes.

When Beantown Bob paused, Jimmi the Pilot stepped out from the hallway and double-tapped each of the men as they tumbled backwards down the steps, landing at the bottom, a heaping pile of corpses.

The gunfight was over in less than sixty seconds and when it was done, Waxy sat stunned on the bar stool, his ears ringing from the shots. His eyes watered from the gunpowder smoke and he struggled to focus again having been blinded by the muzzle flashes. When he could finally see clearly again, Moe the Eskimo was standing over the man with the slashed throat, wiping the blade of his switchblade clean on his black and white checkered pants. When he finished, Moe the Eskimo lit up a Camel.

Beantown Bob held his shotgun at the ready as Jimmi the Pilot confirmed that the other four men were dead at the bottom of the stairs.

Somethin' for Nothin'

"Shit."

"You can say that again." Beantown Bob shouldered the shotgun.

"You okay, kid?" Jimmi the Pilot called out, peering through the smoky haze towards the bar.

Waxy nodded his head, staring at the man on the floor at his feet, bleeding out from the neck.

"Fucking Mexicans." Jimmi the Pilot spat on the pile of bodies at his feet.

"There will be more," Beantown Bob announced grimly.

"Shit. This one didn't even take the tag off his L.L. Bean jacket."

Moe the Eskimo blew a smoke ring, then asked, "Now what?"

Jimmi the Pilot looked at Moe the Eskimo, then up the steps at Beantown Bob.

"Now we get our shit off that fucking glacier and get the hell out of Dodge," barked Beantown Bob.

Just then, Waxy saw Emma appear in the hallway behind Jimmi the Pilot. She gasped at the sight of death.

Jimmi the Pilot reflexively raised his pistol and began to turn.

"Jimmi, *no!*" Waxy called out.

Jimmi the Pilot lowered his Beretta. When Emma bolted towards Waxy, he grabbed her and blocked her way. He eased her back into the hallway and nodded over his shoulder at Waxy, who carefully stepped around the pool of blood and went to her.

"Get her out of here. We've got a mess to clean up."

As Waxy led Emma outside, he saw Moe the Eskimo

dragging the body of the man whose throat he had cut to the kitchen like a dead seal.

Bahammy Mammy Glacier

Moe the Eskimo and Waxy watched as Jimmi the Pilot turned the Cessna back down the glacier and departed to retrieve Albert and Beantown Bob.

Jimmi the Pilot declared that they were in an *"All Hands On Deck"* situation, which meant everyone had to heave to and help get the gold and cash off Bahammy Mammy Glacier in an airlift that would consume every daylight hour of every day with clear enough weather for him to land and depart. And on those days that precluded flying with storms or just the irritatingly low scud of clouds that filled the valleys and obscured the mountain peaks, they used ATVs to get to the anonymous bend in the river and spent their time building and camouflaging bunkers and lean-tos scattered haphazardly throughout the woods where they could cache the treasure retrieved from the *Globemaster*.

All outsiders had to go, so at night, Albert was back behind the bar at *Fenway Park West*, while Waxy and Moe the Eskimo manned the kitchen. Solo again, like her Seattle coffeehouse days, CiCi sang mournful tunes by Linda Ronstadt, Karla Bonoff and Carole King, while Dylan, his arm in a cast, watched, sulked and drank at a back booth, impatiently waiting for what he was sure would be a mere pittance of what everyone else would get out of the cargo plane. Sometimes Beantown Bob watched and listened to CiCi from the catwalk, wondering if he could or even should keep her, after he had taken care of Albert.

Jimmi the Pilot stood guard on the bar stool nearest the door with his Beretta in his belt and a shotgun within easy reach just behind the bar, watching for more Mexicans.

Emma quit the *Lucky Wishbone Diner* to run the bar during the day, supervising Nordo and Graham from *Torchlight,* who Beantown Bob now paid to bartend and wash dishes, since the band could no longer perform after Dylan broke his arm.

"We're getting close to getting it all," Waxy said to Moe the Eskimo.

Moe the Eskimo nodded.

"What are you going to do?"

With a shrug of the shoulders, he lit up a Camel and looked down the length of the glacier and towards the valley where his village had once stood.

"Are you going to stay in Alaska?" Waxy asked.

"I got no quarrel with the Mexicans. That's Bob and Jimmi's problem. They can work it out without me."

"So, you're going to stay?"

"It's my home. I won't stay in Anchorage. Too city for me. I may move North."

Waxy nodded.

"If I survive."

"Huh?" Waxy looked over at Moe the Eskimo. "What are you talking about?"

"Call it a premonition. A vision."

"A vision of what?"

Moe the Eskimo blew out smoke and watched it swirl into nothingness in the clear mountain air. He looked over at Waxy.

Somethin' for Nothin'

"What vision?"

"Beware the wolf." Moe the Eskimo flicked the ash off his Camel. "You know what they intend to do to you. To Albert."

Waxy nodded and murmured, "Yeah. Leave us up here to die."

"And me, too." Moe the Eskimo took a deep draw and exhaled slowly. "I won't die up here. I know that much. But I don't know if I'll survive the journey down. I don't know if my journey will take me back or somewhere beyond."

"What journey? Beyond what?"

The sound of the Cessna's Continental engine purred off in the distance. It drew their eyes as it grew louder. They strained to see the plane out over the valley.

"Do this—on the last load, make sure you and Albert get off the mountain first."

"How?"

Moe the Eskimo shrugged. He saw the Cessna on long final approach to Bahammy Mammy Glacier and pointed it out to Waxy.

"Just do it that way." Moe the Eskimo tossed his cigarette butt into the snow. "Or die."

Moe the Eskimo tracked the approach of the Cessna with his eyes.

Waxy stared at him then turned to watch Jimmi the Pilot flare and touch down. The Cessna slid up just past Waxy and Moe the Eskimo, where it turned ninety degrees to place the skis sideways to the slope of the glacier. The engine shut down and the doors flung open.

"I swear, I shit my pants every time I land up here with you," Beantown Bob declared, getting out of the right front seat.

Albert followed him out from the back seat, not saying a word, but holding his nose and waving his hand in front of his face. He caught Waxy's look and rolled his eyes back into his head.

Jimmi the Pilot finished flipping off switches and let gravity help slide him out of the cockpit. "Bad news, men. That winter storm is moving a lot faster than forecast. This might be our last chance before we get pounded with snow, so we gotta work fast."

It was Sunday, so with *Fenway Park West* closed they would spend the night on the glacier to save time. They would work into the night and start flying again at first light. So, Moe the Eskimo set up their camp site, while the others got the tripod, winch and sleds out and set up.

Once everything was ready they stationed themselves and got to work in the grueling routine that they had been following for nearly a month now: one man inside the plane passed ingots and bags of cash out to another man on the wing, who loaded it into duffel bags to be winched out of the crevasse. Up top, a sled was used to shuttle the treasure up the slope to the plane where Jimmi the Pilot carefully placed it into the Cessna in every available space, trying to max out the load up to and sometimes even beyond the gross weight limit of the aircraft, figuring that the fuel burn and the descent down off the mountain to denser air would allow some margin for error. When Jimmi the Pilot decided the plane was full and ready to airlift their treasures down to the bend in the river, Waxy, Albert or Moe the Eskimo—on a rotating basis— would accompany him down to the cache location along the river to help unload. Since Beantown Bob hated to fly, the only trips he made were to get on and off the glacier.

Somethin' for Nothin'

Those left behind used to rest and eat while they waited for the Cessna's return. But with the threat of the coming storm, they silently watched Jimmi the Pilot depart, swapped stations, and got back to work right away, now in a desperate rush to greedily retrieve all the rest of the gold bullion, even though they had already airlifted millions and millions off Bahammy Mammy Glacier.

The crew worked like busy ants pulling gold bars out of one plane and into the other until darkness fell and made landing and departing off the mountain impossible. Without a meeting or a group decision made, though, they kept working into the night with Coleman Lanterns casting eerie, flickering shadows in the crevasse. It was almost midnight when fatigue caught up with them. Moe the Eskimo served a hot meal of stew, which was eaten in silence. Beantown Bob and Jimmi the Pilot retired to their tent. Albert crawled into his sleeping bag and lay on his back staring up at nothing, waiting for Waxy to finish helping Moe the Eskimo clean up the camp site.

Like in the kitchen at *Fenway Park West,* Waxy and Moe the Eskimo worked in silent harmony, as if their movements were choreographed, pausing only when the conspiratorial whispers between Beantown Bob and Jimmi the Pilot crescendoed to carry incoherently across the glacier, then ebbed back to breathy, scratchy whispers.

By the time Moe the Eskimo and Waxy finished, Beantown Bob was snoring loudly. As was their ritual, Moe the Eskimo lit up a Camel cigarette. He sipped and passed a flask of whiskey to Waxy, as they whispered out their own plans.

Waxy left Moe the Eskimo smoking his third Camel and went into the tent he shared with Albert to tell him that they

M.T. Bass

would have some help tomorrow, their last day before the storm hit.

By dawn, Moe was already up and had warmed the left over stew for breakfast. After eating, Jimmi the Pilot and Waxy fueled up the plane from the stash of gas cans they brought up and stored on the glacier over the previous weeks to save even more time. They took the first load down they had mined in the dark the night before.

"Shit, we might not even get the whole day in," Jimmi the Pilot said after getting a weather report over the radio from Flight Service. "That cold front is clipping along."

"I think we'll get it all," Waxy answered, his voice scratchy through the intercom. "It looks like there's only a couple more loads to go."

Jimmi the Pilot nodded. He spotted the cache site and reduced power.

"You know, I'm glad for you and Emma."

"Thanks."

"Good for you." Jimmi the Pilot echoed himself so faintly, the intercom did not pick up his voice, "Good for you."

"So, what do you think Bob's going to do?"

Jimmi the Pilot scanned the horizon. "He wants to go tropical, I think. For a while anyway. Maybe Thailand—probably to look up an old friend of mine I've told him about…who knows."

"I don't think CiCi will want to go there."

Jimmi the Pilot chuckled. "She ain't going with him no matter where he goes. You know that."

Waxy slowly nodded his head.

"Be careful. Even though I really don't think he cares much anymore, he's still pissed off about it. You know Bob."

Somethin' for Nothin'

Waxy studied Jimmi the Pilot's face. "I like you, Jimmi."

"You, too, kid."

"I hope everything works out for you with, you know, everything."

"Fuck them spics. I'll be fine."

"Hope so."

"Let finish this bitch."

Jimmi landed on the sandbar. They unloaded and flew back to Bahammy Mammy Glacier.

~~

Waxy was right: only took two more trips before they had pulled the last of the gold and money bags out of the *Globemaster*. Moe the Eskimo reeled Waxy, then Albert out of the crevasse, then they all worked to pull the last of the loot uphill to the Cessna.

"Okay, that's it. Two more hops and we're home free," said Jimmi the Pilot, clapping his hands together. "I'll take Bob down and then be back in a flash to get you guys."

"Yeah," Albert drawled deliberately, reaching into his parka. "I don't think so."

Albert and Waxy had deliberately spread apart from one another. Moe the Eskimo was off on his own as usual.

"Hey, fuck you," said Beantown Bob. "Get in fucking line, barkeep."

"Like I said," Albert growled, pulling his Walther out of his parka. "I don't *fucking* think so."

"Seriously? Seriously? I ought to—"

Albert raised the pistol. "Hands where I can see them."

"Come on, you asshole. We don't have time for this. We're losing the light. And the storm's coming," Jimmi the Pilot shouted impatiently. "Besides, punk, you ain't got the *cajones* to put us down, you shit."

"Don't, Jimmi," Waxy said pulling out his Walther as Jimmi took a step towards Albert. "I can pull the trigger. You know that. You saw it."

Albert gave Waxy a curious look at the new information he had just heard.

"God damn it." Beantown Bob stamped his feet and hollered. "Moe—talk some sense into these asshole friends of yours."

"Moe, get their guns," Waxy said.

"Seriously? You, too?" Beantown Bob asked Moe the Eskimo as he relieved first Jimmi the Pilot, then him of their guns. He looked at them both, then pocketed Jimmi the Pilot's Beretta in favor of Beantown Bob's Thirty-eight Special revolver, which he held on his employer.

"I heard you talk," Moe the Eskimo said so low that only Beantown Bob could hear, then backed away.

"Boys, the light. The storm. The light," Jimmi the Pilot pleaded. "We don't have time for this shit."

"Fine. Here's how it's going to go," Albert said calmly. "Everybody puts their car keys into this bag and we leave it up here on the ice, while Jimmi takes me and Waxy down. You drop us off, come back for Bob and Moe and our keys, then we can all live happily ever after."

"I don't know if I can take two passengers with this load," said Jimmi the Pilot. "I only planned on one."

"Then take some of it out," Albert said through his gritted teeth. "This is how it's going to go."

Somethin' for Nothin'

"NO! Goddamn it, no," Beantown Bob screamed helplessly. "Just get them the fuck out of here and get me off this God damned mountain once and for all."

Waxy, Albert and Jimmi the Pilot got into the Cessna. A few moments later, the engine fired up. Jimmi the Pilot gave a two fingered wave to Beantown Bob, goosed the power and spun the tail around with the rudder to head down the glacier. It slowly gathered speed on the take off run, but kept going and going and going, far further than it usually took to get airborne.

Beantown Bob watched the Cessna struggle to get into the air, then disappear as if falling off the edge of Bahammy Mammy Glacier. They had gotten used to seeing Jimmi the Pilot fly off the ice and maintain altitude before reducing power to descend into the valley, so he immediately knew something was wrong, that something was very wrong. The engine screaming at full power echoed off the mountains, but the plane was nowhere to be seen. Beantown Bob suddenly came to the realization that the plane was going to crash and his fate was sealed up there on the ice.

"You turncoat son-of-a-bitch," Beantown Bob growled at Moe the Eskimo.

Before he could even take a step forward, Moe the Eskimo shot Beantown Bob in the chest.

Beantown Bob collapsed to his knees, coughing up blood, then fell to his face, gasping as he bled out on the glacier.

Moe the Eskimo wondered whether he should put Beantown Bob out of his misery with a shot to the head, but decided he might need every bullet he had for his long journey. He turned his back on Beantown Bob and went to get his snowshoes and the backpack stuffed with supplies he had stashed just in case he would ever need to hike down off the mountain.

~~

Jimmi the Pilot knew, even before Beantown Bob, that the flight was doomed. He had chewed up way too much ice trying to get airborne and now, with the speed and the slope, there was too little of Bahammy Mammy Glacier left to stop on. One way or another they were going to be airborne, so he might as well go down flying, instead of falling.

Jimmi the Pilot reflexively tried to push the already firewalled throttle forward. At the last minute, he dropped a half a notch of flaps to get airborne, which worked fine until the Cessna reached the end of the ice and the helpful aerodynamic cushion of ground effect was suddenly thousands of feet below them on the valley floor. The Cessna dropped with a sudden lurch and Jimmi the Pilot had no choice but to lower the nose to keep the wings from stalling. His only hope was to use the altitude he had to make a safe crash landing somewhere below along the river.

When the Cessna fell off Bahammy Mammy Glacier, Albert sensed immediately that things might not be all right. Waxy—after all the time he had spent in the cockpit with Jimmi the Pilot—knew for sure their situation was dire. He knew they were going to crash.

"Jimmi—Fix it, Jimmi, fix it!" Waxy hollered into his mic.

Jimmi the Pilot flipped off the intercom. He didn't need the distraction of panic filling his headsets. He dialed one-twenty-one point five into the radio and transmitted, "Mayday, Mayday, Mayday—Six-Six-Golf going down four-five miles south-southeast of Denali near the Tamalaheena River."

Somethin' for Nothin'

Jimmi the Pilot had not noticed that the valley was filling with thick dark clouds from the approaching winter storm and he inadvertently descended into instrument conditions in a snow squall.

"Fuck me. Fuck me. Fuck me," Jimmi the Pilot said to himself as he went "Popeye," trying to keep the Cessna flying by instruments alone.

They broke out of the clouds above the river. There, Jimmi the Pilot made the last conscious decision of his life. He figured that if he turned up stream towards the bend in the river, search and rescue teams might not only find them but the cash and the gold they had hidden there, so he gently banked the sinking Cessna downstream, careful not to stall the wing. He peered hard through the snow squall for a clearing to set down in without going into the river. He saw a length of sandbar that might just be long enough, even though their speed was high. He frantically worked the lever on the hydraulic pump to lift the skis to land on the wheels.

"Come on you bitch come on you bitch come on you bitch, *come on,*" Jimmi the Pilot chanted as he coaxed the plane a little further, one 'bitch' at a time, until the wheels bit the hard sand and gravel.

But there was too much speed. And they were descending way too fast. And with both Waxy and Albert, along with the last load of gold bullion and nearly full fuel tanks, there was way too much weight and momentum to stop on the short strip of shore before the Cessna plunged into the woods, shearing off the wings and slamming head-on into a spruce tree, killing Jimmi the Pilot instantly.

~~~

Epilogue

"But Jimmi the Pilot was dead," Waxy said in a low, hushed voice, then paused for dramatic effect. He leaned in and looked his small semi-circle of an audience directly in the eye, one-by-one.

"But you didn't die, did you Grandpa?"

Waxy glanced towards Emma sitting at the other end of the couch. He winked at her and smiled.

"No, Savannah. I didn't die."

July 22, 1977—The first barrel of oil reached Valdez from Prudhoe Bay via the Trans Alaska Pipeline System

Waxy and Albert never had to work another day for the rest of their lives.

~~~

Thank you for reading my story.

About M.T. Bass

M.T. Bass lives, writes, flies and plays music in Mudcat Falls, USA.

www.MTBass.net

Available in Paperback & eBook

Kansas City, 1965 — Y.T. Erp, Jr. can't wait to leave for college at the University of California, Berkeley to escape not only the work, but especially all the phlegm-brained idiots at his father's aerospace company. Leaving behind a pregnant auburn-haired cheerleader, a sensuous red-headed siren plotting to usurp his familial ties, and his two best friends—one who ends up in Vietnam and the other in the Weather Underground—his "trip" on the wild side of the Generation Gap takes him from the psychedelic scene of Haight-Ashbury to the F.B.I.'s Ten Most Wanted list. Meanwhile his father is consumed by the task of managing his unmanageable corporate team in the quest to help fulfill a President's challenge to "land a man on the moon."

www.MTBass.net

Available in eBook

Lodging — bending of the stalk of a plant (stalk lodging)
or the entire plant (root lodging)

While World War II engulfs every nation on the globe, Sarah and her high school friend Rebecca can only dream of escaping a dreary, wind-blown existence in western Kansas, until their boring, stodgy old hometown fills with handsome young men learning to fly Army Air Corps bombers known as *Liberators*, and their lives are suddenly filled with temptation and, perhaps, true love.

www.MTBass.net

CROSSROADS

A Novel by M.T. Bass

Available in eBook

Cleveland, 1977 — Grappling with a foreign policy crisis, the U.S. Government targets a hapless rock-'n'-roller as a Russian spy in a classic case of mistaken identity for an innocent, 'Wrong Man' hero...or *is he?* Think of an unholy fictional union between the Rolling Stones and Alfred Hitchcock's *North by Northwest*. Unlike any novel you have ever read, this one has a soundtrack. After all, a story whose characters are musicians should have...well...*music.* Right?

www.MTBass.net

Available in Paperback & eBook

Hollywood, 1950 — Former P-51 fighter pilot A. Gavin Byrd is on location for a movie shoot, when he gets a call from the police that his older brother, a prominent Beverly Hills plastic surgeon, has been found dead on his boat. The Lieutenant in charge of the investigation is ready to close the case as a suicide from the start, but "Hawk" doesn't buy it and decides to find out what really happened for himself.

With help from a former starlet ex-girl friend, a friendly police sergeant whose life was saved in the war by his brother and a nosy Los Angeles Times reporter, Hawk's search for the truth takes him through cross-fire, dog fights and mine fields in Hollywood, Beverly Hills, Burbank and Las Vegas, and leads him into some of the darker corners of his brother's patient files and private life that he never knew existed.

CPSIA information can be obtained at www.ICGtesting.com
Printed in the USA
LVOW06s0830151215

466675LV00001B/1/P